Fool

Fool

Christopher Moore

HARPER LUXE

An Imprint of HarperCollins*Publishers*

LP
FiC
Moore

FOOL.. Copyright © 2009 by Christopher Moore. All rights reserved. Printed in the United States of America. No part of this book may be used or reproduced in any manner whatsoever without written permission except in the case of brief quotations embodied in critical articles and reviews. For information address HarperCollins Publishers, 10 East 53rd Street, New York, NY 10022.

HarperCollins books may be purchased for educational, business, or sales promotional use. For information please write: Special Markets Department, HarperCollins Publishers, 10 East 53rd Street, New York, NY 10022.

FIRST HARPERLUXE EDITION

HarperLuxe™ is a trademark of HarperCollins Publishers

Library of Congress Cataloging-in-Publication Data is available upon request.

ISBN: 978-0-06-171987-5

09 10 11 12 13 ID/RRD 10 9 8 7 6 5 4 3 2 1

WARNING

This is a bawdy tale. Herein you will find gratuitous shagging, murder, spanking, maiming, treason, and heretofore unexplored heights of vulgarity and profanity, as well as non-traditional grammar, split infinitives, and the odd wank. If that sort of thing bothers you, then gentle reader pass by, for we endeavor only to entertain, not to offend. That said, if that's the sort of thing you think you might enjoy, then you have happened upon the perfect story!

Contents

Cast of Characters

Lear—King of Britain

Goneril—oldest daughter of Lear, Duchess of Albany. Wife of the Duke of Albany.

Regan—second daughter of Lear, Duchess of Cornwall. Wife of the Duke of Cornwall.

Cordelia—youngest daughter of Lear, Princess of Britain.

Cornwall—Duke of Cornwall, Regan's husband.

Albany—Duke of Albany, Goneril's husband.

Gloucester—Earl of Gloucester, a friend of King Lear.

Edgar—eldest son of Gloucester, the heir to the earldom.

Edmund—bastard son of Gloucester.

The Anchoress—a holy woman.

Kent—Earl of Kent, close friend of King Lear.

Pocket—a fool.

Burgundy—Duke of Burgundy, a suitor to Cordelia.

France—Prince of France, a suitor to Cordelia.

Curan—captain of Lear's guard.

Drool—an apprentice fool.

A Ghost—there's always a bloody ghost.

Great Britain

N

50 miles

Scotland

Goneril's Castle

Great Birnam
Wood

Albany

Edinburgh

Ireland

York

Abbey at Dog Snogging

River Ouse

Dog Snogging

Wales

Castle Gloucester

Gloucester

The White Tower

River Thames

London

Kent

Dover

Regan's Castle

Cornwall

Calais

English Channel

Fucking France

The Stage

The stage is a more or less mythical thirteenth-century Britain, with vestiges of British culture reaching back to pre-Roman times still loitering about. Britain encompasses what is now modern Great Britain, including England, Wales, Ireland, and Scotland, of which Lear is king. Generally, if not otherwise explained, conditions may be considered damp.

ACT I

When we are born, we cry that we are come
To this great stage of fools.

—King Lear, Act IV, Scene 5

1.

Always a Bloody Ghost

Tosser!" cried the raven.

There's always a bloody raven.

"Foolish teachin' him to talk, if you ask me," said the sentry.

"I'm duty-bound foolish, yeoman," said I. I am, you know? A fool. Fool to the court of Lear of Britain. "And you *are* a tosser,"[1] I said.

"Piss off!" said the raven.

The yeoman took a swipe at the bird with his spear and the great black bird swooped off the wall and went cawing out over the Thames. A ferryman looked up from his boat, saw us on the tower, and waved. I jumped onto the wall and bowed—at your fucking

---

1. Tosser—one who tosses, a wanker.

service, thank you. The yeoman grumbled and spat after the raven.

There have always been ravens at the White Tower. A thousand years ago, before George II, idiot king of Merica, destroyed the world, there were ravens here. The legend says that as long as there are ravens at the Tower, England will stand strong. Still, it may have been a mistake to teach one to talk.

"The Earl of Gloucester approaches!" cried a sentry on the west wall. "With his son Edgar and the bastard Edmund!"

The yeoman by me grinned. "Gloucester, eh? Be sure you do that bit where you play a goat and Drool plays the earl mistaking you for his wife."

"That would be unkind," said I. "The earl is newly widowed."

"You did it the last time he was here and she was still warm in the grave."

"Well, yes. A service that—trying to shock the poor wretch out of his grief, wasn't it?"

"Good show, too. The way you was bleatin' I thought ol' Drool was givin' it to you right proper up the bung."

I made a note to shove the guard off the wall when opportunity presented.

"Heard he was going to have you assassinated, but he couldn't make a case to the king."

"Gloucester's a noble, he doesn't need a case for murder, just a whim and a blade."

"Not bloody likely," the yeoman said, "everyone knows the king's got a wing o'er you."

That was true. I enjoy a certain license.

"Have you seen Drool? With Gloucester here, there'll be a command performance." My apprentice, Drool—a beef-witted bloke the size of a draught horse.

"He was in the kitchen before the watch," said the yeoman.

The kitchen buzzed—the staff preparing for a feast.

"Have you seen Drool?" I asked Taster, who sat at the table staring sadly at a bread trencher[2] laid out with cold pork, the king's dinner. He was a thin, sickly lad, chosen, no doubt, for his weakness of constitution, and a predisposition toward dropping dead at the slightest provocation. I liked to tell him my troubles, sure that they would not travel far.

"Does this look poisoned to you?"

"It's pork, lad. Lovely. Eat up. Half the men in England would give a testicle to feast thus, and it only mid-day. I'm tempted myself." I tossed my head—gave him a grin and a bit of a jingle on the ol' hat bells to

---

2. Trencher—a thick, wide slice of stale bread, used like a plate.

cheer him. I pantomimed stealing a bit of his pork. "After you, of course."

A knife thumped into the table by my hand.

"Back, Fool," said Bubble, the head cook. "That's the king's lunch and I'll have your balls before I'll let you at it."

"My balls are yours for the asking, milady," said I. "Would you have them on a trencher, or shall I serve them in a bowl of cream, like peaches?"

Bubble harrumphed, yanked her knife from the table and went back to gutting a trout at the butcher block, her great bottom rolling like thunderclouds under her skirt as she moved.

"You're a wicked little man, Pocket," said Squeak, waves of freckles riding o'er her shy smile. She was second to the cook, a sturdy, ginger-haired girl with a high giggle and a generous spirit in the dark. Taster and I often passed pleasant afternoons at the table watching her wring the necks of chickens.

Pocket is my name, by the way. Given to me by the abbess who found me on the nunnery doorstep when I was a tiny babe. True, I am not a large fellow. Some might even say I am diminutive, but I am quick as a cat and nature has compensated me with other gifts. But wicked?

"I think Drool was headed to the princess's chambers," Squeak said.

"Aye," said Taster, glumly. "The lady sent for a cure for melancholy."

"And the git went?" Jest on his own? The boy wasn't ready. What if he blundered, tripped, fell on the princess like a millstone on a butterfly? "Are you sure?"

Bubble dropped a gutless trout into a bushel of slippery cofishes.[3] "Chanting, 'Off to do ma duty,' he was. We told him you'd be looking for him when we heard Princess Goneril and the Duke of Albany was coming."

"Albany's coming?"

"Ain't he sworn to string your entrails from the chandelier?" asked Taster.

"No," corrected Squeak. "That was Duke of Cornwall. Albany was going to have his head on a pike, I believe. Pike, wasn't it, Bubble?"

"Aye, have his head on a pike. Funny thing, thinkin' about it, you'd look like a bigger version of your puppet-stick there."

"Jones," said Taster, pointing to my jester's scepter, Jones, who is, indeed, a smaller version of my own handsome countenance, fixed atop a sturdy handle of polished hickory. Jones speaks for me when even my tongue needs to exceed safe license with knights and nobles, his head pre-piked for the wrath of the dull and

3. Cofishes—other fish in a group, coworkers, cohorts, etc. Shut up, it's a word.

humorless. My finest art is oft lost in the eye of the subject.

"Yes, that would be right hilarious, Bubble—ironic imagery—like the lovely Squeak turning you on a spit over a fire, an apple up both your ends for color—although I daresay the whole castle might conflagrate in the resulting grease fire, but until then we'd laugh and laugh."

I dodged a well-flung trout then, and paid Bubble a grin for not throwing her knife instead. Fine woman, she, despite being large and quick to anger. "Well, I've a great drooling dolt to find if we are to prepare an entertainment for the evening."

Cordelia's chambers lay in the North Tower; the quickest way there was atop the outer wall. As I crossed over the great main gate-house, a young spot-faced yeoman called, "Hail, Earl of Gloucester!" Below, the greybeard Gloucester and his retinue were crossing the drawbridge.

"Hail, Edmund, you bloody bastard!" I called over the wall.

The yeoman tapped me on the shoulder. "Beggin' your pardon, sirrah,[4] but I'm told that Edmund is sensitive about his bastardy."

4. Sirrah—form of address, "dude."

"Aye, yeoman," said I. "No need for prodding and jibe to divine that prick's tender spot, he wears it on his sleeve." I jumped on the wall and waved Jones at the bastard, who was trying to wrench a bow and quiver from a knight who rode beside him. "You whoreson scalawag!" said I. "You flesh-turd dropped stinking from the poxy arsehole of a hare-lipped harlot!"

The Earl of Gloucester glowered up at me as he passed under the portcullis.[5]

"Shot to the heart, that one," said the yeoman.

"Too harsh, then, you reckon?"

"A bit."

"Sorry. Excellent hat, though, bastard," I called, by way of making amends. Edgar and two knights were trying to restrain the bastard Edmund below. I jumped down from the wall. "Haven't seen Drool, have you?"

"In the great hall this morning," said the yeoman. "Not since."

A call came around the top of the wall, passing from yeoman to yeoman until we heard, "The Duke of Cornwall and Princess Regan approach from the south."

---

5. Portcullis—a heavy vertical grate, usually spiked on the bottom and made of or clad in iron to resist fire. Typically the inner gate of a fortress, an open grate so attackers could be hit with arrows or spears if they broke through the outer gates.

"Fuckstockings!" Cornwall: polished greed and pure born villainy; he'd dirk[6] a nun for a farthing,[7] and short the coin, for the fun.

"Don't worry, little one, the king'll keep your hide whole."

"Aye, yeoman, he will, and if you call me *little one* in company, the king'll have you walking watch on the frozen moat all winter."

"Sorry, Sir Jester, sir," said the yeoman. He slouched then as not to seem so irritatingly tall. "Heard that tasty Princess Regan's a right bunny cunny, eh?" He leaned down to elbow me in the ribs, now that we were best mates and all.

"You're new, aren't you?"

"Just two months in service."

"Advice, then, young yeoman: When referring to the king's middle daughter, state that she is fair, speculate that she is pious, but unless you'd like to spend your watch looking for the box where your head is kept, resist the urge to wax ignorant on her naughty bits."

"I don't know what that means, sir."

6. Dirk—a knife, especially a dagger, or the act of using a dagger on someone.

7. Farthing—the smallest denomination of English coinage, equal to one quarter of a penny.

"Speak not of Regan's shaggacity, son. Cornwall has taken the eyes of men who have but looked upon the princess with but the spark of lust."

"The fiend! I didn't know, sir. I'll say nothing."

"And neither shall I, good yeoman. Neither shall I."

And thus are alliances made, loyalties cemented. Pocket makes a friend.

The boy was right about Regan, of course. And why I hadn't thought to call her *bunny cunny* myself, when I of all people should know—well, as an artist, I must admit, I was envious of the invention.

Cordelia's private solar[8] lay at the top of a narrow spiral staircase lit only with the crosses of arrow loops. I could hear giggling as I topped the stairs.

"So I am of no worth if not on the arm and in the bed of some buffoon in a codpiece?" I heard Cordelia say.

"You called," said I, stepping into the room, codpiece in hand.

The ladies-in-waiting giggled. Young Lady Jane, who is but thirteen, shrieked at my presence—disturbed, no doubt, by my overt manliness, or perhaps

---

8. Solar—a sitting room or parlor in the top story of a tower. The tower unblocked by outer walls receives a lot of sun, thus the name.

by the gentle clouting on the bottom she received from Jones.

"Pocket!" Cordelia sat at the center of the circle of girls—holding court, as such—her hair down, blond curls to her waist, a simple gown of lavender linen, loosely laced. She stood and approached me. "You honor us, Fool. Did you hear rumors of small animals to hurt, or were you hoping to accidentally surprise me in my bath again?"

I tipped my hat, a slight, contrite jingle there. "I was lost, milady."

"A dozen times?"

"Finding my way is not my strong suit. If you want a navigator I'll send for him, but hold me blameless should your melancholy triumph and you drown yourself in the brook, your gentle ladies weeping damply around your pale and lovely corpse. Let them say, 'She was not lost in the map, confident as she was in her navigator, but lost in heart for want of a fool.' "

The ladies gasped as if I'd cued them. I'd have blessed them if I were still on speaking terms with God.

"Out, out, out, ladies," Cordelia said. "Give me peace with my fool so that I might devise some punishment for him."

The ladies scurried out of the room.

"Punishment?" I asked. "For what?"

"I don't know yet," she said, "but by the time I've thought of the punishment, I'm sure there'll be an offense."

"I blush at your confidence."

"And I at your humility," said the princess. She grinned, a crescent too devious for a maid of her tender years. Cordelia is not ten years my junior (I'm not sure, exactly, of my own age), seventeen summers has she seen, and as the youngest of the king's daughters, she's always been treated as if fragile as spun glass. But, sweet thing that she is, her bark could frighten a mad badger.

"Shall I disrobe for my punishment?" I offered. "Flagellation? Fellation? Whatever. I am your willing penitent, lady."

"No more of that, Pocket. I need your counsel, or at least your commiseration. My sisters are coming to the castle."

"Unfortunately, they have arrived."

"Oh, that's right, Albany and Cornwall want to kill you. Bad luck, that. Anyway, they are coming to the castle, as are Gloucester and his sons. Goodness, *they* want to kill you as well."

"Rough critics," said I.

"Sorry. And a dozen other nobles as well as the Earl of Kent are here. Kent doesn't want to kill you, does he?"

"Not that I know of. But it *is* only lunchtime."

"Right. And do you know why they are all coming?"

"To corner me like a rat in a barrel?"

"Barrels do not have corners, Pocket."

"Does seem like a lot of bother for killing one small, if tremendously handsome fool."

"It's not about you, you dolt! It's about me."

"Well, even less effort to kill you. How many can it take to snap your scrawny neck? I worry that Drool will do it by accident someday. You haven't seen him, have you?"

"He stinks. I sent him away this morning." She waved a hand furiously to return to her point. "Father is marrying me off!"

"Nonsense. Who would have you?"

The lady darkened a bit, then, blue eyes gone cold. Badgers across Blighty[9] shuddered. "Edgar of Gloucester has always wanted me and the Prince of France and Duke of Burgundy are already here to pay me troth."

"Troth about what?"

"Troth!"

"About what?"

"Troth, troth, you fool, not truth. The princes are here to marry me."

9. Blighty—Britain, Great Britain; slang.

"Those two? Edgar? No." I was shaken. Cordelia? Married? Would one of them take her away? It was unjust! Unfair! Wrong! Why, she had never even seen me naked.

"Why would they want to troth you? I mean, for the night, to be sure, who wouldn't troth you cross-eyed? But permanently, I think not."

"I'm a bloody princess, Pocket."

"Precisely. What good are princesses? Dragon food and ransom markers—spoiled brats to be bartered for real estate."

"Oh no, dear fool, you forget that sometimes a princess becomes a queen."

"Ha, princesses. What worth are you if your father has to tack a dozen counties to your bum to get those French poofters to look at you?"

"Oh, and what worth a fool? Nay, what worth a fool's second, for you merely carry the drool cup for the Natural.[10] What's the ransom for a jester, Pocket? A bucket of warm spittle."

I grabbed my chest. "Pierced to the core, I am," I gasped. I staggered to a chair. "I bleed, I suffer, I die on the forked lance of your words."

She came to me. "You do not."

---

10. A Natural—the "Natural" jester was one who had some physical deformity or anomaly, a hunchback, a dwarf, a giant, Down's syndrome, etc. Naturals were thought to have been "touched" by God.

"No, stay back. Blood stains will never come out of linen—they are stubborned with your cruelty and guilt . . ."

"Pocket, stop it now."

"You have kilt me, lady, most dead." I gasped, I spasmed, I coughed. "Let it always be said that this humble fool brought joy to all whom he met."

"No one will say that."

"Shhhh, child. I grow weak. No breath." I looked at the imaginary blood on my hands, horrified. I slid off a chair, to the floor. "But I want you to know that despite your vicious nature and your freakishly large feet, I have always—"

And then I died. Bloody fucking brilliantly, I'd say, too, hint of a shudder at the end as death's chilly hand grabbed my knob.

"What? What? You have always what?"

I said nothing, being dead, and not a little exhausted from all the bleeding and gasping. Truth be told, under the jest I felt like I'd taken a bolt to the heart.

"You're absolutely no help at all," said Cordelia.

The raven landed on the wall as I made my way back to the common house in search of Drool. No little vexed was I by the news of Cordelia's looming nuptials.

"Ghost!" said the raven.

"I didn't teach you that."

"Bollocks!" replied the raven.

"That's the spirit!"

"Ghost!"

"Piss off, bird," said I.

Then a cold wind bit at my bum and at the top of the stairs, in the turret ahead, I saw a shimmering in the shadows, like silk in sunlight—not quite in the shape of a woman.

And the ghost said:

"With grave offense to daughters three,
Alas, the king a fool shall be."

"Rhymes?" I inquired. "You're looming about all diaphanous in the middle of the day, puking cryptic rhymes? Low craft and tawdry art, ghosting about at noon—a parson's fart heralds darker doom, thou babbling wisp."

"Ghost!" cried the raven, and with that the ghost was gone.

There's always a bloody ghost.

2.

Now, Gods, Stand up for Bastards!¹

I found Drool in the laundry resolving a wank, spouting great gouts of git-seed across the laundry walls, floors, and ceiling, giggling, as young Shanker Mary wagged her tits at him over a steaming cauldron of the king's shirts.

"Put those away, tart, we've a show to do."

"I was just giving 'im a laugh."

"If you wanted to show charity you could have bonked him honest and there'd be a lot less cleaning to do."

"That'd be a sin. Besides, I'd as soon straddle a gateman's halberd as try to get a weapon that girth up me."

1. *King Lear*, Act I, Scene 2, Edmund.

Drool pumped himself dry and sat down on the floor splay-legged, huffing like a great dribbling bellows. I tried to help the lout repack his tackle, but getting him into a codpiece against his firm enthusiasm was like trying to pound a bucket over a bull's head—a scenario I thought comical enough to perhaps work into the act tonight, should things get slow.

"Nothing stopping you from givin' the lad a proper cleavage toss, Mary. You had 'em out and all soaped up, a couple of jumps and a tickle and he'd have carried water for you for a fortnight."

"He already does. And I don't even want that thing near me. A Natural, he is. There's devils in his jizm."

"Devils? Devils? There's no devils in there, lass. Chock full o' nitwits, to be sure, but no devils." A Natural was either blessed or cursed, never just an accident of nature, as the name implied.

Sometime during the week, Shanker Mary had gone Christian on us, despite being a most egregious slut. You never knew anymore who you were dealing with. Half the kingdom was Christian, the other half paid tribute to the old gods of Nature, who were always showing promise on the moonrise. The Christian God with his "day of rest" was strong with the peasants come Sunday, but by Thursday when there was drinking and fucking to be done, Nature had her kit off, legs aloft, and a flagon of ale in each hand, taking converts for the Druids as fast as they could come. They were a solid majority when the holiday was about, dancing, drinking, shagging the virgins, and sharing the harvest, but on the human sacrifice or burn-down-the-King's-forest days, there was none but crickets cavorting 'round the Stonehenge—the singers having forsaken Mother Earth for Father Church.

"Pretty," said Drool, trying to wrestle back control of his tool. Mary had commenced to stirring the laundry but had neglected to pull her dress up. Had the git's attention hostage, she did.

"Right. She's a bloody vision of loveliness, lad, but you've buffed yourself to a gleam already and we've work to do. The castle's awash in intrigue, subterfuge, and villainy—they'll be wantingcomic relief between the flattery and the murders."

"Intrigue and villainy?" Drool displayed a gape-toothed grin. Imagine soldiers dumping hogsheads of spittle through the crenellations atop the castle wall—thus is Drool's grin, as earnest in expression as it is damp in execution—a slurry of good cheer. He loves intrigue and villainy, as they play to his most special ability.

"Will there be hiding?"

"There will most certainly be hiding," said I, as I shouldered an escaped testicle into his cod.

"And listening?"

"Listening of cavernous proportions—we shall hang on every word as God on Pope's prayers."

"And fuckery? Will there be fuckery, Pocket?"

"Heinous fuckery most foul, lad. Heinous fuckery most foul."

"Aye, that's the dog's bollocks,[2] then!" said Drool, slapping his thigh. "Did you hear, Mary? Heinous fuckery afoot. Ain't that the dog's bollocks?"

"Oh yeah, the dog's bloody B. it is, love. If the saints are smilin' on us, maybe one of them nobles will hang your wee mate there like they been threatening."

"Two fools well-hung we'd have then, wouldn't we?" said I, elbowing my apprentice in the ribs.

"Aye, two fools well-hung, we'd have, wouldn't we?" said Drool, in my voice, tone to note coming out his great maw as like he'd caught an echo on his tongue and coughed it right back. That's the oaf's gift—not only can he mimic perfectly, he can recall whole conversations, hours long, recite them back to you in the original speakers' voices, and not

2. The dog's bollocks!—excellent! The bee's knees! The cat's pj's. Literally, the dog's balls, which doesn't seem to be that great a thing, yet, there you are.

comprehend a single word. He'd first been gifted to Lear by a Spanish duke because of his torrential dribbling and the ability to break wind that could darken a room, but when I discovered the Natural's keener talent, I took him as my apprentice to teach him the manly art of mirth.

Drool laughed. "Two fools well-hung—"

"Stop that!" I said. "It's unsettling." Unsettling indeed, to hear your own voice sluicing pitch-perfect out of that mountain of lout, stripped of wit and washed of irony. Two years I'd had Drool under my wing and I was still not inured to it. He meant no harm, it was simply his nature.

The anchoress at the abbey had taught me of nature, making me recite Aristotle: "It is the mark of an educated man, and a tribute to his culture, that he look for precision in a thing only as its *nature* allows." I would not have Drool reading Cicero or crafting clever riddles, but under my tutelage he had become more than fair at tumbling and juggling, could belch a song, and was, at court, at least as entertaining as a trained bear, with slightly less proclivity for eating the guests. With guidance, he would make a proper fool.

"Pocket is sad," said Drool. He patted my head, which was wildly irritating, not only because we were face-to-face—me standing, him sitting bum-to-floor—

but because it rang the bells of my coxcomb in a most melancholy manner.

"I'm not sad," said I. "I'm angry that you've been lost all morning."

"I weren't lost. I were right here, the whole time, having three laughs with Mary."

"Three?! You're lucky you two didn't burst into flames, you from friction and her from bloody thunderbolts of Jesus."

"Maybe four," said Drool.

"You do look the lost one, Pocket," said Mary. "Face like a mourning orphan what's been dumped in the gutter with the chamber pots."

"I'm preoccupied. The king has kept no company but Kent this last week, the castle is brimming with backstabbers, and there's a girl-ghost rhyming ominous on the battlements."

"Well, there's always a bloody ghost, ain't there?" Mary fished a shirt out of the cauldron and bobbed it across the room on her paddle like she was out for a stroll with her own sodden, steaming ghost. "You've got no cares but making everyone laugh, right?"

"Aye, carefree as a breeze. Leave that water when you're done, would you, Mary? Drool needs a dunking."

"Nooooooo!"

"Hush, you can't go before the court like that, you smell of shit. Did you sleep on the dung heap again last night?"

"It were warm."

I clouted him a good one on the crown with Jones. "Warm's not all, lad. If you want warm you can sleep in the great hall with everyone else."

"He ain't allowed," offered Mary. "Chamberlain[3] says his snoring frightens the dogs."

"Not allowed?" Every commoner who didn't have quarters slept on the floor in the great hall—strewn about willy-nilly on the straw and rushes—nearly dog-piled before the fireplace in winter. An enterprising fellow with night horns aloft and a predisposal to creep might find himself accidentally sharing a blanket or a tumble with a sleepy and possibly willing wench, and then be banished for a fortnight from the hall's friendly warmth (and indeed, I owe my own modest apartment above the barbican[4] to such nocturnal proclivity), but put out for *snoring*? Unheard of. When night's inky cape falls o'er the great

3. Chamberlain—a servant usually in charge of running a castle or household.

4. Barbican—a gatehouse, or extension of a castle wall beyond the gatehouse, used for defense of the main gate, often connected to a drawbridge.

hall, a gristmill it becomes, the machines of men's breath grind their dreams with a frightful roar, and even Drool's great gears fall undistinguished among the chorus. "For snoring? Not allowed in the hall? Balderdash!"

"And for having a wee on the steward's wife," Mary added.

"It were dark," explained Drool.

"Aye, and even in daylight she is easily mistaken for a privy, but have I not tutored you in the control of your fluids, lad?"

"Aye, and with great success," said Shanker Mary, rolling her eyes at the spunk-frosted wall.

"Ah, Mary, well said. Let's make a pact: If you do not make attempts at wit, I will refrain from becoming a soap-smelling prick-pull. What say ye?"

"You said you liked the smell of soap."

"Aye, well, speaking of smell. Drool, fetch some buckets of cold water from the well. We need to cool this kettle down and get you bathed."

"Nooooooo!"

"Jones will be very unhappy with you if you don't hurry," said I, brandishing Jones in a disapproving and somewhat threatening manner. A hard master is Jones, bitter, no doubt, from being raised as a puppet on a stick.

A half-hour later, a miserable Drool sat in the steaming cauldron, fully-clothed, his natural broth having turned the lye-white water to a rich, brown oaf-sauce. Shanker Mary stirred about him with her paddle, being careful not to stir him beyond suds to lust. I was quizzing my student on the coming night's entertainments.

"So, because Cornwall is on the sea, we shall portray the duke how, dear Drool?"

"As a sheep-shagger," said the despondent giant.

"No, lad, that's Albany. Cornwall shall be the fish-fucker."

"Aye, sorry, Pocket."

"Not a worry, not a worry. You'll still be sodden from your bath, I suspect, so we'll work that into the jest. Bit of sloshing and squishing will but add to the merriment, and if we can thus imply that Princess Regan is herself, a fishlike consort, well I can't think of anyone who won't be amused."

" 'Cepting the princess," said Mary.

"Well, yes, but she is very literal-minded and often has to be explained the thrust of the jest a time or two before lending her appreciation."

"Aye, remedial thrusting's the remedy for Regan's stubborn wit," said the puppet Jones.

"Aye, remedial thrusting's the remedy for Regan's stubborn wit," said Drool in Jones's voice.

"You're dead men," sighed Shanker Mary.

"You're a dead man, knave!" said a man's voice from behind me.

And there stood Edmund, bastard son of Gloucester, blocking the only exit, sword in hand. Dressed all in black, was the bastard: a simple silver brooch secured his cape, the hilts of his sword and dagger were silver dragon heads with emerald eyes. His jet beard was trimmed to points. I do admire the bastard's sense of style—simple, elegant, and evil. He owns his darkness.

I, myself, am called the Black Fool. Not because I am a Moor, although I hold no grudge toward them (Moors are said to be talented wife-stranglers) and would take no offense at the moniker were that the case, but my skin is as snowy as any sun-starved son of England. No, I am called so because of my wardrobe, an argyle of black satin and velvet diamonds—not the rainbow motley of the run-a-day fool. Lear said: "After thy black wit shall be thy dress, fool. Perhaps a new outfit will stop you tweaking Death's nose. I'm short for the grave as it is, boy, no need to anger the worms before my arrival." When even a king fears irony's twisted blade, what fool is ever unarmed?

"Draw your weapon, fool!" said Edmund.

"Sadly, sir, I have none," said I. Jones shook his head in un-armed woe.

We both were lying, of course. Across the small of my back I wore three wickedly-pointed throwing daggers—fashioned for me by the armorer to be used in our entertainments—and while I had never used them as weapons, truly flung they had spitted apples off the head of Drool, nipped plums from his outstretched fingers, and yea, even speared grapes out of the air. I had little doubt that one might find its way into Edmund's eye and thus vent his bitter mind like a lanced boil. If he needed to know he would know soon enough. If not, well, why trouble him?

"If not a fight, then a murder it is," said Edmund. He lunged, his blade aimed for my heart. I sidestepped and knocked his blade away with Jones, who lost a bell from his coxcomb for his trouble.

I hopped up onto the lip of the cauldron.

"But, sir, why spend your wrath on a poor, helpless fool?"

Edmund slashed. I leapt. He missed. I landed on the far side of the cauldron. Drool moaned. Mary hid in the corner.

"You shouted bastard at me from the battlements."

"Aye, they announced you as bastard. You, sir, are a bastard. And a bastard most unjust to make me die with the foul taste of truth still on my tongue. Allow me a lie before you strike: You have such kind eyes."

"But you spoke badly of my mother as well." He put himself between me and the door. Bloody bad planning, building a laundry with only one exit.

"I may have implied that she was a poxy whore, but from what your father says, that, too, is not breaking the bonds of verity."

"What?" asked Edmund.

"What?" asked Drool, a perfect parrot of Edmund.

"What?" inquired Mary.

"It's true, you git! Your mother *was* a poxy whore!"

"Beggin' your pardon, sir, poxiness ain't so bad," said Shanker Mary, shining a ray of optimism on these dark ages. "Unfairly maligned, the poxy are. Methinks a spot o' the pox implies experience. Worldliness, if you will."

"The tart makes an excellent point, Edmund. But for the slow descent into madness and death with your bits dropping off along the way, the pox is a veritable blessing," said I, as I skipped just out of blade's reach from the bastard, who stalked me around the great cauldron. "Take Mary here. In fact, there's an idea. Take Mary. Why spend your energy after a long journey murdering a speck of a fool when you can enjoy the pleasures of a lusty wench who is not only ready, but willing, and smells pleasantly of soap?"

"Aye," said Drool, expelling froth as he spoke. "She's a bloody vision of loveliness."

Edmund let his sword point drop and looked at Drool for the first time. "Are you eating soap?"

"Just a wee sliver," bubbled Drool. "They weren't saving it."

Edmund turned back to me. "Why are you boiling this fellow?"

"Couldn't be helped," said I. (How dramatic, the bastard, the water was barely steaming. What appeared to be boiling was Drool venting vapors.)

"Common fuckin' courtesy, ain't it?" said Mary.

"Speak straight, both of you." The bastard wheeled on one heel and before I knew what was happening, he had the point of his blade at Mary's throat. "I've been nine years in the Holy Land killing Saracens, killing one or two more makes no difference to me."

"Wait!" I leapt back to the lip of the cauldron, reaching to the small of my back with my free hand. "Wait. He's being punished. By the king. For attacking me."

"Punished? For attacking a fool?"

" 'Boil him alive,' the king said." I jumped down to Edmund's side of the cauldron—moved toward the doorway. I'd needed a clear line of sight, and should he move, I didn't want the blade to hit Mary.

"Everyone knows how fond the king is of his dark little fool," said Mary, nodding enthusiastically.

"Bollocks!" shouted Edmund, as he pulled the sword back to slash.

Mary screamed. I flipped a dagger in the air, caught it by the blade, and was readying to send it to Edmund's heart when something hit him in the back of the head with a thud and he went bum over eyebrows into the wall, his blade clanging across the floor to my feet.

Drool had stood up in the cauldron and was holding Mary's laundry paddle—a bit of dark hair and bloody scalp clung to the bleached wood.

"Did you see that, Pocket? Smashing fall he did." All of it a pantomime to Drool.

Edmund was not moving. As far as I could see, he was not breathing either.

"God's bloody balls, Drool, you've kilt the earl's son. We'll all be hung, now."

"But he were going to hurt Mary."

Mary sat on the floor by Edmund's prostrate body and began stroking his hair on a spot where there was no blood. "I was going to shag him docile, too."

"He would have killed you without a thought."

"Ah, blokes have their tempers, don't they? Look at him, he's a fair form of a fellow, innit he? And rich, too." She took something from his pocket. "What's this?"

"Well done, lass, not so much as a comma between grief and robbery, and much the better when he's still so fresh his fleas have not sailed to livelier ports. The Church wears well on you."

"No, I'm not robbing. Look, it's a letter."

"Give it here."

"You can read?" The tart's eyes widened as if I had confessed the ability to turn lead into gold.

"I was raised in a nunnery, wench. I am a walking library of learning—bound in comely leather and suitable for stroking—at your service, should you fancy a bit of culture to go with your lack of breeding, or vice versa, of course."

Then Edmund gasped and stirred.

"Oh fuckstockings. The bastard's alive."

3.

Our Darker Purpose[1]

Well this is a downy lot of goose toss if I've ever read it," said I. I sat on the bastard's back, cross-legged, reading the letter he'd written to his father. " '*And my lord must understand how unjust it is that I, the issue of true passion, is shorn of respect and position while deference is given my half brother, who is the product of a bed made of duty and drudgery.*' "

"It's true," said the bastard. "Am I not as true of shape, as sharp of mind, a—"

"You're a whiny little wanker,[2] is what you are," said I, my brashness perhaps spurred by the weight of Drool, who was sitting on the bastard's legs. "What did

1. *King Lear*, Act I, Scene 1, King Lear.

2. Wanker—one who wanks, a tosser.

you think you would possibly gain by giving this letter to your father?"

"That he might relent and give me half my brother's title and inheritance."

"Because your mother was a better boff than Edgar's? You're a bastard *and* an idiot."

"You could not know, little man."

It was tempting then, to clout the knave across the head with Jones, or better, slit his throat with his own sword, but as much as the king might favor me, he favors the order of his power more. The murder of Gloucester's son, no matter how deserved, would not go unpunished. But I was fast on my way to fool's funeral anyway if I let the bastard up before his anger cooled. I'd sent Shanker Mary away in hope that any wrath that fell might pass her by. I needed a threat to stay Edmund's hand, but I had none. I am the least powerful of all about the court. My only influence is raising others' ire.

"I do know what it is to be deprived by the accident of birth, Edmund."

"We are not the same. You are as common as field dirt. I am not."

"I could not know then, Edmund, what it is to have my title cast as an insult? If I call you bastard, and you call me fool, can we answer as men?"

"No riddles, fool. I can't feel my feet."

"Why would you want to feel your feet? Is that more of the debauchery of the ruling class I hear so much about? So blessed are you with access to the flesh's pleasures that you have to devise ingenious perversions to get your withered, inbred plumbing to come to attention—need to feel your feet and whip the stable boy with a dead rabbit to scratch your scurvy, libidinous itch, is it?"

"What are you on about, fool? I can't feel my feet because there's a great oaf sitting on my legs."

"Oh. Quite right, sorry. Drool, lift off a bit, but don't let him up." I climbed from the bastard's back and walked to the laundry doorway where he could see me. "What you want is property and title. Do you imagine that you will get it by begging?"

"The letter's not begging."

"You want your brother's fortune. How much better would a letter from *him* convince your father of your worth?"

"He would never write such a letter, and besides, he does not play for favor, it is his already."

"Then perhaps the problem is moving favor from Edgar to you. The right letter from him would do it. A letter wherein he confesses his impatience with waiting for his inheritance, and asks for your help in usurping your father."

"You're mad, fool. Edgar would never write such a letter."

"I didn't say he would. Do you have anything written in his hand?"

"I do, a letter of credit he was to grant to a wool merchant in Barking Upminster."

"Do you, sweet bastard, know what a scriptorium is?"

"Aye, it's a place in the monastery where they copy documents—bibles and such."

"And so my accident of birth is the remedy of yours, for because I hadn't even one parent to lay claim to me, I was brought up in a nunnery that had just such a scriptorium, where, yes, they taught a boy to copy documents, but for our darker purpose, they taught him to copy it in exactly the hand that he found on the page, and the one before that, and the one before that. Letter to letter, stroke for stroke, the same hand as a man long gone to the grave."

"So you are a skilled forger? If you were raised in a nunnery how is it you are a fool and not a monk or a priest?"

"How is it that you, the son of an earl, must plead mercy from under the arse of an enormous nitwit? We're all Fate's bastards. Shall we compose a letter, Edmund?"

I'm sure I would have become a monk, but for the anchoress. The closest to court I would have come would have been praying for the forgiveness of some noble's war crimes. Was I not reared for the monastic life from the moment Mother Basil found me squirming on the steps of the abbey at Dog Snogging[3] on the Ouze?

I never knew my parents, but Mother Basil told me once that she thought my mother might have been a madwoman from the local village who had drowned in the river Ouze shortly after I appeared on the doorstep. If that were so, the abbess told me, then my mother had been touched by God (like the Natural) and so I was given to the abbey as God's special child.

The nuns, most of whom were of noble birth, second and third daughters who could not find a noble husband, doted on me like a new puppy. So tiny was I that the abbess would carry me with her in her apron pocket, and thus I was given the name of Pocket. Little Pocket of Dog Snogging Abbey. I was much the novelty, the only male in that all-female world, and the nuns competed to see who might carry me in their apron pocket, although I do not remember it. Later, after I learned

3. Snogging, to snog—kissing, making out, swapping spit, sucking face.

to walk, they would stand me on the table at mealtime and have me parade up and down waving my winky at them, a unique appendage in those feminine environs. I was seven before I realized that you could eat breakfast with your pants on. Still, I always felt separate from the rest of them, a different creature, isolated.

I was allowed to sleep on the floor in the abbess's chambers, as she had a woven rug given her by the bishop. On cold nights I was permitted to sleep under her covers to keep her feet warm, unless one of the other nuns had joined her for that purpose.

Mother Basil and I were constant companions, even after I grew out of her marsupial affection. I attended the masses and prayers with her every day from as long as I could remember. How I loved watching her shave every morning after sunup, stropping her razor on a leather strap and carefully scraping the blue-black whiskers from her face. She would show me how to shave the little spot under your nose, and how she pulled aside the skin on her neck, so as not to nick her Adam's apple. But she was a stern mistress, and I had to pray every three hours like all the other nuns, as well as carry water for her bath, chop wood, scrub floors, work in the garden, as well as take lessons in maths, catechism, Latin and Greek, and calligraphy. By the time I was nine I could read and write three languages and recite *The Lives of the Saints* from memory. I lived to serve God and the nuns of Dog Snogging, hoping that one day I might be ordained as a priest myself.

And I might have, but then one day workmen came to the abbey, stonecutters and masons, and in a matter of days they had built a cell off of one of the abandoned passages in the rectory. We were going to have our very own anchorite, or in our case, anchoress. An acolyte so devoted to God that she would be walled up in a cell with only a small opening through which she would be passed food and water, and there she would spend the rest of her life, literally part of the church, praying and dispensing wisdom to the people of the village through her window until she was taken into the bosom of the Lord. Next to being martyred, it was the most holy act of devotion a person could perform.

Daily I crept out of Mother Basil's quarters to check on the progress of the cell, hoping to somehow bask in the glory that would be bestowed upon the anchoress. But as the walls rose, I saw there was no window left to the outside, no place for the villagers to receive blessings, as was the custom.

"Our anchoress will be very special," Mother Basil explained in her steady baritone voice. "So devout is she that she will only lay eyes on those who bring her food. She will not be distracted from her prayers for the king's salvation."

"She is the charge of the king?"

"No other," said Mother Basil. The rest of us were bound by payment to pray for the forgiveness of the Earl of Sussex, who had slaughtered thousands of innocents in the last war with the Belgians and was bound to toast on the coals of Hell unless we could fulfill his penance, which had been pronounced by the Pope himself to be seven million Hail Marys per peasant. (Even with a dispensation and a half-price coupon purchased at Lourdes, the earl was getting no more than a thousand Hail Marys to the penny, so Dog Snogging was becoming a very rich monastery on his sins.) But our anchoress would answer for the sins of the king himself. He was said to have perpetrated some jollygood wickedness, so her prayers must be very potent indeed.

"Please, Mother, please let me take food to the anchoress."

"No one is to see or speak to her."

"But someone has to take her food. Let me do it. I promise not to look."

"I shall consult the Lord."

I never saw the anchoress arrive. The rumor simply passed that she was in the abbey and the workmen had set the stones around her. Week's went by with me begging the abbess to allow me the holy duty of feeding the anchoress, but it was not until one evening when Mother Basil needed to spend the night alone with young sister Mandy, praying in private for the forgiveness of what the abbess called a "Smashing Horny Weekender," that I was allowed to attend to the anchoress.

"In fact," said the Reverend Mother, "you stay there, outside her cell until morning, and see if you can learn some piety. Don't come back until morning. Late morning. And bring tea and a couple of scones with you when you come back. And some jam."

I thought I would burst, I was so excited when I first made my way down that long, dark hallway— carrying a plate of cheese and bread, and a flagon of ale. I half expected to see the glory of God shining through the window, but when I got there, it wasn't a window at all, but an arrow loop, like in a castle wall, cut in the shape of a cross, the edges tapered so that the broad stone came to a point at the opening. It was as if the masons only knew one window they could put in a thick wall. (Funny that arrow loops and sword hilts, mechanisms of death, form the sign of the cross—a symbol of mercy—but on second thought, I guess it was a mechanism of death in itself.) The opening was barely wide enough to pass the flagon through; the plate would just fit through at the cross. I waited. No light came from inside the cell. A single candle on the wall across from the opening was the only illumination.

I was terrified. I listened, to see if I could hear the anchoress reciting novenas. There wasn't even the sound of breathing. Was she sleeping? What kind of sin was it to interrupt the prayers of someone so holy? I put the plate and ale on the floor and tried to peer into the darkness of the cell, perhaps see her glow.

Then I saw it. The dim sparkle of the candle reflecting in an eye. She was sitting there, not two feet from the opening. I jumped back against the far wall, knocking over the ale on the way.

"Did I frighten you?" came a woman's voice.

"No. No, I was just, I am—forgive me. I am awed by your piety."

Then she laughed. It was sad laughter, as if it had been held a long time and then let out in almost a sob, but she was laughing and I was confused.

"I'm sorry, mistress—"

"No, no, no, don't be sorry. Don't you dare be sorry, boy."

"I'm not. I won't be."

"What is your name?"

"Pocket, mum."

"Pocket," she repeated, and she laughed some more. "You've spilled my ale, Pocket."

"Aye, mum. Shall I fetch you some more?"

"If you don't want the glory of my bloody godliness burning us both down, you better had, hadn't you, friend Pocket? And when you come back, I want you to tell me a story that will make me laugh."

"Yes, mum,"

And that was the day that my world changed.

Remind me, why is it we're not just murdering my brother?" asked Edmund. From whimpering scribblings to conspiracy to murder in the course of an hour, Edmund was a quick study when it came to villainy.

I sat, quill in hand, at the table in my small apartment above the great gatehouse in the outer wall of the castle. I have my own fireplace, a table, two stools, a bed, a cupboard for my things, a hook for my coxcomb and clothes, and in the middle of my room a large cauldron for heating and pouring boiling oil upon a siege force through gutters in the floor. But for the clanking of the massive chains when the drawbridge is raised or lowered, it is a cozy den in which to pursue slumber or other horizontal sport. Best of all, it is private, with a thumping big bolt on the door. Even among the nobles, privacy is rare, as conspiracy thrives there.

"While that is an attractive course, unless Edgar is disgraced, disinherited, and his properties willfully given to you, the lands and title could pass to some legitimate cousin, or worse, your father might set about trying to sire a new legitimate heir."

I shuddered a bit then—along with, I'm sure, a dozen maidens about the kingdom—at the mental vision of Gloucester's withered flanks, bared and about the business of making an heir upon their nubile nobility. They would be clawing at the nunnery door to escape the honor.

"I hadn't thought of that," said Edmund.

"Really, you, not think? How shocking. Although a simple poisoning does seem cleaner, the letter is the sharper sword." If I gave the scoundrel proper rope, perhaps he could hang for both our purposes. "I can craft such a letter, subtle, yet condemning. You'll be the Earl of Gloucester before you can get dirt shoveled on your father's still twitching body. But the letter may not do all."

"Speak your mind, fool. As much as I'd love to silence your yammering, speak."

"The king favors your father *and* your brother, which is why they were called here. If Edgar becomes betrothed to Cordelia, which could happen before the morrow—well, with the princess's dowry in hand, there'll be no cause for him to resort to the treachery we are about to craft around him. You'll be left with your fangs showing, noble Edmund, and the legitimate son will be all the richer."

"I'll see he is not betrothed to Cordelia."

"How? Will you tell him horrid things? I have it on good authority that her feet are like ferryboats. They strap them up under her gown to keep them from flapping when she walks."

"I will see to it that there is no marriage, little man, don't you worry. But you must see to this letter. Tomorrow Edgar goes on to Barking to deliver the letters of credit and I'll return to Gloucester with my father. I'll let the letter slip to him then, so his anger has time to fester in Edgar's absence."

"Quick, before I waste parchment, promise you'll not let Edgar marry Cordelia."

"Fine, fool, promise you'll not tell anyone that you ever penned this letter, and I will."

"I promise," said I. "By the balls of Venus."

"Then, so do I," said the bastard.

"All right, then," said I, dipping my quill in ink, "although murder would be a simpler plan." I've never cared for the bastard's brother Edgar, either. Earnest and open-faced is he. I don't trust anyone who appears so trustworthy. They must be up to something. Of course, Edmund hanging black-tongued for his brother's murder would make for a festive chandelier as well. A fool does enjoy a party.

In a half-hour I had crafted a letter so wily and peppered with treachery that any father might strangle his son at the sight of it and, if childless, bastinade his own bollocks with a war hammer to discourage conspirators yet to be born. It was a masterpiece of both forgery and manipulation. I blotted it well and held it up for Edmund to see.

"I'll need your dagger, sir," said I.

Edmund reached for the letter and I danced away from him. "First the knife, good bastard."

Edmund laughed. "Take my dagger, fool. You're no safer, I still have my sword."

"Aye, which I handed you myself. I need your dagger to razor the seal off that letter of credit so I may affix it to this missive of ours. You'll need to break it only in your father's presence, as if you yourself are only then discovering your brother's black nature."

"Oh," said Edmund.

He gave me the knife. I performed the deed with sealing wax and candle and handed the blade back with the letter. (Could I have used one of my own knives for the task? Of course, but it was not time for Edmund to know of them.)

The letter was barely in his pocket before Edmund had drawn his sword and had it leveled at my throat. "I think I can assure your silence better than a promise."

I didn't move. "So, you lament being born out of favor, what favor will you court by killing the king's fool? A dozen guards saw you come in here."

"I'll take my chances."

Just then the great chains that ran through my room began to shake, rattling as if a hundred suffering prisoners were shackled to them rather than a slab of oak and iron. Edmund looked around and I scampered to the far side of the room. Wind rushed through the arrow loops that served as my windows and extinguished the candle I had used for the sealing wax. The bastard spun to face the arrow loops and the room went dark, as if a cape had been thrown over the day. The golden form of a woman shimmered in the air at the dark wall.

The ghost said,

"A thousand years of torture rule,
The knave who dares to harm a fool."

I could only see Edmund by the glow of the spirit, but he was moving crablike toward the door that led out onto the west wall, reaching frantically for the latch. Then he threw the bolt and was through the door in an instant. Light filled my little apartment and I could again view the Thames through the slits in the stone.

"Well rhymed, wisp," said I to the empty air. "Well rhymed."

4.

The Dragon and His Wrath[1]

D on't despair, lad," I said to Taster. "It's not as grim as it looks. The bastard will stay Edgar and I'm relatively sure that France and Burgundy are buggering each other and would never let a princess come between them—although I'll wager they'd borrow her wardrobe were it not guarded—so the day is saved. Cordelia will remain in the White Tower to torment me as always."

We were in an antechamber off the great hall. Taster sat, head in hands, looking paler than normal, a mountain of food piled before him on the table.

"The king doesn't like dates, does he?" asked Taster. "Not likely he'll eat any of the dates that were brought as gifts, right?"

1. *King Lear*, Act I, Scene 1, King Lear.

"Did Goneril or Regan gift them?"

"Aye, a whole larder they brought with them."

"Sorry, lad, you've work ahead, then. How it is you're not as fat as a friar, with all you're required to eat, is beyond me."

"Bubble says I must have a city of worms living up my bum, but that ain't it. I've a secret, if you won't tell anyone—"

"Go on lad, I'm hardly paying attention."

"What about him?" He nodded to Drool, who was sitting in the corner petting one of the castle cats.

"Drool," I called, "is Taster's secret safe with you?"

"As dim as a snuffed candle, he is," said the git in my voice. "Telling a secret to Drool is like casting ink in the night sea."

"See there," said I.

"Well," said Taster, looking around as if anyone would want to be in our miserable company. "I'm sick a lot."

"Of course you are, it's the bloody Dark Ages, everyone has the plague or the pox. It's not like you're leprous and dropping fingers and toes like rose petals, is it?"

"No, not sick like that. I just vomit nearly every time I eat."

"So you're a little chunder-monkey. Not to worry, Taster, you keep it down long enough for it to kill you, don't you?"

"I reckon." He nibbled at a stuffed date.

"Duty done, then. All's well that ends well. But back to my concerns: Do you think France and Burgundy are poofters,[2] or are they, you know, just fucking French?"

"I've never even seen them," Taster said.

"Oh, quite right. What about you, Drool? Drool? Stop that!"

Drool pulled the damp kitten out of his mouth. "But it were licking me first. You said it was only proper manners—"

"I was talking about something completely different. Put the cat down."

The heavy door creaked open and the Earl of Kent slipped into the room, as stealthy as a church bell rolling down stairs. Kent's a broad-shouldered bull of a fellow, and while he moves with great strength for his grandfather years, Grace and Subtlety remain blushing virgins in his retinue.

"There you are, boy."

"What boy?" said I. "I see no boy here." True, I only stand to Kent's shoulder, and it would take two of me and a suckling pig to balance him on a scale, but even a fool requires some respect, except from the king, of course.

2. Poofter—homosexual.

"Fine, fine. I just wanted to tell you not to make sport of feebleness nor age tonight. The king's been brooding all week about 'crawling unburdened to the grave.' I think it's the weight of his sins."

"Well, if he weren't so dog-fuckingly old there would be no temptation toward mirth, would there? Not my fault, that."

Kent grinned then. "Pocket, you would not willfully hurt your master."

"Aye, Kent, and with Goneril and Regan and their lords in the hall there'll be no need to jest geriatric. Is that why the king has kept company only with you this week, brooding upon his years? He hasn't been planning on marrying off Cordelia then?"

"He's spoken of it, but only as part of his entire legacy, of property and history. He seemed set on a course to hold the kingdom steady when I last left him. He bade me leave while he gave private audience to the bastard, Edmund."

"He's talking to Edmund? Alone?"

"Aye. The bastard drew on his father's years of service for the favor."

"I must go to the king. Kent, stay here with Drool, if you would. There's food and drink to hold you. Taster, show good Kent the best of those dates. Taster? Taster? Drool, shake Taster, he appears to have fallen asleep."

Fanfare sounded then, a single anemic trumpet, the other three trumpeters having recently succumbed to herpes. (A sore on the lip is as bad as an arrow in the eye to a trumpeter. The chancellor had them put down, or maybe they'd just been made drummers. They weren't blowing bloody fanfare, that's all I'm saying.)

Drool put down his kitten and climbed to his feet.

"With grave offense to daughters three,

Alas, the king a fool shall be," said the giant in a lilting female voice.

"Where did you hear that, Drool? Who said that?"

"Pretty," said Drool, massaging the air with his great meaty paws as if caressing a woman's breasts.

"Time to go," said Kent. The old warrior threw open the door into the hall.

They stood all around the great table—round after the tradition of some long forgotten king—the center open to the floor where servants served, orators orated, and Drool and I performed. Kent took his place near the king's throne. I stood with some yeomen to the side of the fire and motioned for Drool to find a place to hide behind one of the stone pillars that supported the vault. Fools do not have a place at the table. Most times I served at the foot of the king, providing quips, criticisms, and brilliant observations through the meal, but only after he had called for me. Lear had not called for a week.

He came into the room head up, scowling at each of his guests until his eye lit on Cordelia and he smiled. He motioned for everyone to sit and they did.

"Edmund," said the king, "fetch the princes of France and Burgundy."

Edmund bowed to the king and backed toward the main entrance of the hall, then looked to me, winked, and motioned for me to come join him. Dread rose in my chest like a black serpent. What had the bastard done? I should have cut his throat when I'd had the chance.

I sidled down the side wall, the bells on the tips of my shoes conspicuously unhelpful in concealing my movement. The king looked to me, then away, as if the sight of me might cause rot on his eye.

Once through the door Edmund pulled me roughly aside. The big yeoman at the threshold lowered the blade of his halberd an inch and frowned at the bastard. Edmund released me and looked bewildered, as if his own hand had betrayed him.

(I bring food and drink to the guards when they are on post during feasts. I believe it is written in the *Obfuscations of St. Pesto:* "In nine cases out of ten, a large friend with a poleax shall truly a blessing be.")

"What have you wrought, bastard?" I whispered with great fury and no little spit.

"Only what you wanted, fool. Your princess will have no husband, that I can assure, but even your sorceries won't keep you safe if you reveal my strategy."

"My sorceries? What? Oh, the ghost."

"Yes, the ghost, and the bird. When I was crossing the battlement, a raven called me a tosser and shat on my shoulder."

"Right, my minions are everywhere," said I, "and you're right to fear my canny mastery of the heavenly orbs and command of spirits and whatnot. But lest I unleash something unpleasant upon you, tell me, what did you say to the king?"

Edmund smiled then, which I found more unsettling than his blade. "I heard the princesses speaking amongst themselves about their affections for their father earlier in the day, and was enlightened to their character. I merely hinted to the king that he might ease his burden with the same knowledge."

"What knowledge?"

"Go find out, fool. I'm off to fetch Cordelia's suitors."

And he was away. The guard held the door and I slipped back into the hall and to a spot near the table.

The king, it seemed, had only then finished a roll call of sorts, naming each of his friends and family at court, proclaiming his affection for each, and in the cases of Kent and Gloucester, recalling their long history of battles and conquests together. Bent, white-haired, and slight is the king, but there is a cold fire in his eye still—his visage puts one in mind of a hunting bird fresh unhooded and set for its kill.

"I am old, and my burdens of responsibility and property weigh heavily on me, so to avoid conflict in the future, I propose to divide my kingdom among younger strengths now, so I may crawl to the grave light of heart."

"What better than a light-hearted grave crawl?" I said softly to Cornwall, villainous twat that he is. I crouched between him and his duchess, Regan. Princess Regan: tall, fair, raven-haired, with a weakness for plunging red velvet gowns and another for rascals, both grievous faults had they not played out so pleasurably for this teller of tales.

"Oh, Pocket, did you get the stuffed dates I sent you?" Regan asked.

And generous to a fault as well.

"Shhhhhh, bunny cunny," I shushed. "Father is speaking."

Cornwall drew his dagger and I moved along the table to Goneril's side.

Lear went on: "These properties and powers I will divide between my sons-in-law, the Duke of Albany and the Duke of Cornwall, and that suitor who takes the hand of my beloved Cordelia, but so I may determine who shall have the most bounteous share, I ask of my daughters: Which of you loves me most? Goneril, my eldest born, speak first."

"No pressure, pumpkin," I whispered.

"I have this, fool," she snapped, and with a great smile and no little grace, she made her way around the outside of the round table and to the opening at the center, bowing to each of the guests as she went. She is shorter and rather more round than her sisters, more generously padded in bosom and bustle, her eyes a grey sky short of emerald, her hair a yellow sun short of ginger. Her smile falls on the eye like water on the tongue of a thirst-mad sailor.

I slid into her chair. "A handsome creature is she," I said to the Duke of Albany. "That one breast, the way it juts a bit to the side—when she's naked, I mean— does that bother you at all? Make you wonder what it's looking at over there—bit like a wall-eyed man you think is always talkin' to someone else?"

"Hush, fool," Albany said. He is nearly a score years older than Goneril, goatish and dull, methinks, but somewhat less of a scoundrel than the average noble. I do not loathe him.

"Mind you, it's obviously part of the pair, not some breast-errant off on a quest of its own. I like a bit of asymmetry in a woman—makes me suspicious when Nature's too evenhanded—fearful symmetry and all. But it's not like you're shaggin' a hunchback or anything—I mean, once she's on 'er back it's hard to get either one of them to look you in the eye, innit?"

"Shut up!" barked Goneril, having turned her back on her father—which one is never supposed to do—in order to scold me. Bloody clumsy etiquette that.

"Sorry. Go on," said I, waving her on with Jones, who jingled gaily.

"Sir," she addressed the king, "I love you more than words can say. I love you more than eyesight, space, and liberty. I love you beyond anything that can be valued, rich or rare. No less than life itself, with grace, health, beauty, and honor. As much as any child or father has loved, so I love thee. A love that takes my breath away and makes me scarcely able to speak. I love you above all things, even pie."

"Oh bollocks!"

Who had said it? I was relatively sure it was not my voice, as it hadn't come from the normal hole in my face, and Jones had been silent as well. Cordelia? I scooted out of Goneril's chair and scampered to the junior princess's side, staying low to avoid attention or flying cutlery.

"Bloody buggering bollocks!" said Cordelia.

Lear, refreshed from his shower of flowered bullshit, said, "What?"

I stood then. "Well, sirrah, lovable as thou art, the lady's profession strains credibility. It's no secret how much the bitch loves pie." I crouched again quickly.

"Silence, fool! Chamberlain, bring me the map."

The distraction had worked, the king's ire had turned from Cordelia to me. She took the opportunity to poke me in the earlobe with her fork.

"Ouch!" Whispered, yet emphatic. "Tart."

"Knave."

"Harpy."

"Rodent."

"Whore."

"Whoremonger."

"Do you have to pay to be a whoremonger? Because strictly speaking—"

"Shhh," she said, grinning. She poked me in the ear again, then nodded toward the king, that we should pay attention.

The king pointed to the map with a bejeweled dagger. "All these lands, from here to here, with rich farmlands, bounteous rivers, and deep forests, I do grant to Goneril and her husband, Albany, and to their offspring in perpetuity. Now, we must hear from our second daughter. Dearest Regan, wife to Cornwall. Speak."

Regan made her way to the center floor, looking down at her older sister, Goneril, as she passed, as if to say, "I'll show you."

She raised her arms out to her sides, trailing the long, velvet sleeves down to the floor so she described the shape of a grand and bosomy crucifix. She looked to the ceiling as if drawing inspiration from the heavenly orbs themselves, then pronounced: "What she said."

"Huh?" said the king, and verily "huh" was echoed around the room.

Regan seemed to realize that she should probably go on. "My sister has expressed my thoughts exactly—as if she may have looked at my notes even before we here entered. Except I love thee more. In the list of all senses, all fall short, and I am touched by nothing but your love." She bowed then, looking up a bit to see if anyone was buying it.

"I'm going to be sick," said Cordelia, probably louder than was really necessary, as were the coughing and gagging noises she perpetrated thereafter.

Deflecting, I stood and said, "She's been touched by a bit more than his majesty's love, I dare say. I mean, in this very room I can name—"

The king shot me his best *Must I chop off your head?* look and I fell silent. He nodded and looked to the map. "To Regan and Cornwall I leave this third of

the kingdom, no smaller or less valuable than that bestowed upon Goneril. Now, Cordelia, our joy, who is
courted by so many eligible young nobles, what can you
say to receive a third more opulent than your sisters?"

Cordelia stood at her chair, not making her way to
the middle of the room as her sisters had. "Nothing,"
she said.

"Nothing?" asked the king.

"Nothing."

"You'll get nothing for nothing," said Lear. "Speak
again."

"Well, you can't blame her, really, can you?" I in-
terjected. "I mean you've given all the good bits to
Goneril and Regan, haven't you? What's left, a bit of
Scotland rocky enough to starve a sheep and this poxy
river near Newcastle?" I'd taken the liberty of going
over to the map. "I'd say nothing is a fair start for bargaining. You should counter with Spain, majesty."

Now Cordelia moved to the center of the room.
"I'm sorry, Father, that I can't heave my heart into my
mouth like my sisters. I love you according to my bond
as a daughter, no more, no less."

"Be careful what you say, Cordelia," said Lear.
"Your dowry is draining away with every word."

"My lord, you have sired me, raised me, and loved
me. I return those duties back, as is proper: I obey you,

love you, and most honor you. But how can my sisters say they love you above all? They have husbands. Don't they have to reserve some love for them?"

"Yes, but have you met their husbands?" said I. There was growling from various points around the table. How can you call yourself a noble if you'll just start growling for no reason. Uncivilized, it is.

"When I shall marry, you can rest assured that my husband will get at least half my care and half my love as well. To say anything else I'd be lying to you."

This was Edmund's doing, I was sure of it. Somehow he'd known that Cordelia would answer this way and had convinced the king to ask the question. And she did not know that her father had been wrestling with his own mortality and worth for the week. I hopped over to the princess and whispered, "Lying now would be the better part of valor. Repent later. Throw the old gent a bone, lass."

"So this is how you feel?" asked the king.

"Aye, my lord. It is."

"So young and so untender," said Lear.

"So young, my lord, and true," said Cordelia.

"So young, and so bloody stupid," said the puppet Jones.

"Fine, child. So be it. Let your truth be your dowry, then. For by the radiance of the sun, the dark of the night, all the saints, the Holy Mother, the orbs of the sky, and Nature herself, I disown you."

In his spirituality Lear is—well—flexible. When pressed for a curse or a blessing he will sometimes invoke gods from a half-dozen pantheons, just to be sure to catch the ear of whichever might be on watch that day.

"No property, land, or title shall be yours. Cannibals of darkest Merica, who would sell their own young in the meat market, shall be closer to me than you, my used-to-be daughter."

I wondered about that. No one had ever seen a Merican, being as they are mythical. Legend goes that in the name of profit they did sell the limbs of their own children as food—that was before they burned the world, of course. Since I didn't expect a state visit from the merchant cannibals of the apocalypse anytime soon, it appeared my liege was either herniating the metaphor or speaking the tongue of a frothing nutter.

Kent stood then. "My liege!"

"Sit down, Kent!" the king barked. "Come not between the dragon and his wrath. I loved her the best, and hoped that she would take care of me in my dotage, but since she doesn't love me enough, only in the grave will there be peace for Lear."

Cordelia looked more confused than hurt. "But, Father—"

"Out of my sight! Where is France? Where is Burgundy? Finish this business! Goneril, Regan, your younger sister's share of the kingdom shall be divided between you. Let Cordelia marry her own pride. Cornwall and Albany shall divide the power and property of a king evenly. I shall retain only my title and enough of a stipend to maintain one hundred knights and their carriers. You shall keep me from month to month in your own castles, but the kingdom shall be yours."

"Royal Lear, this is madness!" Kent again, now making his way around the table to the center floor.

"Careful, Kent," said Lear. "The bow of my anger is bent, don't make me loose the arrow."

"Loose it if you must. You'd kill me for being bold enough to tell you that you're mad? The best of loyalty is that a loyal man has the courage to speak plainly when his leader moves to folly. Reverse your decision, sir. Your youngest daughter doesn't love you least because she's quiet, any more than those who speak loudest are the most sincere."

The older sisters and their husbands were on their feet at that. Kent glared at them.

"No more, Kent," the king warned. "On your life, not another word."

"What has my life ever been, but a thing I risked in service for you? Protecting you? Threaten my life as you will, it will not stop me from telling you that you do wrong, sir!"

Lear started to draw his sword then and I knew he had truly lost all sense of judgment, if turning on his favorite daughter and closest advisor and friend hadn't shown it already. If Kent decided to defend himself he'd go through the old man like a scythe through a wheat straw. It was unfolding too fast, even for a fool to stay the king's blade with wit. I could only watch. But Albany moved quickly down the table and stayed the king's hand, pushing his sword back down into the scabbard.

Kent grinned then, the old bear, and I saw that he wouldn't have drawn blade on the old man at all. He would have died to make his point to the king. What's more, Lear knew it, too, but there was no mercy in his eye and the madness had gone cold. He shook himself free of Albany's grasp, and the duke backed away.

When Lear spoke again his voice was low, restrained, but palsied with hate: "Hear me, thou traitorous ferret. No one challenges my authority, my decisions, or my vows—to do so on British land is death, and in the rest of the known world is war. I'll not have it. Your years of service noted, I give you your life, but only your life, and never again in my sight. You have five days, Kent, to provision yourself, and on the sixth day, turn your back on our kingdom forever. If twelve days pass and you are still in the land, your life is forfeit. Now go, this is my decree and it shall not be revoked."

Kent was shaken. This was not the blade he had braced for. He bowed then. "Fare thee well, king. I go, for I dare to question a power so high that you give it away for a flattering tongue." He turned to Cordelia then: "Take heart, girl, you've spoken truly and done nothing wrong. May the gods protect you." He turned on a heel, putting his back to the king, something I'd never seen him do before, and marched out, pausing only a second to look at Regan and Goneril. "Well lied, you spiteful bitches."

I wanted to cheer the old brute, write a poem for him, but the hall had fallen silent and the sound of the great oaken door closing behind Kent echoed through the hall like the first thunder of a world-breaking storm.

"Well," said I, dancing to the middle of the floor. "I think that went about as well as could be expected."

5.

Pity the Fool

Kent banished, Cordelia disinherited, the king having given away his property and power, but most important, my home, the White Tower; the two older sisters insulted by Kent, the dukes ready to cut my throat, well—getting a laugh might be a challenge. Royal succession, it seemed, would not be a prudent subject to broach, and I was lost for a transition to slapstick or pantomime after Lear's high drama, so Drool was but a millstone on comedy's neck. I juggled apples and sang a little song about monkeys while I pondered the problem.

The king was, of late, leaning decidedly pagan, while the elder sisters favored the Church. Gloucester and Edgar were devout to the Roman pantheon, and Cordelia, well, she thought the whole lot was shit and

England should have her own church with women in the clergy. Quaint. So the high-minded comedy of religious satire it would be . . .

I tossed my apples around the table and said, "Two popes are shagging a camel behind a mosque, when this Saracen comes up—"

"There is only one, true pope!" shouted Cornwall, great tower of malignant smegma that he is.

"It's a jest, you wanker," said I. "Suspend fucking disbelief for a bit, would you?"

He was right, in a way (although not for the purpose of the camel bit). For the last year there had only been one pope, in the holy city of Amsterdam. But for the prior fifty years there had been two popes, the Retail Pope and the Discount Pope. After the Thirteenth Holy Crusade, when it was decided that to avoid future strife, the birthplace of Jesus would be moved to a different city every four years, holy shrines lost their geographical importance. There arose a great price war in the Church, with shrines offering pilgrims dispensation at varying competitive rates. Now there didn't need to be a miracle declared on the spot; anywhere could basically be declared a holy site, and often was. Lourdes would still sell dispensation coupons with the healing waters—but also some bloke in Puddinghoe could plant some pansies and hawk, "Jesus had a wee right on this very spot when he was a lad—two pennies and a spliff of Cardiff chronic 'ill get you out o' purgatory for an con, mate."

Soon a whole guild of low-priced shrine keepers around Europe named their own Pope—Boldface the Relatively Shameless, Discount Pope of Prague. The price war was on. If the Dutch pope would give you a hundred years out of purgatory for a shilling and a ferryman's ticket, the Discount Pope would let you out for two hundred years and send you home with the femur of a minor saint and a splinter of the True Cross. The Retail Pope would offer cheesy bacon toppings on the Host with communion and the Discount Pope would counter with topless-nun night for midnight mass.

It came to a head, though, when St. Matthew appeared in a vision to the Retail Pope, telling him that the faithful were more interested in the quality of their religious experience, not just the quantity. Thus inspired, the Retail Pope moved Christmas to June when the weather wasn't so shit for shopping, and the Discount Pope, not realizing the game had changed, responded by forgiving hell altogether for anyone who gave a priest a hand job. Without hell, there was no fear, and without fear, there was no further need for the Church to supply redemption, and more important, no means for the Church to modify behavior.

The Discount faithful defected in droves, either to the Retail branch of the Church, or to a dozen different pagan sects. Why not get pissed and dance naked around a pole all Sabbath if the worst of it was a rash on the naughty bits and the dropping of the odd bastard now and then? Pope Boldface was burned in a wicker man the next Beltane and cats shat in his ashes.

So, yes, a two-pope joke was untimely, but fuck all, it was dire times, and I sallied forth, for a bit: "So the second pope says, 'Your sister? I thought she was kosher?' "

And no one laughed. Cordelia rolled her eyes and made a raspberry sound.

The pathetic one-trumpet fanfare dribbled, the great doors were thrown open, and France and Burgundy ponced[1] into the hall followed by the bastard Edmund.

"Silence, fool," commanded Lear, with great superfluity. "Hail, Burgundy, hail, France."

"Hail, Edmund the bloody bastard!" said I.

Lear ignored me and motioned for France and Burgundy to come before him. They were both fit, taller than me but not tall, a few years south of thirty. Burgundy had dark hair and the sharp features of a

---

1. Ponced—verb form of "ponce," a gay man, meaning to walk in a gay manner. Could possibly be a real word.

Roman. France, sandy hair and softer features. Each wore sword and dagger that I doubted had been ever drawn but for ceremony. Fucking frogs.

"Lord Burgundy," said Lear, "you have rivaled for the hand of our youngest daughter. What dowry do you require for her?"

"No less than your highness has offered," said the dark poofter.

"Alas, that is no more, good Burgundy. What we offered, was offered when she was dear to us. Now she has roused our anger and betrayed our love and her dowry is nothing. If you want her as she is there, take her, but there will be no dowry."

Burgundy was stunned. He backed away, nearly stepping on France's feet. "I'm sorry, then, sir, but I must tend to property and power in my choice of duchess."

"She shall have neither," said Lear.

"So be it," said Burgundy. He nodded, bowed, and stepped back. "I am sorry, Cordelia."

"No worry, sir," said the princess. "If Burgundy's heart is wed only to property and power, then it could never be to me truly. Peace be with you."

I breathed half a sigh of relief. We might be driven from our home, but if Cordelia was driven out with us—

"I'll take her!" said Edgar.

"You will not, you blubbering, beetle-browed, dog-buggering dolt!" I may have accidentally exclaimed.

"You will not," said Gloucester, pushing his son back into his seat.

"Well, I will have her," said the Prince of France. "For she is a dowry in herself."

"Oh for fuck's sake!"

"Pocket, that's enough," said the king. "Guard, take him outside and hold him until our will is done."

Two yeomen stepped up behind me and seized me under the armpits. I heard Drool moan and looked over to see him cowering behind a column. This had never happened before—nothing like it. I was the all-licensed fool! I of all people could speak truth to power—I am chief cheeky monkey to the King of Bloody Britain!

"You don't know what you're getting into, France. Have you seen her feet? Or perhaps that is your game, put her to work in the vineyards crushing wine grapes. Majesty, the poofter means to force servitude on her, mark my words."

But no one heard the last of it, the yeomen had dragged me from the room and held me in the hall outside. I sought to brain one with Jones but he caught the puppet stick and tucked him in his belt at the small of his back.

"Sorry, Pocket," said Curan, the captain of the guard, a grizzled bear in chain mail who held me by my right arm. "'Twas a direct order, and you were fast cutting your throat with your own tongue."

"Not me," said I. "He wouldn't hurt me."

"I'd have said he'd not banish his best friend or disown his favorite daughter before this night. Hanging a fool's an easy leap, lad."

"Aye," said I. "You're right. Let me go, then."

"Not until the king's business is done," said the old yeoman.

The doors came open, fanfare trickled anemic through the portal, and out came the Prince of France, on his arm, Cordelia, radiant and wearing a grim smile. I could see her jaw clenched, but she relaxed when she saw me and some of the fire of anger left her eyes.

"So, you're off with the frog Prince?" said I.

France laughed at that, bloody buggering French fuck that he is. Is there anything so irritating as a noble who actually behaves nobly?

"Yes, I am leaving, Pocket, but there is one thing you must always remember and never forget—"

"Both at once?"

"Shut up!"

"Aye, milady."

"You must always remember, and you must never forget, that while you are the Black Fool, the dark fool, the Royal Fool, the all-licensed fool, and the King's Fool, you were not brought here to be those things. You were brought here to please me. Me! So when you put your titles aside, a fool still shall there reside, and now and forever, you are *my* fool."

"Oh my, you are going to do well in France—they hold unpleasantness to be a virtue."

"Mine!"

"Now and forever, milady."

"You may kiss my hand, fool."

The yeoman released me and I bent to take her hand. She pulled it away, and turned, her gown fanning out around her as she walked away. "Sorry, having you on."

I smiled into the floor. "You bitch."

"I'll miss you, Pocket," she said over her shoulder, and she hurried down the corridor.

"Take me with you. Take us both with you. France, you could use a brilliant fool and a great lumbering bag of flatulence like Drool, couldn't you?"

The prince shook his head, entirely too much pity in his eyes for my tastes. "You are Lear's fool, with Lear you shall stay."

"That's not what your wife just said."

"She will learn," said the prince. He turned on his heel and followed Cordelia down the corridor. I started after them but the captain yanked me back by the arm.

"Let her go, lad."

Next out of the hall came the sisters and their husbands. Before I could say anything the captain had clamped his hand over my mouth and was lifting me off my feet as I kicked. Cornwall made as to draw his dagger, but Regan pulled him away. "You've just won a kingdom, my duke, killing vermin is a servant's task. Leave the bitter fool stew in his own bile."

She wanted me. It was clear.

Goneril would not look me in the eye, but hurried past, and her husband, Albany, just shook his head as he walked by. A hundred brilliant witticisms died suffocating on the captain's heavy glove. Thus muted, I pumped my codpiece at the duke and tried to force a fart, but my bum trumpet could find no note.

As if the gods had sent down a dim and gaseous avatar to help me, Drool came next through the door, walking rather more straight than was his habit. Then I saw that someone had looped a rope around his neck, the noose fixed to a spear whose point was almost piercing Drool's throat. Edmund stepped into the corridor holding the other end of the spear, two men at arms flanking him.

"The captain havin' a laugh with you, then, Pocket?" said Drool, innocent of his peril.

The captain dropped me to my feet then, but held my shoulder to keep me from going at Edmund, whose father and brother passed behind him.

"You were right, Pocket," said Edmund, poking Drool a bit with the spear for emphasis. "Killing you would be enough to cement my unfavorable position forever, but a hostage—there's a mute I can use. I so enjoyed your performance in there that I prevailed upon the king to provide me with a fool of my own, and look at his gift. He'll be coming to Gloucester with us to assure that you don't forget your promise."

"You don't need the spear, bastard. He'll go if I ask him."

"Are we going on holiday, Pocket?" asked Drool, blood beginning to trickle down his neck then.

I approached the giant. "No, lad," said I. "You're going to go with the bastard here. Do as he says." I turned to the captain. "Give me your knife."

The captain eyed Edmund and the men at arms beside him, who had hands on hilts. "I don't know, Pocket—"

"Give me your bloody knife!" I whirled, pulled the knife from the captain's belt, and before the men at arms could draw I'd cut the rope around Drool's neck and pushed Edmund's spear aside.

"You don't need the spear, bastard." I handed the captain his knife and motioned for Drool to bend down so we were eye-to-eye. "I want you to go with Edmund and don't give him any trouble, you understand?"

"Aye. You ain't comin'?"

"I'll be along, I'll be along. I've business at the White Tower first."

"Shagging to be done?" Drool nodded so enthusiastically you could nearly hear his tiny brain rattling around his gourd. "I'll be helping, right?"

"No, lad, but you'll have your own castle. You'll be the proper fool, won't you? There'll be all kinds of hiding and listening, Drool, do you understand what I'm saying, lad?" I winked, hoping against hope that the git would get my meaning.

"Will there be heinous fuckery, Pocket?"

"Aye, I think you can count on it."

"Smashing!" Drool clapped his hands and danced a little jig then, chanting, "Heinous fuckery most foul, heinous fuckery most foul—"

I looked to Edmund. "You've my word, bastard. But you've also my word that if any harm comes to the Natural, I'll see to it that ghosts ride you into your grave."

A flash of fear showed in Edmund's eye then, but he fought it down and affected his usual swaggering smirk. "His life is on your word, little man."

The bastard turned and strutted down the corridor. Drool looked back, a big tear welling in his eye as he realized what was happening. I waved him on.

"I'd have taken the other two if you'd dirked him," said Curan. The other guard nodded in agreement. "Evil bastard was asking for it."

"Well, now you fucking tell me," said I.

Another guard hurried out of the hall then, and seeing it was only the fool with his captain, reported, "Captain, the king's food taster. He's dead, sir."

Three friends had I.

6.

Friendship and the Odd Bonk

Life is loneliness, broken only by the gods taunting us with friendship and the odd bonk. I admit it, I grieved. Perhaps I am a fool to have expected Cordelia to stay. (Well, yes, I am a fool—don't be overly clever, eh? It's annoying.) But for most of my manly years she had been the lash on my back, the bait to my loins, and the balm of my imagination—my torment, my tonic, my fever, my curse. I ache for her.

There is no comfort in the castle. Drool gone, Taster gone, Lear gone mad. At best, Drool was little more company than Jones, and decidedly less portable, but I worry for him, great child that he is, stumbling about in the circle of so many villains and so much sharp metal. I miss his gape-toothed smile, filled as it was with forgiveness, acceptance, and often, cheddar. And Taster, what did I know of him, really? Just a wan lad from

Hog Nostril on Thames. Yet when I needed a sympathetic ear, he provided, even if he was oft distracted from my woes by his own selfish dietary concerns.

I lay on my bed in the portislodge staring out the cruciform arrow loops at the grey bones of London, stewing in my misery, yearning for my friends.

For my first friend.

For Thalia.

The anchoress.

On a chill autumn day at Dog Snogging, the third time I was allowed to bring food to the anchoress, we became fast friends. I was still in awe of her, and merely being in her presence made me feel base, unworthy, and profane, but in a good way. I passed the plate of rough brown bread and cheese through the cross in the wall with prayers and a plea for her forgiveness.

"This fare will do, Pocket. It will do. I'll forgive you for a song."

"You must be a most pious lady and have great love for the Lord."

"The Lord is a tosser."

"I thought the Lord was a shepherd?"

"Well, that, too. But a bloke needs hobbies. Do you know 'Greensleeves'?"

"I know 'Dona Nobis Pacem.'"

"Do you know any pirate songs?"

"I could sing 'Dona Nobis Pacem' like a pirate."

"It means *give us peace,* in Latin, doesn't it?"

"Aye, mistress."

"Bit of a stretch then, innit, a pirate singing give us bloody peace?"

"I suppose. I could sing you a psalm, then, mistress."

"All right, then, Pocket, a psalm it is—one with pirates and loads of bloodshed, if you have it."

I was nervous, desperate for approval from the anchoress, and afraid that if I displeased her I might be struck down by an avenging angel, as seemed to happen often in scripture. Try as I might, I could not recall any piraty psalms. I cleared my throat and sang the only psalm I knew in English:

"The Lord is my tosser, I shall not want—"

"Wait, wait, wait," said the anchoress. "Doesn't it go, 'the Lord is my shepherd'?"

"Well, yes, mistress, but you said—"

And she started to laugh. It was the first time I heard her truly laugh and it felt as if I was getting approval from the Virgin herself. In the dark chamber, just the single candle on my side of the cross, it seemed like her laughter was all around me, embracing me.

"Oh, Pocket, you are a love. Thick as a bloody brick, but such a love."

I could feel the blood rise in my face. I was proud and embarrassed and ecstatic all at once. I didn't know what to do, so I fell to my knees and prostrated myself before the arrow loop, pushing my cheek against the stone floor. "I'm sorry, mistress."

She laughed some more. "Arise, Sir Pocket of Dog Snogging."

I climbed to my feet and stared into the dark cross-shaped hole in the wall, and there I saw that dull star that was her eye reflecting the candle flame and I realized that there were tears in my own eyes.

"Why did you call me that?"

"Because you make me laugh and you are deserving and valiant. I think we're going to be very good friends."

I started to ask her what she meant, but the iron latch clanked and the door into the passageway swung slowly open. Mother Basil was there, holding a candelabra, looking displeased.

"Pocket, what's going on here?" said the mother superior in her gruff baritone.

"Nothing, Reverend Mother. I've just given food to the anchoress."

Mother Basil seemed reluctant to enter the passageway, as if she was afraid to be in view of the arrow loop that looked into the anchoress's chamber.

"Come along, Pocket. It's time for evening prayers."

I bowed quickly to the anchoress and hurried out the door under Mother Basil's arm.

As the sister closed the door, the anchoress called, "Reverend Mother, a moment, please."

Mother Basil's eyes went wide and she looked as if she'd been called out by the devil. "Go on to vespers, Pocket. I'll be along."

She made her way into the dead-end passageway and closed the door behind her even as the bell calling us to vespers began to toll.

I wondered what the anchoress would discuss with Mother Basil, perhaps some conclusion she had realized during her hours of prayer, perhaps I had been found wanting and she would ask that I not be sent to her again. After just making my first friend, I was sorely afraid of losing her. While I repeated the prayers in Latin after the priest, in my heart I prayed to God to not take my anchoress away, and when mass ended, I stayed in the chapel and prayed until well after the midnight prayers.

Mother Basil found me in the chapel.

"There are going to be some changes, Pocket."

I felt my spirit drop into my shoe soles.

"Forgive me, Reverend Mother, for I know not what I do."

"What are you on about, Pocket? I'm not scolding you. I'm adding duties to your devotion."

"Oh," said I.

"From now on, you are to take food and drink to the anchoress in the hour before vespers, and there in the outer chamber, shall you sit until she has eaten, but upon the bell for vespers you are to leave there, and not return until the next day. No longer than an hour shall you stay, do you understand?"

"Yes, mum, but why only the hour?"

"More than that and you will interfere with the anchoress's own communion with God. Further, you are never to ask her about where she was before this, about her family, or her past in any way. If she should speak of these things you are to immediately put your fingers in your ears, and verily sing 'la, la, la, la, I can't hear you, I can't hear you,' and leave the chamber immediately."

"I can't do that, mum."

"Why not?"

"I can't work the latch to the outer door with my fingers in my ears."

"Ah, sweet Pocket, I do so love your wit. I think you shall sleep on the stone floor this night, the rug shields you from the blessed cooling of your fevered imagination, which God finds an abomination. Yes, a light beating and the bare stone for you and your wit tonight."

"Yes, mum."

"And so, you must never speak with the anchoress about her past, and if you should, you shall be excommunicated and damned for all eternity with no hope for redemption, the light of the Lord shall never fall upon you, and you shall live in darkness and pain for ever and ever. And in addition, I shall have Sister Bambi feed you to the cat."

"Yes, mum," said I. I was so thrilled I nearly peed. I would be blessed by the glory of the anchoress every single day.

"Well that's a scaly spot o' snake wank," said the anchoress.

"No, mum, it's a cracking big cat."

"Not the cat, the hour a day. Only an hour a day?"

"Mother Basil doesn't want me to disturb your communion with God, Madame Anchoress." I bowed before the dark arrow loop.

"Call me Thalia."

"I daren't, mum. And neither may I ask you about your past or from whence you come. Mother Basil has forbidden it."

"She's right on that, but you may call me Thalia, as we are friends."

"Aye, mum. Thalia."

"And you may tell me of your past, good Pocket. Tell me of your life."

"But, Dog Snogging is all I know—all I have ever known."

I could hear her laughing in the dark. "Then, tell me a story from your lessons, Pocket."

So I told the anchoress of the stoning of St. Stephen, of the persecution of St. Sebastian, and the beheading of St. Valentine, and she, in turn, told me stories of the saints I had never heard of in catechism.

"And so," said Thalia, "that is the story of how St. Rufus of Pipewrench was licked to death by marmots."

"That sounds a most horrible martyring," said I.

"Aye," said the anchoress, "for marmot spit is the most noxious of all substances, and that is why St. Rufus is the patron of saliva and halitosis unto this day. Enough martyring, tell me of some miracles."

And so I did. I told of the magic, self-filling milk pail of St. Bridgid of Kildare, of how St. Fillan, after his ox was killed by a wolf, was able to compel the same wolf to pull a cart full of materials for building a church, and how St. Patrick drove the snakes out of Ireland.

"Aye," said Thalia, "and snakes have been grateful ever since. But let me apprise you of the most wondrous miracle of how St. Cinnamon drove the Mazdas out of Swinden."

"I've never heard of St. Cinnamon," said I.

"Well, that is because these nuns at Dog Snogging are base and not worthy to know such things, and why you must never share what you learn here with them lest they become overwhelmed and succumb to an ague."

"An ague of over-piety?"

"Aye, lad, and you will be the one to have killed them."

"Oh, I would never want to do that."

"Of course you wouldn't. Did you know, in Portugal they canonize a saint by actually shooting him out of a cannon?"

And so it went, day in, day out, week in, week out, trading secrets and lies with Thalia. You might think that it was cruel of her to spend her only time in contact with the outside world telling lies to a little boy, but then, the first story that Mother Basil had told me was about a talking snake who gave tainted fruit to naked people, and the bishop had made her an abbess. All along what Thalia was teaching me was how to entertain her. How to share a moment in story and laughter—how you could become close to someone, even when separated from them by a stone wall.

Once a month for the first two years the bishop came from York to check on the anchoress, and she would seem to lose her spirit for a day, as if he were skimming it off and taking it away, but soon she would recover and our routine of chat and laughter would go on. After a few years the bishop stopped coming, and I was afraid to ask Mother Basil why, lest it be a reminder and the dour prelate resume his spirit-sucking sojourns.

The longer the anchoress was in her chamber, the more she delighted in my conveying the most mundane details from the outside.

"Tell me of the weather today, Pocket. Tell me of the sky, and don't skip a single cloud."

"Well, the sky looked like someone was catapulting giant sheep into the frosty eye of God."

"Fucking winter. Crows against the sky?"

"Aye, Thalia, like a vandal with quill and ink set loose to randomly punctuate the very dome of day."

"Ah, well spoken, love, completely incoherent imagery."

"Thank you, mistress."

While about my chores and studies I tried to take note of every detail and construct metaphors in my head so I might paint word pictures for my anchoress, who depended on me to be her light and color.

My days seemed to begin at four when I came to Thalia's chamber, and end at five, when the bell rang for vespers. Everything before was in preparation for that hour, and everything after, until sleep, was in sweet remembrance.

The anchoress taught me how to sing—not just the hymns and chants I had been singing from the time I was little, but the romantic songs of the troubadours. With simple, patient instruction, she taught me how to dance, juggle, and perform acrobatics, and all by verbal description—not once in those years had I laid eyes on the anchoress, or seen more than her partial profile at the arrow loop.

I grew older and fuzz sprouted on my cheek—my voice broke, making me sound as if a small goose was trapped in my gullet, honking for her supper. The nuns at Dog Snogging started to take notice of me as something other than their pet, for many were sent to the abbey when they were no older than I. They would flirt and ask me for a song, a poem, a story, the more bawdy the better, and the anchoress had taught me many of those. Where she had learned them, she would never say.

"Were you an entertainer before you became a nun?"

"No, Pocket. And I am not a nun."

"But, perhaps your father—"

"No, my father was not a nun either."

"I mean, was he an entertainer?"

"Sweet Pocket, you mustn't ask about my life before I came here. What I am now, I have always been, and everything I am is here with you."

"Sweet Thalia," said I. "That is a fiery flagon of dragon toss."

"Isn't it, though?"

"You're grinning, aren't you?"

She held the candle close to the arrow loop, illuminating her wry smile. I laughed, and reached through the cross to touch her cheek. She sighed, took my hand and pressed it hard against her lips, then, in an instant, she had pushed my hand away and moved out of the light.

"Don't hide," said I. "Please don't hide."

"Fat lot of choice I have about whether I hide or not. I live in a bloody tomb."

I didn't know what to say. Never before had she complained about her choice to become the anchoress of Dog Snogging, even if other expressions of her faith seemed—well—abstract.

"I mean don't hide from me. Let me see you."

"You want to see? You want to see?"

I nodded.

"Give me your candles."

She had me hand four lit candles through the arrow loop. Whenever I performed for her she had me set them in holders around the outer chamber so she could see me dance, or juggle, or do acrobatics, but never had she asked for more than one candle in her own chamber. She placed the candles around her chamber and for the first time I could see the stone pallet where she slept on a mattress of straw, her meager possessions laid out on a heavy table, and Thalia, standing there in a tattered linen frock.

"Look," she said. She pulled her frock over her head and dropped it on the floor.

She was the most beautiful thing I had ever seen. She looked younger than I had imagined, thin, but womanly—her face was that of a mischievous Madonna, as if carved by a sculptor inspired more by desire than the divine. Her hair was long and the color of buckskin, catching the candlelight as if a single ray of sunlight might make it explode in golden fire. I felt a heat rise in my face, and another kind of rise in my trousers. I was excited and confused and ashamed all at once, and I turned my back on the arrow loop and cried out.

"No!"

Suddenly, she was right behind me, and I felt her hand on my shoulder, then rubbing my neck.

"Pocket. Sweet Pocket, don't. It's all right."

"I feel like the Devil and the Virgin are doing battle in my body. I didn't know you were like that."

"Like a woman, you mean?"

Her hand was warm and steady, kneading the muscles in my shoulder through the cross in the wall and

I leaned into it. I wanted to turn and look, I wanted to run out of the chamber, I wanted to be asleep, or just waking—ashamed that the Devil had visited me in the night with a damp dream of temptation.

"You know me, Pocket. I'm your friend."

"But you are the anchoress."

"I'm Thalia, your friend, who loves you. Turn around, Pocket."

And I did.

"Give me your hand," said she.

And I did.

She put it on her body, and she put her hands on mine, and pressed against the cold stone. Through the cross in the wall, I discovered a new universe—of Thalia's body, of my body, of love, of passion, of escape—and it was a damn sight better than bloody chants and juggling. When the bell rang for vespers we fell away from the cross, spent and gasping, and we began to laugh. Oh, and I had chipped a tooth.

"One for the Devil, then, love?" said Thalia.

When I arrived with the anchoress's supper the next afternoon she was waiting with her face pressed nearly through the center of the arrow cross—she looked like one of the angel-faced gargoyles that flanked the main doors of Dog Snogging, except they always seemed to be weeping and she was grinning. "So, didn't go to confession today, did you?"

I shuddered. "No, mum, I worked in the scriptorium most of the day."

"Pocket, I think I would prefer you not call me mum, if it's not too much to ask. Given the new level of our friendship it seems—oh, I don't know—unsavory."

"Yes, m—uh—mistress."

"*Mistress* I can work with. Now, pass me my supper and see if you can fit your face in the opening the way that I have."

Thalia's cheekbones were wedged in the arrow loop, which was little wider than my hand.

"Doesn't that hurt?" I'd been finding abrasions on my arms and various bits all day from our adventure the night before.

"It's not the flaying of St. Bart, but, yes, it stings a bit. You can't confess what we did, or what we do, love? You know that, right?"

"Then am I going to have to go to hell?"

"Well—" She pulled back, rolled her eyes as if searching the ceiling for an answer. "—not alone. Give us our supper, lad, and get your face in the loop, I have something to teach you."

And so it went for weeks and months. I went from being a mediocre acrobat to a talented contortionist, and Thalia seemed to regain some of the life that I had thought sure she'd lost. She was not holy in the sense that the priests and nuns taught, but she was full of spirit and a different kind of reverence. More concerned with this life, this moment, than an eternity beyond the reach of the cross in the wall. I adored her, and I wanted her to be out of the chamber, in the world, with me, and I began to plan her escape. But I was but a boy, and she was bloody barking, so it was not meant to be.

"I've stolen a chisel from a mason who passed by on his way to work on the minster at York. It will take some time, but if you work on a single stone, you might escape in summer."

"You are my escape, Pocket. The only escape I can ever allow myself."

"But we could run off, be together."

"That would be smashing, except I can't leave. So, hop up and get your tackle in the cross. Thalia's a special treat for you."

I never seemed to make my point once my tackle went in the cross. Distracted, I was. But I learned, and while I was forbidden confession—and to tell the truth, I didn't feel that badly about it—I began to share what I had learned.

"Thalia, I must confess to you, I have told Sister Nikki about the little man in the boat."

"Really? Told her or showed her?"

"Well, showed her, I reckon. But she seems a bit thick. She kept making me show her over and over—asked me to meet her in the cloisters to show her again after vespers tonight."

"Ah, the joy of being slow. Still, it's a sin to be selfish with one's knowledge."

"That's what I thought," said I, relieved.

"And speaking of the little man in the boat, I believe there is one on this side of the loop who has been naughty and requires a thorough tongue-lashing."

"Aye, mistress," said I, wedging my cheeks into the arrow loop. "Present the rascal for punishment."

And so it went. I was the only person I knew who had calluses on his cheekbones, but I had also developed the arms and grip of a blacksmith from suspending myself with my fingertips wedged between the great stones to extend my bits through the arrow loop. And thus I hung, spread spiderlike across the wall, my business being tended to, frantic and friendly, by the anchoress, when the bishop entered the antechamber.

(The bishop entered the antechamber? The bishop entered the antechamber? At this point you're going coy on us, euphemizing about parts and positions when you've already confessed to mutual violation with a holy woman through a bloody arrow slot? Well, no.)

The actual sodding Bishop of Bloody York entered the sodding antechamber with Mother sodding Basil, who bore a brace of sodding storm lanterns.

And so I let go. Unfortunately, Thalia did not. It appeared that her grip, too, had been strengthened by our encounters on the wall.

"What the hell are you doing, Pocket?" said the anchoress.

"What are you doing?" asked Mother Basil.

I hung there, more or less suspended to the wall by three points, one of them not covered by shoes. "Ahh-hhhhhhh!" said I. I was finding it somewhat difficult to think.

"Give us a little slack, lad," said Thalia. "This is meant to be more of a dance, not a tug-of-war."

"The bishop is out here," said I.

She laughed. "Well, tell him to get in the queue and I'll tend to him when we're finished."

"No, Thalia, he's really out here."

"Oh toss," said she, releasing my knob.

I fell to the floor and quickly rolled onto my stomach.

Thalia's face was at the arrow loop. "Evening, your grace." A big grin there. "Fancy a spot of stony bonking before vespers?"

The bishop turned so quickly his miter went half-past on his head. "Hang him," he said. He snatched one of Mother Basil's lanterns and walked out of the chamber.

"Bloody brown bread you serve tastes like goat scrotum!" Thalia called after. "A lady deserves finer fare!"

"Thalia, please," I said.

"Not a comment on you, Pocket. Your serving style is lovely, but the bread is rubbish." Then to Mother Basil. "Don't blame the boy, Reverend Mother, he's a love."

Mother Basil grabbed me by the ear and dragged me out of the chamber.

"You're a love, Pocket," said the anchoress.

Mother Basil locked me in a closet in her chambers, then mid-way through the night, opened the door and handed in a crust of bread and a chamber pot. "Stay here until the bishop is on his way in the morning, and if anyone asks, you've been hung."

"Yes, Reverend Mother," said I.

She came to get me the next morning and hustled me out through the chapel. I'd never seen her so distraught. "You've been like a son to me, Pocket," she said, fussing about me, strapping a satchel and other bits of kit on me. "So it's going to pain me to send you off."

"But, Reverend Mother—"

"Hush, lad. We'll take you to the barn, hang you in front of a few farmers, then you're off to the south to meet up with a group of mummers[1] who will take you in."

"Beggin' pardon, mum, but if I'm hung, what will mummers do with me, a puppet show?"

"I'll not really hang you, just make it look good. We have to, lad, the bishop ordered it."

"Since when does the bishop order nuns to hang people?"

"Since you shagged the anchoress, Pocket."

At the mention of her I broke away from Mother Basil, ran through the abbey, down the old corridor and into the antechamber. The arrow cross was gone, completely bricked up and mortared in. "Thalia! Thalia!" I called. I screamed and beat the stones until my fists bled, but not a sound came from the other side of the wall. Ever.

The sisters pulled me away, tied my hands, and took me to the barn where I was hanged.

---

1. Mummers—traveling entertainers, often associated with winter solstice celebrations, but could be anything from acrobats to a theatrical troupe.

7.

A Brother Traitor

Am I to be forever alone? The anchoress told me it might be so, trying to comfort me when I felt pushed aside by the sisters of Dog Snogging.

"You're gifted with wit, Pocket, but to cast jibe and jest you must stand separate from the target of your barbs. I fear you may become a lonely man, even in the company of others."

Perhaps she was right. Perhaps it is why I am such an accomplished horn-beast and eloquent crafter of cuckoldry. I seek only succor and solace beneath the skirts of the soft and understanding. And so, sleepless, did I make my way to the great hall to find some comfort among the castle wenches who slept there.

The fire still blazed, logs the size of oxen set in before bed. My sweet Squeak, who had oft opened her heart and whatnot to a wayfaring fool, had fallen asleep in the arms of her husband, who spooned her mercilessly as he snored. Shanker Mary was not to be seen, no doubt servicing the bastard Edmund somewhere, and my other standard lovelies had fallen into slumber in proximity too close to husbands or fathers to admit a lonely fool.

Ah, but the new girl, just in the kitchen a fortnight, called Tess or Kate or possibly Fiona. Her hair was jet and shone like oiled iron; milky skin, cheeks brushed by a rose—she smiled at my japes and had given Drool an apple without his asking. I am relatively sure that I adored her. I tiptoed across the rushes that lined the floor (I had left Jones in my chamber, his hat bells no help in securing stealthy romance), lay down beside her, and introduced my personage to the nether of her blanket. An affectionate nudge at the hip woke her.

"Hello," said she.

"Hello," said I. "Not a papist, are you, love?"

"Christ, no, Druid born and raised."

"Thank God."

"What are you doing under my blanket?"

"Warming up. I'm terribly cold."

"No you're not."

"Brrrr. Freezing."

"It's hot in here."

"All right, then. I'm just being friendly."

"Would you stop prodding me with that?"

"Sorry, it does that when it's lonely. Perhaps if you petted it."

Then, praised be the merciful goddess of the wood, she petted it, tentatively, almost reverentially at first, as if she sensed how much joy it could bring to all who came in contact with it. An adaptable lass, not given to fits of hysteria or modesty—and soon a gentle surety in her grip that betrayed some experience in the handling of manly bits—simply lovely she was.

"I thought it would have a little hat, with bells."

"Ah, yes. Well, given a private place to change, I'm sure that can be arranged. Under your skirt, perhaps. Roll to the side, love, we'll be less obvious if we keep the cuddle on a lateral plane." I popped her bosoms out of her frock, then, freed the roly-poly pink-nosed puppies to the firelight and the friendly ministries of this master juggler, and thought to burble my cheeks softly between them, when the ghost appeared.

The spirit was more substantial now, features describing what must have been a most comely creature before she was shuffled off to the undiscovered country, no doubt by a close relative weary of her irritating nature. She floated above the sleeping form of the cook Bubble, rising and falling on the draft of her snores.

"Sorry to haunt you while you're rogering the help," said the ghost.

"The rogering has not commenced, wisp, I have barely bridled the horse for a moist and bawdy ride. Now, go away."

"Right, then. Sorry to have interrupted your attempted rogering."

"Are you calling me a horse?" asked Possibly Fiona.

"Not at all, love, you pet the little jester and I'll attend to the haunting."

"There's always a bloody ghost about, ain't there?" commented Possibly, a squeeze on my knob for emphasis.

"When you live in a keep where blood runs blue and murder is the favored sport, yes," said the ghost.

"Oh do fuck off," said I. "Thou visible stench, thou steaming aggravation, thou vaporous nag! I'm wretched, sad, and lonely, and trying to raise a modicum of comfort and forgetting here in the arms of, uh—"

"Kate," said Possibly Fiona.

"Really?"

She nodded.

"Not Fiona?"

"Kate since the day me da tied me belly cord to a tree."

"Well, bugger. Sorry. Pocket here, called the Black Fool, charmed I'm sure. Shall I kiss your hand?"

"Double-jointed, then, are ye?" said Kate, a tickle to my tackle making her point.

"Bloody hell, would you two shut up?" said the ghost. "I'm haunting over here."

"Go on," said we.

The ghost boosted her bosom and cleared her throat, expectorating a tiny ghost frog that evaporated in the firelight with a hiss, then said:

"When a second sibling's base derision,
Proffers lies that cloud the vision,
And severs ties that families bind,
Shall a madman rise to lead the blind."

"What?" said the former Fiona.

"What?" said I.

"Prophecy of doom, innit?" said the ghost. "Spot o' the old riddly foreshadowing from beyond, don't you know?"

"Can't kill her again, can we?" asked faux Fiona.

"Gentle spook," said I. "If it is a warning you bring, state it true. If action you require, ask outright. If music you must make, play on. But by the wine-stained balls of Bacchus, speak your bloody business, quick and clear, then be gone, before time's iron tongue licks away my mercy bonk with second thoughts."

"You are the haunted one, fool. It's your business I do. What do you want?"

"I want you to go away, I want Fiona to come along quietly, and I want Cordelia, Drool, and Taster back—now, can you tell me how to make those things come about? Can you, you yammering flurry of fumes?"

"It can be done," said the ghost. "Your answer lies with the witches of Great Birnam Wood."

"Or you could just fucking tell me," said I.

"Nooooo," sang the ghost, all ghosty and ethereal, and with that she faded away.

"Leaves a chill when she goes, don't she?" said formerly Fiona. "Appears to have softened your resolve, if you don't mind my sayin'."

"The ghost saved my life last evening," said I, trying to will life back into the wan and withered.

"Kilt the little one, though, didn't she? Back to your bed, fool, the king's leaving on the morrow and there's a wicked lot of work to do in the morning to prepare for his trip."

Sadly, I tucked away my tackle and sulked back to the portislodge to pack my kit for my final journey from the White Tower.

Well, I won't miss the bloody trumpets at dawn, I can tell you that. And sod the bloody drawbridge chains rattling in my apartment before the cock crows. We might have been going to war for all the racket and goings-on at first light. Through the arrow loop I could see Cordelia riding out with France and Burgundy, standing in the stirrups like a man, like she was off to the hunt, rather than leaving her ancestral home forever. To her credit, she did not look back, and I did not wave to her, even after she crossed the river and rode out of sight.

Drool was not so fickle, and as he was led out of the castle by a rope round his neck, he kept stopping and looking back, until the man at arms to whom he was tethered would yank him back into step. I could not bear to let him see me, so I did not go out onto the wall. Instead I slunk back to my pallet and lay there, my forehead pressed to the cold stone wall, listening as the rest of the royals and their retinues clomped across the drawbridge below. Sod Lear, sod the royals, sod the bloody White Tower. All I loved was gone or soon to be left behind, and all that I owned was packed in a knapsack and hung on my hook, Jones sticking out the top, mocking me with his puppety grin.

Then, a knock at my door. Like dragging myself from the grave, was making my way to open it. There she stood, fresh and lovely, holding a basket.

"Fiona!"

"Kate," said Fiona.

"Aye, your stubbornness suits you, even in daylight."

"Bubble sends her sympathies over Taster and Drool, and sends you these sweet cakes and milk for your comfort, but says to be sure and remind you to not leave the castle without saying your farewells, and further that you are a cur, a rascal, and a scurvy patch."

"Ah, sweet Bubble, when kindness shagged an ogre, thus was she sired."

"And I'm here to offer comfort myself, finishing what was started in the great hall last night. Squeak says to ask you about a small chap in a canoe."

"My my, Fi, bit of a tart, aren't we?"

"Druish, love. My people burn a virgin every autumn—one can't be too careful."

"Well, all right, but I'm forlorn and I shan't enjoy it."

"In that we shall suffer together. Onward! Off with your kit, fool!"

What is it about me that brings out the tyrant in women, I wonder?

"The next morning" stretched into a week of preparation for departure from the White Tower. When Lear pronounced that he would be accompanied by one hundred knights it was not as if one hundred men could mount up and ride out of the gates at sunrise. Each knight—the unlanded second or third son of a noble—would have at least one squire, a page, usually a man to tend his horses, and sometimes a man at arms. Each had at least one warhorse, a massive armored beast, and two, sometimes three animals to carry his armor, weapons, and supplies. And Albany was three weeks' journey to the north, near Aberdeen; with the slow pace set by the old king and so many on foot we'd need a crashing assload of supplies. By the end of the week our column numbered over five hundred men and boys, and nearly as many horses. We would have needed a wagon full of coin to pay everyone if Lear had not conscripted Albany and Cornwall to maintain his knights.

I watched Lear pass under the portislodge at the head of the column before going downstairs and climbing on my own mount, a short, swayback mare named Rose.

"Mud shall not sully my Black Fool's motley, lest it dull his wit as well," said Lear, the day he presented the horse. I did not own the horse, of course. She belonged to the king—or now his daughters, I suppose.

I fell in at the end of the column behind Hunter, who was accompanied by a long train of hounds and a wagon with a cage built on it, which held eight of the royal falcons.

"We'll be raiding farms before we get to Leeds," said Hunter, a stout, leather-clad man, thirty winters on his back. "I can't feed this lot—and they've not enough stowed to last them a week."

"Cry calamity if you will, Hunter, but I'm the one to keep them in good spirits when their bellies are empty."

"Aye, I've no envy for you, fool. Is that why you ride back here with we catch-farts and not at the king's side?"

"Just drawing plans for a bawdy song at supper without the clank of armor in my ear, good Hunter."

I wanted to tell Hunter that I was not overburdened by my duties, but by my disdain for the senile king who had sent my princess away. And I wanted time to ponder the ghost's warnings. The bit about daughters three and the king becoming a fool had come to pass, or at least was in the way of it. So the girl ghost had predicted the *"grave offense"* to *"daughter's three"* even if all the daughters had not seen the offense yet—when Lear arrived at Albany with this rowdy retinue, offense would soon follow. But what of this: *"When a second sibling's base derision, proffers lies that cloud the vision"*?

Did it mean the second daughter? Regan? What did it matter if her lies clouded Lear's vision? The king was nearly blind as it was, his eyes milky with cataract—I'd taken to describing my pantomimes as I performed them so the old man would not miss the joke. And with no power, what tie could be severed that would make a difference now? A war between the two dukes? None of it about me, why do I care?

Why then would the ghost appear to this most irrelevant and powerless fool? I puzzled it, and fell far behind the column, and when I stopped to have a wee, was accosted by a brigand.

He came up from behind a fallen tree, a great bear of a fiend, his beard matted and befouled with food and burrs, a maelstrom of grey hair flying about under a wide-brimmed black hat. I may have screamed in surprise, and a less educated ear might have likened my shriek to that of a little girl, but be assured it was most manly and more for the fair warning of my attacker, for next I knew I had pulled a dagger from the small of my back and sent it flying. His miserable life was saved only by my slight miscalculation of his distance—the butt of my blade bounced off his behatted noggin with a thud.

"Ouch! Fuck's sake, fool. What is wrong with you?"

"Hold fast, knave," said I. "I've two more blades at the ready, and these I'll send pointy end first—the quality of my mercy having been strained and my ire aroused by having peed somewhat upon my shoes." I believed it a serviceable threat.

"Hold your blades, Pocket. I mean you no harm," came the voice under the hat brim. Then, "*Y Ddraig Goch ddyry gychwyn.*"[1]

I wound up to send my second dagger to the scoundrel's heart, "You may know my name, but that gargling with catsick that you're doing will not stop me from dropping you where you stand."

"*Ydych chi'n cymryd cerdynnau credid?*"[2] said the highwayman, no doubt trying to frighten me further, his consonants chained like anal beads strung out of hell's own bunghole.

"I may be small, but I'm not a child to be afraid of a pretended demon speaking in tongues. I'm a lapsed Christian and a pagan of convenience. The worst I can do on my conscience is cut your throat and ask the forest to count it as a sacrifice come the Yule, so

1. *Y Ddraig Goch ddyry gychwyn*—Welsh, "The Red Dragon should go forward!" Originally the Welsh National Motto. Later replaced by "Yes, we have shepherd's pie!"

2. *Ydych chi'n cymryd cerdynnau credid?*—Welsh, "Do you take credit cards?"

cease your nonsense and tell me how you know my name."

"It's not nonsense, it's Welsh," said the brigand. He folded back the brim of his hat and winked. "What say you save your wicked sting for an enemy true? It's me, Kent. In disguise."

Indeed, it was, the king's old banished friend—all of his royal trappings but his sword gone—he looked like he'd slept in the woods the week since I'd last seen him.

"Kent, what are you doing here? You're as good as dead if the king sees you. I thought you'd be in France by now."

"I've no place to go—my lands and title are forfeit, what family I have would risk their own lives to take me in. I have served Lear these forty years, I am loyal, and I know nothing else. My thought is to affect accents and hide my face until he has a change of heart."

"Is loyalty a virtue when paid to virtue's stranger? I think not. Lear has misused you. You are mad, or stupid, or you lust for the grave, but there is no place for you, good greybeard, in the company of the king."

"And there is for you? Or did I not see you restrained and dragged from the hall for that same offense: truth told boldly? Don't preach virtue to me, fool. One voice can, without fear, call the king on his folly, and here he stands, piss-shoed, two leagues back from the train."

Fuckstockings, truth is a surly shrew sometimes! He was right, of course, loudmouthed old bull. "Have you eaten?"

"Not for three days."

I went to my horse and dug into my satchel for some hard cheese and an apple I had left from Bubble's farewell gift. I gave them to Kent. "Come not too soon," said I. "Lear still fumes about Cordelia's honest offense and your supposed treason. Follow behind to Albany's castle. I'll have Hunter leave a rabbit or a duck beside the road for you every day. Do you have flint and steel?"

"Aye, and tinder."

I found the stub of a candle in the bottom of my bag and handed it to the old knight. "Burn this and catch the soot upon your sword, then rub the black into your beard. Cut your hair short and blacken it, too. Lear can't see clearly more than a few feet away, so keep your distance. And carry on with that ghastly Welsh accent."

"Perhaps I'll fool the old man, but what of the others?"

"No righteous man thinks you a traitor, Kent, but I don't know all of these knights, nor which might reveal you to the king. Just stay out of sight and by the time we reach Albany's castle I'll have flushed out any knave who might betray your cause."

"You're a good lad, Pocket. If I've shown you disrespect in the past, I'm sorry."

"Don't grovel, Kent, it doesn't wear well on the aged. A swift sword and a strong shield are allies I can well use with scoundrels and traitors weaving intrigue about like the venomous spider-whore of Killarney."

"Spider-whore of Killarney? I've never heard of her?"

"Aye, well, sit on that downed tree and eat your lunch. I'll spin the tale for you like it was web from her own bloody bum."

"You'll fall behind the column."

"Sod the column, that tottering old tosspot so slows them they'll be leaving a snail trail soon. Sit and listen, greybeard. By the way have you ever heard of Great Birnam Wood?"

"Aye, it's not two miles from Albany."

"Really? How do you feel about witches?"

8.

A Wind from Fucking France

Hunter was right, of course, he wasn't able to feed Lear's train. We imposed on villages along the way for fare and quarter, but north of Leeds the villages had suffered bad harvests and they could not bear our appetites without starving themselves. I tried to foster good cheer among the knights, while keeping distance from Lear—I had not forgiven the old man for disowning my Cordelia and sending away Drool. Secretly I relished the soldiers' complaints about their lack of comfort, and made no real effort to dampen their rising resentment for the old king.

On the fifteenth day of our march, outside of Lint-upon-Tweed, they ate my horse.

"Rose, Rose, Rose—would a horse by any other name taste so sweet?" the knights chanted. They thought themselves clever, slinging such jests while spraying roasted bits of my mount from their greasy lips.

The dull always seek to be clever at the fool's expense, to somehow repay him for his cutting wit, but never are they clever, and often are they cruel. Which is why I may never own things, never care for anyone, nor show desire for anything, lest some ruffian, thinking he is funny, take it away. I have secret desires, wants, and dreams, though. Jones is a fine foil, but I should like someday to own a monkey. I would dress him in a tiny jester's suit, of red silk, I think. I would call him Jeff, and he would have his own scepter, that would be called Tiny Jeff. Yes, I should very much like a monkey. He would be my friend—and it would be forbidden to murder, banish, or eat him. Foolish dreams?

We were met at the gate of Castle Albany by Goneril's steward, adviser, and chief toady, that most pernicious twat, Oswald. I'd had dealings with the rodent-faced muck-sucker when he was but a footman at the White Tower, when Goneril was still princess at court, and I, a humble jongleur, was found wandering naked amid her royal orbs. But that tale is best left for another time, the scoundrel at the gate impedes our progress.

Spidery in appearance as well as disposition, Oswald lurks even when in the open, lurking being his natural state of locomotion. A fine black fuzz he wears for a beard, the same is on his head, when his blue tartan tam is humbled at his heart, which it was not that day. He neither removed his hat nor bowed as Lear approached.

The old king was not pleased. He stopped the train an arrow-shot from the castle and waved me forward.

"Pocket, go see what he wants," said Lear. "And ask why there is no fanfare for my arrival."

"But nuncle,"[1] said I. "Shouldn't the captain of the guard be the one—"

"Go on, fool! A point is to be made about respect. I send a fool to meet this rascal and put him in his place. Spare no manners, remind the dog that he is a dog."

"Aye, majesty." I rolled my eyes at Captain Curan, who almost laughed, then stopped himself, seeing that the king's anger was real.

I pulled Jones from my satchel and sallied forth, my jaw set, as determined as the prow of a warship.

"Hail, Castle Albany," I called. "Hail, Albany. Hail, Goneril."

Oswald said nothing, did not so much as remove his hat. He looked past me to the king, even when I was standing an arm's length from him.

_____
1. Nuncle—archaic, uncle.

I said: "King of bloody Britain here, Oswald. I'd suggest you pay proper respect."

"I'll not lower myself to speak with a fool."

"Primping little whoreson wanker, innit he?" said the puppet Jones.

"Aye," said I. Then I spotted a guard in the barbican, looking down on us. "Hail, Cap'n, seems someone's emptied a privy on your drawbridge and the steaming pile blocks our way."

The guard laughed. Oswald fumed.

"M'lady has instructed me to instruct you that her father's knights are not welcome in the castle."

"That so? She's actually talking to you, then?"

"I'll not have an exchange with an impudent fool."

"He's not impudent," said Jones. "With proper inspiration, the lad sports a woody as stout as a mooring pin. Ask your lady."

I nodded in agreement with the puppet, for he is most wise for having a brain of sawdust.

"Impudent! Impudent! Not impotent!" Oswald frothing a bit now.

"Oh, well, why didn't you say so," said Jones. "Yes, he's that."

"To be sure," said I.

"Aye," said Jones.

"Aye," said I.

"The king's rabble shall not be permitted in the castle."

"Aye. That so, Oswald?" I reached up and patted his cheek. "You should have ordered trumpets and rose petals scattered on our path." I turned and waved the advance to the train, Curan spurred his horse and the column galloped forward. "Now get off the bridge or be trampled, you rat-faced little twat."

I strode past Oswald into the castle, pumping Jones in the air as if I was leading cadence for war drummers. I think I should have been a diplomat.

As Lear rode by he clouted Oswald on the head with his sheathed sword, knocking the unctuous steward into the moat. I felt my anger for the old man slip a notch.

Kent, his disguise now completed by nearly three weeks of hunger and living in the outdoors, fell in behind the train as I had instructed. He looked lean and leathery now, more like an older version of Hunter than the old, overfed knight he had been at the White Tower. I stood to the side of the gate as the column entered and nodded to him as he passed.

"I'm hungry, Pocket. All I had to eat yesterday was an owl."

"Perfect fare for witch finding, methinks. You're with me to Great Birnam Wood tonight, then?"

"After supper."

"Aye. If Goneril doesn't poison the lot of us."

Ah, Goneril, Goneril, Goneril—like a distant love chant is her name. Not that it doesn't summon memories of burning urination and putrid discharge, but what romance worth the memory is devoid of the bittersweet?

When I first met her, Goneril was but seventeen, and although betrothed to Albany from the age of twelve, she had never seen him. A curious, round-bottomed girl, she had spent her entire life in and around the White Tower, and she'd developed a colossal appetite for knowledge of the outside world, which somehow she thought she could sate by grilling a humble fool. It started on odd afternoons, when she would call me to her chambers, and with her ladies-in-waiting in attendance, ask me all manner of questions her tutors had refused to answer.

"Lady," said I, "I am but a fool. Shouldn't you ask someone with position?"

"Mother is dead and Father treats us like porcelain dolls. Everyone else is afraid to speak. You are my fool, it is your duty to speak truth to power."

"Impeccable logic, lady, but truth be told, I'm here as fool to the little princess." I was new to the castle, and did not want to be held accountable for telling Goneril something that the king didn't wish her to know.

"Well, Cordelia is having her nap, so until she wakes you are *my* fool. I so decree it."

The ladies clapped at the royal decree.

"Again, irrefutable logic," said I to the thick but comely princess. "Proceed."

"Pocket, you have traveled the land, tell me, what is it like to be a peasant?"

"Well, milady, I've never been a peasant, strictly speaking, but for the most part, I'm told it's wake early, work hard, suffer hunger, catch the plague, and die. Then get up the next morning and do it all again."

"Every day?"

"Well, if you're a Christian—on Sunday you get up early, go to church, suffer hunger until you have a big meal of barley and swill, then catch the plague and die."

"Hunger? Is that why they seem so wretched and unhappy?"

"That would be one of the reasons. But there's much to be said for hard work, disease, run-of-the-mill suffering, and the odd witch burning or virgin sacrifice, depending on your faith."

"If they are hungry, why don't they just eat something?"

"That is an excellent idea, milady. Someone should suggest that."

"Oh, I shall make a most excellent duchess, I think. The people will praise me for my wisdom."

"Most certainly, milady," said I. "Your father married his sister, then, did he, love?"

"Heavens no, mother was a Belgian princess, why do you ask?"

"Heraldry is my hobby, go on."

Once we were inside the main curtain wall[2] of Castle Albany, it was clear that we would go no farther. The main keep of the castle stood behind yet another curtain wall and had its own drawbridge, over a dry ditch rather than a moat. The bridge was lowering even as the king approached. Goneril walked out on the drawbridge unaccompanied, wearing a gown of green velvet, laced a bit too tightly. If the intent was to lessen the rise of her bosom it failed miserably, and brought gasps and guffaws from several of the knights until Curan raised his hand for silence.

"Father, welcome to Albany," said Goneril. "All hail good king and loving father."

2. Curtain wall—the outer wall of a castle compound, usually surrounding all of the buildings.

She held out her arms and the anger drained from Lear's face. He climbed down from his horse. I scampered to the king's side and steadied him. Captain Curan signaled and the rest of the train dismounted.

As I straightened Lear's cape about his shoulders, I caught Goneril's eye. "Missed you, pumpkin."

"Knave," said she under her breath.

"She was always the most fair of the three," I said to Lear. "And certainly the most wise."

"My lord means to accidentally hang your fool, Father."

"Ah, well, if accident, there's no fault but Fate," said I with a grin—pert and nimble spirit of mirth that I am. "But call then for a spanking of Fate's fickle bottom and hit it good, lady." I winked and smacked the horse's rump.

Wit's arrow hit and Goneril blushed. "I'll see *you* hit, you wicked little dog."

"Enough of that," said Lear. "Leave the boy alone. Come give your father a hug."

Jones barked enthusiastically and chanted, "A fool must hit it. A fool must hit it, hit it good." The puppet knows a lady's weakness.

"Father," said she, "I'm afraid we've accommodation only for you in the castle. Your knights and others will have to make do in the outer bailey.[3] We've quarters and food for them by the stables."

"But what about my fool?"

"Your fool can sleep in the stable with the rest of the rabble."

"So be it." Lear let his eldest lead him into the castle like a milk cow by the nose ring.

"She truly loathes you, doesn't she?" said Kent. He was busy wrapping himself around a pork shoulder the size of a toddler—his Welsh accent actually sounding more natural through the grease and gristle than when clear.

"Not to worry, lad," said Curan, who had joined us by our fire. "We'll not let Albany hang you. Will we, lads!?"

Soldiers all around us cheered, not sure what they were cheering for, beyond the fact that they were enjoying the first full meal with ale that they'd had since leaving the White Tower. A small village was housed inside the bailey and some of the knights were already wandering off in search of an alehouse and a whore. We were outside the castle, but at least we were out of the wind, and we could sleep in the stables, which the pages and squires had mucked out on our arrival.

3. Bailey—courtyard inside a castle wall.

"But if we're not welcome in the great hall, then they are not welcome to the talents of the king's fool," said Curan. "Sing us a song, Pocket."

A cheer went up around the camp: "Sing! Sing! Sing!"

Kent raised an eyebrow. "Go ahead, lad, your witches will wait."

I am what I am. I drained my flagon of ale, set it by the fire, then whistled loudly, jumped up, did three somersaults and laid out into a back-flip, wherefrom I landed with Jones pointed at the moon, and said, "A ballad, then!?"

"Aye!" came the cheer.

And ever so sweetly, I crooned the lilting love song "Shall I Shag My Lady Upon the Shire?" I followed that with a bit of a narrative song by way of a troubadour tradition: "The Hanging of Willie Wagging William." Well, everyone likes a story after supper, and by the one-eyed balls of the Cyclops, that one got them clapping, so I slowed it down a bit with the solemn ballad, "Dragon Spooge Befouled My Bonny Bonny Lass." Bloody inconsiderate to leave a train of fighting men fighting back tears, so I danced my way around the camp while singing the shanty "Alehouse Lilly (She'll Bonk You Silly)."

I was about to say good night and head out when Curan called for silence and a road-worn herald wearing a great golden *fleur-delis* on his chest entered the camp. He unrolled his scroll and read.

"Hear ye, hear ye. Let it be known that King Philip the Twenty-seventh of France is dead. God rest his soul. Long live France. Long live the king!"

No one "long lived the king" back at him and he seemed disappointed. Although one knight did murmur "So?" and another, "Good bloody riddance."

"Well, you British pig dogs, Prince Jeff is now king," said the herald.

We all looked at each other and shrugged.

"And Princess Cordelia of *Britain* is now Queen of France," the herald added, rather huffy now.

"Oh," said many, realizing at last at least a glancing relevance.

"Jeff?" said I. "The bloody frog prince is called Jeff?" I strode to the herald and snatched the scroll out of his hand. He tried to take it back and I clouted him with Jones.

"Calm, lad," said Kent, taking the scroll from me and handing it back to the herald. *"Merci,"* said he to the messenger.

"He took my bloody princess *and* my monkey's name!" said I, taking another swing with Jones, which missed its mark as Kent was dragging me away.

"You should be pleased," said Kent. "Your lady is the Queen of France."

"And don't think she's not going to rub my nose in *that* when I see her."

"Come, lad, let's go find your witches. We'll want to be back by morning in time for Albany to accidentally hang you."

"Oh, she'd like that, wouldn't she?"

9.

Toil and Trouble

S o why is it that we are going to Great Birnam Wood
to look for witches?" asked Kent as we made our
way across the moor. There was only a slight breeze but
it was bloody cold, what with the mist and the gloom
and my despair over King Jeff. I pulled my woolen cape
around me.

"Bloody Scotland," said I. "Albany is possibly
the darkest, dampest, coldest bloody crevice in all of
Blighty. Sodding Scots."

"Witches?" reminded Kent.

"Because the bloody ghost told me I'd find my
answers here."

"Ghost?"

"The girl ghost at the White Tower, keep up, Kent.
Rhymes and riddles and such." I told him of the "*grave*

offense to daughters three" and the "*madman rising to lead the blind.*"

Kent nodded as if he understood. "And I'm along because . . ."

"Because it is dark and I am small."

"You might have asked Curan or one of the others. I'm reticent about witches."

"Nonsense. They're just like physicians, only without the bleeding. Nothing to fear."

"In the day, when Lear was still Christian, we did not do well by witches. I've had a cartload of curses cast on me."

"Not very effective, though, were they? You're child-frighteningly old and still strong as a bull."

"I am banished, penniless, and live under the threat of death upon discovery of my name."

"Oh, good point. Brave of you to come, then."

"Aye, thanks, lad, but I'm not feeling it. What's that light?"

There was a fire ahead in the wood, and figures moving around it.

"Stealthy, now, good Kent. Let us creep up silently and see what is to be seen before revealing ourselves. Now, creep, Kent, you crashing great ox, creep."

And with but two steps my strategy revealed its flaw.

"You're jingling like a coin purse possessed of fits," said Kent. "You couldn't creep up on the deaf nor dead. Silence your bloody bells, Pocket."

I placed my coxcomb on the ground. "I can leave my hat, but I'll not take off my shoes—we'll surrender all stealth if I'm screaming from trodding tender-footed across lizards, thorns, hedgehogs, and the lot."

"Here, then," said Kent, pulling the remains of the pork shoulder from his satchel. "Dampen your bells with the fat."

I raised an eyebrow quizzically—an unappreciated and overly subtle gesture in the dark—then shrugged and began working the suet into the bells at my toes and ankles.

"There!" I shook a leg to the satisfying sound of nothing at all. "Forward!"

Creep we did, until we were just outside the halo of firelight. Three bent-backed hags were walking a slow circle around a large cauldron, dropping in twisted bits of this and that as they chanted.

"Double, double, toil and trouble:
Fire burn, and cauldron bubble."

"Witches," whispered Kent, paying tribute to the god of all things bloody fucking obvious.

"Aye," said I, in lieu of clouting him. (Jones stayed behind to guard my hat.)

"Eye of newt and toe of frog,
Wool of bat and tongue of dog,
Adder's fork and blind-worm's sting,
Lizard's leg and owlet's wing,
For a charm of powerful trouble,
Like a hell-broth boil and bubble."

They double-bubbled the chorus and we were readying ourselves for another verse of the recipe when I felt something brush against my leg. It was all I could do not to cry out. I felt Kent's hand on my shoulder.

"Steady, lad, it's just a cat."

Another brush, and a meow. Two of them now, licking my bells, and purring. (It sounds more pleasant than it was.) "It's the bloody pork fat," I whispered.

A third feline joined the gang. I stood on one foot, trying to hold the other above their heads, but while I am an accomplished acrobat, the art of levitation still eludes me; thus my ground-bound foot became my Achilles' heel, as it were. One of the fiends sank its fangs into my ankle.

"Fuckstockings!" said I, somewhat emphatically. I hopped, I whirled, I made disparaging remarks toward all creatures of the feline aspect. Hissing and yowling ensued. When at last the cats retreated, I was sitting splayed-legged by the fire, Kent stood next to me with his sword drawn and ready, and the three hags stood in ranks across the cauldron from us.

"Back, witches!" said Kent. "You may curse me into a toad, but they'll be the last words out of your mouths while your heads are attached."

"Witches?" said the first witch, who was greenest of the three. "What witches? *We are but humble washer-women, making our way in the wood.*"

"*Rendering laundry service, humble and good,*" said witch two, the tallest.

"*All it be, is as it should,*" said witch three, who had a wicked wart over her right eye.

"By Hecate's[1] night-tarred nipples, stop rhyming!" said I. "If you're not witches, what was that curse you were bubbling about?"

"*Stew,*" said Warty.

"*Stew, stew most true,*" said Tall.

"*Stew most blue,*" said Green.

"It's not blue," said Kent, looking in the cauldron. "More of a brown."

"I know," said Green, "but brown doesn't rhyme, does it, love?"

"I'm looking for witches," said I.

1. Hecate—Greek goddess of witchcraft, sorcery, and ghosts.

"Really?" said Tall.

"I was sent by a ghost."

The hags looked at one another, then back at me. "Ghost told you to bring your laundry here, did it?" said Warty.

"You're not washerwomen! You're bloody witches! And that's not stew, and the bloody ghost of the bloody White Tower said to seek you here for answers, so can we get about it, ye gnarled knots of erect vomitus?"

"Ah, we're toads for sure now," sighed Kent.

"Always a bloody ghost, innit?" said Tall.

"What did she look like?" asked Green.

"Who? The ghost? I didn't say it was a she—"

"What did she look like, fool?" snarled Warty.

"I suppose I shall pass my days eating bugs and hiding under leaves until some crone drops me in a cauldron," mused Kent, leaning on his sword now, watching moths dart into the fire.

"She was ghostly pale," said I, "all in white— vaporous, with fair hair and—"

"She was fit,[2] though?" asked Tall. "Lovely, you might even say?"

"Bit more transparent than I care for in my wenches, but aye, she was fit."

---

2. Fit—British slang, attractive, sexy.

"Aye," said Warty, looking to the others, who huddled with her.

When they came up, Green said, "State your business, then, fool. Why did the ghost send you here?"

"She said you could help me. I am fool to the court of King Lear of Britain. He has sent away his youngest daughter, Cordelia, of whom I am somewhat fond; he's given my apprentice fool, Drool, to that blackguard bastard Edmund of Gloucester, and my friend Taster has been poisoned and is quite dead."

"And don't forget that they're going to hang you at dawn," added Kent.

"Don't concern yourselves with that, ladies," said I. "About to be hanged is my status quo, not a condition that requires your repair."

The hags huddled again. There was much whispering and a bit of hissing. They broke their conference and Warty, who was the apparent coven leader, said, "That Lear's a nasty piece of work."

"Last time he went Christian a score of witches were drowned," said Tall.

Kent nodded, and looked at his shoes. "The Petite Inquisition—not a high point."

"Aye, we were a decade spelling them all back to life for the revenge," said Warty. "Rosemary here still seeps pond-water from the ears on damp days," said Tall.

"Aye, and carps ate my small toes while I was pond-bottom," said Green.

"Her toes thus gefilted,[3] we had to seek an enchanted lynx and take two of his for replacement."

Rosemary (who was Green) nodded gravely.

"Goes through shoes in a fortnight, but there's no better witch to chase a squirrel up a tree," said Tall.

"That's true," said Rosemary.

"Beats the burnings, though," said Warty.

"Aye, that's true," said Tall. "No amount of cat toes'll fix you if you've all your bits burnt off. Lear had him some burnings as well."

"I'm not here on behalf of Lear," said I. "I'm here to correct the madness he's done."

"Well, why didn't you say so?" said Rosemary.

"We're always keen on sending a bit of the mayhem Lear's way," said Warty. "Shall we curse him with leprosy?"

"By your leave, ladies, I don't wish the old man's undoing, only the undoing of his deeds."

"A simple curse would be easier," said Tall. "A bit o' bat spittle in the cauldron and we can have him walking on duck feet before breakfast. Make him quack, too, if you've a shilling or a freshly-strangled infant for the service."

---

3. Gefilte fish—a poached ground fish patty, usually made of carp.

"I just want my friends and my home back," said I.

"Well, if you can't be persuaded, let us have a consult," said Rosemary. "Parsley, Sage, a moment?" She waved the other witches over to an old oak where they whispered.

"Parsley, Sage, and Rosemary?" said Kent. "What, no Thyme?"

Rosemary wheeled on him. "Oh, we've the time if you've the inclination, handsome."

"Jolly good show, hag!" said I. I liked these crones, they had a fine-edged wit.

Rosemary rolled her good eye at the earl, lifted her skirts, aimed her withered bottom at Kent, and rubbed a palsied claw over it. "Round and firm, good knight. Round and firm."

Kent gagged a little and backed away a few steps. "Gods save us! Away you ghastly carbuncled tart!"

I would have looked away, should have, but I had never seen a green one. A weaker man might have plucked out his own eyes, but being a philosopher, I knew the sight could never be unseen, so I persevered.

"Hop on, Kent," said I. "Beast-shagging is thy calling and thou surely have been called."

Kent backed into a tree and half cold-cocked himself. He slid down the trunk, dazed.

Rosemary dropped her skirts. "Just having you on." The crones cackled as they huddled again. "We've a proper toading for you once the fool's business is finished, though. A moment, please . . ."

The witches whispered for a moment, then resumed their march around the cauldron.

"Nose of Turk, and Tartar's lips,
Griffin spunk and monkey hips,
Mandrake rubbed with tiger nads,
To divine undoing for the old king mad."

"Oh bollocks," said Sage, "we're all out of monkey hips."

Parsley looked into the cauldron and gave it a stir. "We can make do without them. You can substitute a fool's finger."

"No," said I.

"Well, then, get a finger from that comely hunk of man-meat with the bootblack on his beard—he seems foolish enough."

"No," said Kent, still a tad dazed. "And it's not bootblack, it's a clever disguise."

The witches looked to me. "There's no counting on accuracy without the monkey hips or fool's finger," said Rosemary.

I said: "Let us make do and gallantly bugger on, shall we, ladies?"

"All right," said Parsley, "but don't blame us if we bollocks-up your future."

There was more stirring and chanting in dead languages, and no little bit of wailing, and finally, when I was about to doze off, a great bubble rose in the cauldron and when it burst it released a cloud of steam that formed itself into a giant face, not unlike the tragedy mask used by traveling players. It glowed against the misty night.

"'Ello," said the giant face, sounding Cockney and a little drunk.

"Hello, large and steamy face," said I.

"Fool, Fool, you must save the Drool,
Quick to Gloucester, or blood will pool."

"Oh, for fuck's sake, this one rhymes, too?" said I to the witches. "Can't a bloke find a straightforward prose apparition?"

"Quiet, fool!" snapped Sage, who I was back to thinking of as Warty. To the face, she said, "Apparition of darkest power, we're clear on the *where* and the *what*, but the fool was hoping for some direction of the *how* variety."

"Aye. Sorry," said large steamy face. "I'm not slow, you know, your recipe was short a monkey hip."

"We'll use two next time," said Sage.

"Well, all right, then . . .

"To reverse the will of a flighty king,
Remove his train to clip his wings.
To eldest daughters knights be dower,
And soon a fool will yield the power."

The steamy face grinned.

I looked at the witches. "So I'm to somehow get Goneril and Regan to take Lear's knights in addition to everything else they have?"

"He never lies," said Rosemary.

"He's often wildly fucking inaccurate," said Parsley, "but not a liar."

"Again," said I to the apparition, "good to know what to do and all, but a method to the madness would be most welcome as well. A strategy, as it were."

"Cheeky little bastard, ent 'e?" said Steamy to the witches.

"Want us to put a curse on him?" asked Sage.

"No, no, the lad's a rocky road ahead without adding a curse to slow him." The apparition cleared his throat (or at least made the throat-clearing noise, as, strictly speaking, he had no throat).

"A princess to your will shall bend,
If seduction in a note, you send,
And fates of kings and queens shall tell,
When bound are passions with a spell."

With that, the apparition faded away.

"That's it, then?" I asked. "A couple of rhymes and we're finished? I have no idea what I'm to do."

"Bit thick yourself, then, are you?" said Sage. "You're to go to Gloucester. You're to separate Lear from his knights and see that they're under the power of his daughters. Then you're to write letters of seduction to the princesses and bind their passions with a magic spell. Couldn't be any clearer if it was rhymed."

Kent was nodding and shrugging as if the bloody obviousness of it all had sluiced through the wood in an illuminating deluge, leaving me the only one dry.

"Oh, do fuck off, you grey-bearded sot. Where would you get a magic spell to bind the bitches' passion?"

"Them," said Kent, pointing rudely at the hags.

"Us," said the hags in chorus.

"Oh," said I, letting the flood wash over me. "Of course."

Rosemary stepped forward and held forth three shriveled grey orbs, each about the size of a man's eye.

I did not take them, fearing they might be something as disgusting as they appeared to be—desiccated elf scrotums or some such.

"Puff balls, from a fungus that grows deep in the wood," said Rosemary.

"In lover's breath these spores release
An enchanting charm you shall unleash
Passion which can be never broken
For him whose name next is spoken."

"So, to recap, simply and without rhyme?"

"Squeeze one of these bulbs under your lady's nose, then say your name and she will find your charms irresistible and become overwhelmed with desire for you," explained Sage.

"Redundant then, really?" said I with a grin.

The hags laughed themselves into a wheeze-around, then Rosemary dropped the puff balls into a small silk pouch and handed it to me.

"There's the matter of payment," said she, as I reached for the purse.

"I'm a poor fool," said I. "All we have between us is my scepter and a well-used shoulder of pork. I suppose I could wait while each of you takes Kent for a roll in the hay, if that will do."

"You will not!" said Kent.

The hag held up a hand. "A price to be named later," said she. "Whenever we ask."

"Fine, then," said I, snatching the purse away from her.

"Swear it," she said.

"I swear," said I.

"In blood."

"But—" As quick as a cat she scratched the back of my hand with her ragged talon. "Ouch!" Blood welled in the crease.

"Let it drip in the cauldron and swear," said the crone.

I did as I was told. "Since I'm here, is there any chance I could get a monkey?"

"No," said Sage.

"No," said Parsely.

"No," said Rosemary. "We're all out of monkeys, but we'll put a glamour on your mate so his disguise isn't so bloody pathetic."

"Go to it, then," said I. "We must be off."

ACT II

How sharper than a serpent's tooth it is
to have a thankless child.

—*King Lear,* Act I, Scene 4

10.

All Your Dread Pleasures

The sky threatened a dismal dawn as we reached Castle Albany. The drawbridge was up.

"Who goes there?" shouted the sentry.

"'Tis Lear's fool, Pocket, and his man at arms, Caius." Caius is the name the witches gave Kent to use to bind his disguise. They'd cast a glamour on him: his beard and hair were now jet black, as if by nature, not soot, his face lean and weathered, only his eyes, as brown and gentle as a moo cow's, showed the real Kent. I advised him to pull down the wide brim of his hat should we encounter old acquaintances.

"Where in bloody hell have you been?" asked the sentry. He signaled and the bridge ground down. "The old king's nearly torn the county apart looking for you. Accused our lady of tying a rock to you and casting you in the North Sea, he did."

"Seems a spot o' bother. I must have grown in her esteem. Just last night she was only going to hang me."

"Last night? You drunken sot, we've been looking for you for a month."

I looked at Kent and he at me, then we at the sentry. "A *month*?"

"Bloody witches," said Kent under his breath.

"If you turn up we're to take you to our lady immediately," said the sentry.

"Oh, please do, gentle guard, your lady does so love seeing me at first light."

The sentry scratched his beard and seemed to be thinking. "Well spoken, fool. Perhaps you lot could do with some breakfast and a wash-up before I take you to my lady."

The drawbridge thumped into place. I led Kent across, and the sentry met us by the inner gate.

"Beggin' your pardon, sir," the sentry said, directing his speech to Kent. "You wouldn't mind waiting until eight bells to reveal the fool's return, would you?"

"That when you're off watch, lad?"

"Aye, sir. I'm not sure I want to be the bearer of the joyous news of the wayward fool's arrival. The king's knights have been raising rabble round the castle for a fortnight and I've heard our lady cursing the Black Fool as part of the cause."

"Blamed even in my absence?" said I. "I told you, Caius, she adores me."

Kent patted the sentry on the shoulder. "We'll escort ourselves, lad, and tell your lady we came through the gate with the merchants in the morning. Now, back to your post."

"Thank you, good sir. But for your rough clothes, I'd take you for a gentleman."

"But for my clothes, I'd be one," said Kent, his grin a dazzle amid his newly-black beard.

"Oh, for fuck's sake, would you two just have a gobble on each other's knob and be done with it," said I.

The two soldiers leapt back as if each was on fire.

"Sorry, just having you on," said I, as I breezed by them and into the castle. "You poofters are such a sensitive lot."

"I'm not a poofter," said Kent as we approached Goneril's chambers.

Midmorning. The time in between allowed us to eat, wash, do some writing, and ascertain that we had, indeed, been gone for over a month, despite it seeming only overnight to us. Perhaps that was the hags' payment? To extract a month from our lives in exchange for the spells, potions, and prognostication—it seemed a fair price, but bloody complicated to explain.

Oswald sat at a scribe's desk outside the duchess's chambers. I laughed and wagged Jones under his nose.

"Still guarding the door like a common footman, then, Oswald? Oh, the years have been good to you."

Oswald wore only a dagger at his belt, no sword, but his hand fell to it as he stood.

Kent dropped his hand to his sword and shook his head gravely. Oswald sat back down on his stool.

"I'll have you know that I'm both steward and chamberlain, as well as trusted adviser to the duchess."

"A veritable quiver of titles she's given you to sling. Tell me, do you still answer to toady and catch-fart, or are those titles only honorary now?"

"All better than common fool," Oswald spat.

"True, I am a fool, and also true, I am common, but I am no common fool, catch-fart. I am the Black Fool, I have been sent for, and I shall be given entry to your lady's chambers, while you, fool, sit by the door. Announce me."

I believe Oswald growled then. A new trick he'd learned since the old days. He'd always tried to cast my title as an insult, and boiled that I took it as a tribute. Would he ever understand that he found favor with Goneril not because of his groveling or devotion, but because he was so easily humiliated? Good, I suppose, that he'd learned to growl, beaten down dog that he was.

He stormed through the heavy door, then returned a minute later. He would not look me in the eye. "My lady will see you now," he said. "But only you. This ruffian can wait in the kitchen."

"Wait here, ruffian," said I to Kent. "And make some effort not to bugger poor Oswald here, no matter how he should beg for it."

"I'm not a poofter," said Kent.

"Not with this villain, you're not," said I. "His bum is property of the princess."

"I'll see you hanged, fool," said Oswald.

"Aroused by the thought, are you, Oswald? No matter, you'll not have my ruffian. *Adieu.*"

Then I was through the doors, and into Goneril's chambers. Goneril sat to the back of a great, round room. Her quarters were housed in a full tower of the castle. Three floors: this hall for meeting and business, another floor above it would have rooms for her ladies, her wardrobe, bathing and dressing, the top would be where she slept and played, if she still played.

"Do you still play, pumpkin?" I asked. I danced a tight-stepped jig and bowed.

Goneril waved her ladies away.

"Pocket, I'll have you—"

"Oh, I know, hanged at dawn, head on a pike, guts for garters, drawn and quartered, impaled, disemboweled, beaten, and made into bangers and mash—all your dread pleasures visited on me with glorious cruelty—all stipulated, lady—duly noted and taken as truth. Now, how may a humble fool serve before his hour of doom descends?"

She twisted up her lip as if to snarl, then burst out laughing and quickly looked around to make sure that no one saw her. "I will, you know—you horrible, wicked little man."

"Wicked? *Moi?*" said I in perfect fucking French.

"Tell no one," she said.

It had always been that way with Goneril. Her "*tell no one,*" however, applied only to me, not to her, I had found out.

"Pocket," she once said, brushing her red-gold hair near a window, where it caught the sun and seemed to shine as if from within. She was perhaps seventeen then, and had gotten in the habit of calling me to her chambers several times a week and questioning me mercilessly.

"Pocket, I am to be married soon, and I am mystified by man bits. I've heard them described, but that's not helping."

"Ask your nurse. Isn't she supposed to teach you about such things?"

"Auntie's a nun, and married to Jesus. A virgin."

"You don't say? She went to the wrong bloody convent, then."

"I need to talk to a man, but not a proper man. You are like one of those fellows that Saracens have look over their harems."

"A eunuch?"

"See, you are worldly and know of things. I need to see your willie."

"Pardon? What? Why?"

"Because I've never seen one, and I don't want to seem naïve on my wedding night when the depraved brute ravages me."

"How do you know he's a depraved brute?"

"Auntie told me. All men are. Now, out with your willie, fool."

"Why my willie? There's willies aplenty you can look at. What about Oswald? He may even have one, or knows where you can get hold of one, I'll wager." (Oswald was her footman then.)

"I know, but this is my first, and yours will be small and not so frightening. It's like when I was learning to ride, and first father gave me a pony, but then, as I got older . . ."

"All right, then, shut up. Here."

"Oh, would you look at that."

"What?"

"That's it, then?"

"Yes. What?"

"Nothing really to be afraid of then, was there? I don't know what all the fuss is about. It's rather pitiful if you ask me."

"It is not."

"Are they all this small?"

"Most are smaller, in fact."

"May I touch it?"

"If you feel you must."

"Well, would you look at that."

"See, now you've angered it."

Where in God's name have you been?" she said. "Father's been a madman looking for you. He and his captain have gone out on patrol every day and well into the evening, leaving the rest of his knights to wreak havoc on the castle. My lord has sent soldiers as far as Edinburgh asking after you. I should have you drowned for all the worry you've caused."

"You did miss me, didn't you?" I cradled the silk purse at my belt, wondering when best to spring the spell. And once she was bewitched, how exactly would I use the power?

"He was supposed to be in Regan's care, but by the time he moves his bloody hundred knights all the way to Cornwall it will be my turn again. I can't abide the rabble in my palace."

"What does Lord Albany say?"

"He says what I tell him to say. It's all intolerable."

"Gloucester," said I, offering the very model of a non sequitur wrapped in an enigma.

"Gloucester?" asked the duchess.

"The king's good friend is there. It's mid-way between here and Cornwall, and the Earl of Gloucester daren't deny the request of the dukes of both Albany and Cornwall. You wouldn't be leaving the king without care, yet you wouldn't have him underfoot, either." With the witches' warning about Drool in danger there, I was determined for all the drama to descend on Gloucester. I sat down on the floor near her feet, held Jones across my knees, and waited, both I and the puppet wearing jolly grins.

"Gloucester . . ." said Goneril, letting a bit of a smile seep out. She really could be lovely when she forgot she was cruel.

"Gloucester," said Jones, "the dog's bollocks of western bloody Blighty."

"Do you think he'll agree to it? It's not how he laid out his legacy."

"He won't agree to Gloucester, but he'll agree to go to Regan's by way of Gloucester. The rest will be up to your sister." Should I have felt myself a traitor? No, the old man brought this on himself.

"But if he doesn't agree, and he has all these men?" She looked me in the eye now. "It's too much power in the hands of the feeble."

"And yet, he had all the power of the kingdom not two months ago."

"You've not seen him, Pocket. The legacy and banishment of Cordelia and Kent was just the beginning. Since you went away he's gotten worse. He searches for you, he hunts, he rails about his days as a soldier of Christ one minute, then calls to the gods of Nature the next. With a fighting force of that size—if he should feel that we've betrayed him—"

"Take them," said I.

"What? I couldn't."

"You have seen my apprentice, Drool? He eats with his hands or with a spoon, we dare not let him have a knife or fork, lest the points imperil all."

"Don't be obtuse, Pocket. What of Father's knights?"

"You pay them? Take them. For his own good. Lear with his train of knights is like a child running with a sword. Are you cruel to relieve him of deadly force, when he is neither strong enough, nor wise enough to wield it? Tell Lear he must dismiss fifty of his knights and their attendants and keep them here.

Tell him they will be at his beck and call when he is in residence."

"Fifty? Just fifty?"

"You must leave some for your sister. Send Oswald to Cornwall with your plan. Have Regan and Cornwall make haste to Gloucester so they are there upon Lear's arrival. Perhaps they can bring Gloucester into the fold. With Lear's knights dismissed, the two whitebeards can reminisce about their glory days and crawl together to the grave in peaceful nostalgia."

"Yes!" Goneril was becoming breathless now, excited. I'd seen it before. It wasn't always a good sign.

"Quickly," said I, "send Oswald to Regan while the sun is high."

"No!" Goneril sat forward quickly, her bosom nearly spilling out of her gown, which captured my attention more than her fingernails digging into my arm.

"What?" said I, the bells of my coxcomb but a finger's breath from jingling her *décolletage*.[1]

"There is no peace for Lear in Gloucester. Haven't you heard? The earl's son Edgar is a traitor."

Had I heard? Had I heard? Of course, the bastard's plan was afoot. "Of course, lady, where do you think I've been?"

---

1. *Décolletage*—the road to Hooterville; cleavage. From the fucking French.

"You've been all the way to Gloucester?" She was panting now.

"Aye. And back. I've brought you something."

"A present?" She showed the delighted, wide grey-green eyes she'd had when she was a girl. "Perhaps I won't hang you, but punishment is due you, Pocket."

Then the lady grabbed me and pulled me across her lap, face-down. Jones rolled to the floor beside me. "Lady, perhaps—"

Smack! "There, fool, I've hit it. Hit it. Hit it. Hit it. So give it. Give it. Give it." A smack with every iamb.[2]

"Bloody hell, you insane tart!" I squirmed. My ass burned with her handprint.

Smack! "Oh good God!" said Goneril. "Yes!" She wiggled under me now.

Smack!

"Ouch! It's a letter! A letter," said I.

"I'll see your little bum as red as a rose!"

Smack!

I squirmed in her lap, turned, grabbed her bosoms and pulled myself upright until I was sitting in her lap. "Here." I pulled the sealed parchment out of my jerkin and held it out.

"Not yet!" said she, trying to roll me over and get back to smacking my bum.

2. Iamb—in poetry, a metrical foot consisting of an unstressed syllable followed by a stressed syllable. Hit *IT*, Give *IT*.

She honked my codpiece.

"You honked my codpiece."

"Aye, give it up, fool." She tried to get a hand under my codpiece.

I reached into the silk purse and retrieved one of the puffballs as I tried to keep my manhood out of her grasp. I heard a door open.

"Surrender the willie!" said the duchess.

She had it then, there was nothing I could do. I squoze the puffball under her nose.

"It's from Edmund of Gloucester," said I.

"Milady?" said Oswald, who was standing in the doorway.

"Let us down, pumpkin," said I. "The catch-fart needs his task set."

It all smacked of history.

The game had progressed further that first day, when Oswald first interrupted us, all those years ago, but it had begun, as always, with one of Goneril's query sessions.

"Pocket," said she, "since you were raised in an abbey, I should think you know much about punishment."

"Aye, lady. I had my share, and it didn't end there. I still endure an inquisition almost daily in these very chambers."

"Gentle Pocket, surely you jest?"

"That *is* part of the job, mum."

She stood then, and dismissed the ladies from her solar with a minor tantrum. When they were gone she said, "I've never been punished."

"Aye, lady, well, you're Christian, there's always time." I'd left the Church with a curse after they walled up my anchoress and I was leaning heavily pagan at the time.

"No one is allowed to strike me, so there's always been a girl to take my punishment for me. My spankings."

"Aye, mum, as it should be. Spare the royal withers and all."

"And I feel funny about it. Just last week I mentioned during mass that Regan might be a bit of a cunt, and my whipping girl was soundly spanked for it."

"Might as well have whipped her for your calling the sky blue, eh? A beating for talking truth, of course you felt funny about it."

"Not that kind of funny, Pocket. Funny like when you taught me about the little man in the boat."

It had been a verbal lesson only, shortly after she'd insisted I teach her about manly bits. But it had kept her amused, on and off, for a fortnight. "Oh, of course," said I. "Funny."

"I need to be spanked," said Goneril.

"A constant, I'd agree, lady, but again we're declaring the sky blue, aren't we?"

"I *want* to be spanked."

"Oh," said I, eloquent and quick-witted rascal that I am. "*That's* different."

"By you," said the Princess.

"Fuckstockings," I thus declared my doom.

Well, by the time Oswald came into the room that first time, both the princess and I were as red-bottomed as Barbary monkeys, quite naked (except for my hat, which Goneril had donned) and administering rhythmically to each other's front sides. Oswald was somewhat less than discreet about it all.

"Alarm! Alarm! My lady is ravaged by a fool! Alarm!" said Oswald, fleeing from the room, to raise the alarm through the castle.

I caught up to Oswald as he entered the great hall, where Lear was sitting on his throne, Regan sitting at his feet to one side, doing needlepoint, Cordelia at the other, playing with a doll.

"The fool has violated the princess!" Oswald announced.

"Pocket!" said Cordelia, dropping her doll and running to my side, sporting a great, goofy grin. She was perhaps eight then.

Oswald stepped in front of me. "I found the fool rutting the princess Goneril like a rapacious goat, sire."

"'Tis not true, nuncle," said I. "I was called to the lady's solar this morning only to jest her out of a morning funk, which can be smelt upon her breath if you have doubts."

At that point Goneril came running into the room, trying to arrange her skirts as she moved. She stopped beside me and curtsied before her father. She was breathless, barefoot, and one breast peeked Cyclopean out the bodice of her gown. I snatched my coxcomb off her head with a jingle and concealed it behind my back.

"There, fresh as a flower," said I.

"Hello, sister," said Cordelia.

"Morning, lamb," said Goneril, blindfolding the pink-eyed Cyclops with a quick tuck.

Lear scratched his beard and glared at his eldest daughter.

"What ho, daughter," said he. "Hast thou shagged a fool?"

"Methinks any wench who shags a man hath shagged a fool, Father."

"That was a distinct no," said I.

"What is shagged?" asked Cordelia.

"I saw it," said Oswald.

"Shag a man and shag a fool, one is the same as another," said Goneril. "But this morning I have your Fool shagged, righteous and rowdy. I bonked him until he cried out for gods and horses to pull me off."

What was this? Was she hoping for more punishment?

"That is so," said Oswald. "I heard the call."

"Shagged, shagged, shagged!" said Goneril. "Oh, what is this I feel? Tiny bastard fools stirring in my womb. I can hear their tiny bells."

"You lying tart," said I. "A fool is no more born with bells than a princess with fangs, both must be earned."

Lear said, "If that were true, Pocket, I'd have a halberd run up your bum."

"You can't kill Pocket," said Cordelia. "I'll need him to cheer me when I'm visited by the red curse, and a horrible melancholy comes over me," said Cordelia.

"What are you on about, child?" said I.

"All women get it," said Cordelia. "They must be punished for Eve's treachery in the garden of evil. Nurse says it makes you ever so miserable."

I patted the child's head. "For fuck's sake, sire, you've got to get the girls some teachers who aren't nuns."

"I should be punished!" said Goneril.

"I've had my curse for simply months," said Regan, not even bothering to look up from her needlepoint. "I find that if I go to the dungeon and have some prisoners tortured I feel better."

"No, I want my Pocket," said Cordelia, starting to whine now.

"You can't have him," said Goneril. "He's to be punished, too. After what he's done."

Oswald bowed for no particular reason. "May I suggest his head on a pike on the London Bridge, sire, to discourage any more debauchery?"

"Silence!" said Lear, standing. He came down the steps, walked past Oswald, who fell to his knees, and stood before me. He put his hand on Cordelia's head.

The old king locked his hawk's gaze upon me. "She didn't speak for three years before you came," he said.

"Aye, sire," said I, looking down.

He turned to Goneril. "Go to your quarters. Have your nurse tend to your illusions. She will see that there is no issue from it."

"But, Father, the fool and I—"

"Nonsense, you're a maid," said Lear. "We have agreed to deliver you thus to the Duke of Albany and so it is true."

"Sire, the lady has been violated," said Oswald, desperate now.

"Guards! Take Oswald to the bailey and flog him twenty lashes for lying."

"But, sire!" Oswald squirmed as two guards seized his arms.

"Twenty lashes to show my mercy! Another word of this, ever, and *your* head will decorate London Bridge."

We watched, stunned, as the guards dragged Oswald away, the unctuous footman weeping and red-faced from trying to hold his tongue.

"May I go watch?" Goneril asked.

"Go," Lear said. "Then to your nurse."

Regan was on her feet now and had skipped to her father's side. She looked at him hopefully, up on her toes, clapping her hands lightly in anticipation.

"Yes, go," said the king. "But you may only watch."

Regan streamed out of the hall after her older sister, her raven hair flying behind her like a dark comet.

"You're my fool, Pocket," said Cordelia, taking my hand. "Come, help me. I'm teaching Dolly to speak French." The little princess led me away. The old king watched us go without another word, one white eyebrow raised and his hawk eye burning under it like a distant frozen star.

11.

A Sweet and Bitter Fool

Goneril dumped me on the floor as if she'd suddenly found a bag of drowned kittens in her lap. She snapped open the letter and began reading without even bothering to tuck her bosoms back into her gown.

"Milady," said Oswald again. He'd learned from that first whipping. He acted as if he didn't even see me. "Your father is in the great hall, asking after his fool."

Goneril looked up, irritated. "Well, then, take him. Take him, take him, take him." She waved us away like flies.

"Very well, milady." Oswald turned on his heel and marched away. "Come, fool."

I stood and rubbed my bum as I followed Oswald out of the solar. Yes, my backside was bruised, but there was pain in my heart as well. What a bitter bitch to cast me out while my bum still burned with the blows of her passion. The bells on my coxcomb drooped in despair.

Kent fell in beside me in the hall. "So, is she smitten with you?"

"With Edmund of Gloucester," said I.

"Edmund? She's smitten with the bastard?"

"Aye, the fickle whore," said I.

Kent looked startled and folded back the brim of his hat to better see me. "But you bewitched her to do so, didn't you?"

"Oh, yes, I suppose I did," said I. So, she was only immune to my charms by means of dark and powerful magic. Ha! I felt better. "She reads the letter I forged in his hand even now."

"Your fool," Oswald announced as we entered the hall.

The old king was there, with Captain Curan and a dozen other knights who looked like they'd just returned from the hunt—for me, no doubt.

"My boy!" Lear called, throwing his arms wide.

I walked into his embrace, but did not return it. I found no tenderness in my heart at the sight of him, but my anger boiled still.

"Oh joy," said Oswald, his disdain dripping like venom in his voice. "The prodigal git returns."

"See here," said Lear. "My men have yet to be paid. Tell my daughter I will see her."

Oswald did not acknowledge the old man, but kept walking.

"You, sir!" roared the king. "Did you hear me?"

Oswald turned slowly, as if he'd heard his name carried in faintly on the wind. "Aye, I heard you."

"Do you know who I am?"

Oswald picked a front tooth with the nail of his small finger. "Aye, my lady's father."

He smirked. The rascal had cheek, that I will give him, that or a burning desire to be catapulted cod over cap into the afterlife.

"Your lady's father!" Lear pulled off his heavy leather hunting gauntlet and backhanded it across Oswald's face. "You knave! You whoreson dog! You slave! You cur!"

The metal studs on Lear's glove were beginning to draw blood where they struck Oswald. "I am none of these things. I will not be struck by you." Oswald was backing toward the great double doors as Lear worried at him with the glove, but when the steward turned to run Kent threw out a leg and swept him off his feet.

"Or tripped, neither, you tosser!" said Kent.

Oswald rolled into a heap at the foot of one of Goneril's guards, then scrambled to his feet and ran out. The guards pretended they'd seen nothing.

"Well done, friend," said Lear to Kent. "Are you the one who brought my fool home?"

"Aye, he is, nuncle," said I. "Rescued me from the darkest heart of the forest, fought off brigands, pygmies, and a brace of tigers to bring me here. But don't let him talk his Welsh at you, one tiger was vanquished in a sluice of phlegm and mortally beaten with consonants."

Lear looked closely now at his old friend, then shivered—guilt's chill claws scuttling across his spine, no doubt. "Welcome, then, sir. I thank thee." Lear handed Kent a small purse of coin. "Earnest payment for your service."

"My thanks and my sword," said Kent, bowing.

"What is your name?" asked Lear.

"Caius," said Kent.

"And whence do you hail?"

"From Bonking, sire."

"Well, yes, lad, as do we all," said Lear, "but from what town?"

"Bonking Ewe on Worms Head," I offered with a shrug. "Wales—"

"Fine, then, join my train," said Lear. "You're hired."

"Oh, and allow me to hire you as well," said I, removing my hat and handing it to Kent with a jingle.

"What's this?" asked Kent.

"Who but a fool would work for a fool?"

"Watch your tongue, boy," said Lear.

"You'll have to get your own hat, fool," said I to the king. "Mine is already promised."

Captain Curan turned to conceal a smile.

"You call me a fool?"

"Oh, should I not call you fool? All your other titles you have given away, along with your land."

"I'll have you whipped."

I rubbed my burning bottom. "That is the only legacy you have left, nuncle."

"You've become a bitter fool in your absence," said the king.

"And you the sweet one," said I. "The fool who makes a jest of his own fate."

"The boy is not altogether fool," said Kent.

Lear turned on the old knight, but not in anger. "Perhaps," said he, weakly, his eye drifting to the stones of the floor as if searching for an answer there. "Perhaps."

"The lady, Goneril, Duchess of Albany!" announced one of the guards.

"Craven hose-beast!" I added, relatively certain the guard would forget that part.

Goneril breezed into the room, no notice of me, she went right to her father. The old man opened his arms but she stopped short, a sword-length away.

"Did you strike my man for chiding your fool?" Now she scowled at me.

I rubbed my bum and blew her a kiss.

Oswald peeked through the doors to the hall, as if waiting for the answer.

"I struck the knave for being impudent. I but asked him to fetch you. My fool has only just returned from being lost. This is not a time for frowns, daughter."

"There're no smiles for you, sire," said I. "Not now that you've nothing to offer. The lady has only bile for fools and those with no title at all."

"Quiet, boy," said the king.

"You see," said Goneril. "Not just your all-licensed fool, but your whole train treats my palace like a tavern and a brothel. They fight and eat all day, drink and carouse all night, and you care for nothing but your precious fool."

"As it should be," said Jones, albeit softly—when royal ire is raging, even the spittle sprayed from their lips can rain down death on the common puppet or person.

"I care for much, and my men are the best in the land. And they have not been paid since we left London. Perhaps if you—"

"They will not be paid!" said Goneril, and suddenly all the knights in the hall came to attention.

"When I gave you all, 'twas on the condition of you maintaining my retinue, daughter. "

"Aye, Father, and they shall be maintained, but not in your charge, and not in their full number."

Lear was growing red-faced now, and shaking with anger as with palsy. "Speak clearly, daughter, these old ears deceive."

Now Goneril went to her father and took his hand. "Yes, Father, you are old. Very old. Really, really, extraordinarily, mind-bogglingly—" She turned to me for a cue.

"Dog-fuckingly," I suggested.

"—dog-fuckingly old," said the duchess. "You are feebly, incontinently, desiccatedly, smelling-of-boiled-cabaggely old. You are brain-rottingly, balls-draggingly—"

"I'm fucking old!" said Lear.

"We'll stipulate that," said I.

"And," continued Goneril, "while you, in your dotage, should be revered for your wisdom and grace, you piss on your legacy and reputation by keeping this train of ruffians. They are too much for you."

"They are my loyal men and you have agreed to maintain them."

"And I shall. I shall pay your men, but half will stay here at Albany, under my charge, under my orders, in soldiers' quarters, not running about the bailey like marauders."

"Darkness and devils," cursed Lear. "It shall not be! Curan, saddle my horses, call my train together. I have another daughter."

"Go to her, then," said Goneril. "You strike my servants and your rabble makes servants of their betters. Be gone, then, but half your train shall remain."

"Prepare my horses!" said Lear. Curan hurried out of the hall, followed by the other knights, passing the Lord Albany as he entered, the duke looking more than somewhat confused.

"Why does the king's captain exit with such urgency?" asked the duke.

"Do you know of this harpy's intent to strip me of my train?" asked Lear.

"This is the first I've heard of it," said Albany. "Pray, be patient, sire. My lady?" Albany looked to Goneril.

"We do not strip him of his knights. I have offered to maintain them here, with our own force, while Father goes on to my sister's castle. We shall treat his men as our own, with discipline, as soldiers, not as guests and revelers. They are out of the old man's control."

Albany turned back to Lear and shrugged.

"She lies!" said Lear, now wagging a finger under Goneril's nose. "Thou detested viper. Thou ungrateful fiend. Thou hideous—uh—"

"Slag!"[1] I offered. "Thou piteous prick-pull. Thou vainglorious virago. Thou skunk-breathed licker of dog scrotums. Do jump in, Albany, I can't go on forever, no matter how inspired. Surely you've years of suppressed resentment to vent. Thou leprous spunk-catch. Thou worm-eaten—"

"Shut up, fool," said Lear.

"Sorry, sirrah, I thought you were losing your momentum."

"How could I have given preference to this villainess over my sweet Cordelia?" asked Lear.

"Doubtless that question was lost worse in the wood than I, seeing as it has only caught up with you now, sire. Shall we take cover against the impact of the revelation that you've awarded your kingdom to the best liars of your loins?" Who would have thought it, but I'd felt more charity toward the old man before he realized his folly. Now—

He turned his eyes skyward and began to invoke the gods:

"Hear me, nature, dear goddess hear.
Convey sterility onto this creature,
Dry up her womb

---

1. Slag—British slang for slut, tramp.

And never let a babe spring from

Her body to honor her.

Instead create in her a child of spleen and bile.

Let it torment her, and stamp wrinkles in her youthful
  brow

Let it turn all of her mother's benefits

To laughter and contempt, that she may feel

How sharper than a serpent's tooth

It is to have a thankless child!"

With that the old man spat at Goneril's feet and stormed out of the hall.

"I think he took that as well as could reasonably be expected," said I. I was ignored, despite my positive tone and sunny smile.

"Oswald!" called Goneril. The smarmy steward slithered forth. "Quickly, take the letter to my sister and Cornwall. Take two of the fastest horses and alternate them. Do not rest until it is in her hand. And then take you to Gloucester and deliver that other message as well."

"You have given me no other message, lady," said the worm.

"Yes, right, come with me. We shall draft a letter." She led Oswald out of the great hall leaving the Duke of Albany looking to me for some sort of explanation.

I shrugged. "She can be a whirlwind of tits and terror when she puts her mind to a purpose, can't she, sir?"

Albany didn't seem to notice my comment, somewhat forlorn, he looked. His beard seemed to be greying with worry as he stood there. "I don't approve of her treatment of the king. The old man has earned more respect. And what of these messages, to Cornwall and Gloucester?"

I started to speak, thinking it a perfect opportunity to mention her newfound affection for Edmund of Gloucester, my recent session of bawdy discipline with the duchess, and a half-dozen metaphors for illicit shagging that had come to mind while the duke mused, when Jones said:

"Sex and cuckoldry
You've mastered those jokes
For a more challenging jape
A new seal should be broke."

"What?" said I. Whenever Jones has spoken before it has been in my own voice—smaller and muted sometimes, from the art of throwing it, but my voice alone, unless Drool is mimicking the puppet. And it is I who works the little ring and string that move Jones's mouth. But this was not my voice, and I had not moved the puppet. It was the voice of the girl ghost from the White Tower.

"Don't be tedious, Pocket," said Albany. "I've no patience for puppets and rhymes."

Jones said:

"A thousand rough nights
To call the lady a whore,
Only today may a fool,
Jest the land into war?"

And like a shooting star cutting brilliant across the ignorant night of my mind, I saw the ghost's meaning.

I said: "I know not what the lady sends to Cornwall, good Albany, but while I was this last month in Gloucester, I heard soldiers talk of Cornwall and Regan gathering forces by the sea."

"Gathering an army? Whatever for? With gentle Cordelia and Jeff now on the throne in France, it would be folly to cross the channel. We've a safe ally there."

"Oh, they aren't gathering forces against France, they are gathering forces against you, my lord. Regan would be queen of all of Britain. Or so I heard said."

"You heard this from soldiers? Under whose flag, these soldiers?"

"Mercenaries, lord. No flag but fortune for them, and the word was there is coin aplenty for a free lance fighter in Cornwall. I have to be off. The king will need someone to whip for your lady's rude announcements."

"That doesn't seem fair," said Albany. He had a spark of decency in him, really, and somehow Goneril had not yet been able to smother it. Plus, he seemed to have forgotten about accidentally hanging me.

"Don't worry for me, good duke. You have worries of your own. Someone must take a hit for your lady, let it be this humble fool. Pray, tell her I said that someone must always hit it. Fare thee well, duke."

And merrily I was off, bottom stinging, to let slip the dogs of war. Hi ho!

Lear sat on his horse outside Castle Albany, howling at the sky like a complete lunatic.

"May Nature's nymphs bring great lobster-sized vermin to infest the rotted nest of her woman bits, and may serpents fix their fangs in her nipples and wave there until her poisoned dugs[2] go black and drop to the ground like overripe figs!"

I looked at Kent. "Built up a spot of steam, hasn't he?" said I.

---

2. Dugs—breasts, teats.

"May Thor hammer at her bowels and produce flaming flatulence that wilts the forest and launches her off the battlements into a reeking dung heap!"

"Not really adhering to any particular pantheon, is he?" said Kent.

"Oh, Poseidon, send your one-eyed son to stare into her bituminous heart and ignite it with flames of most hideous suffering."

"You know," said I, "the king seems to be leaning rather heavily on curses, for someone with his unsavory history with witches."

"Aye," said Kent. "Seems to have steered his wrath toward the eldest daughter, if I'm not mistaken."

"Oh, you don't say?" said I. "Sure, sure, that could be it, I suppose."

We heard horses galloping and I pulled Kent back from the drawbridge as two riders, leading a train of six horses, thundered across.

"Oswald," said Kent.

"With extra horses," said I. "He's gone to Cornwall."

Lear broke with his cursing and watched the riders take out across the moor. "What business has that rascal in Cornwall?"

"He carries a message, nuncle," said I. "I heard Goneril order him to report her mind to her sister, and for Regan and her lord to go to Gloucester and not to be in Cornwall when you arrive."

"Goneril, thou foul monstress!" said the king, clouting himself on the forehead.

"Indeed," said I.

"Oh, evil monstress!"

"To be sure," said Kent.

"Oh, pernicious monstress, perfect in her perfidy!"

Kent and I looked at each other, knowing not what to say.

"I said," said Lear, "most pernicious monstress, perfect in her perfidy!"

Kent mimed a set of generous bosoms on himself and raised an eyebrow as if to ask, "Boobs?"

I shrugged as if to say, "Aye, boobs sounds right."

"Aye, most pernicious perfidy indeed, sire," said I.

"Aye, most bouncy and jiggling perfidy,"[3] said Kent.

Then, as if coming out of a trance, Lear snapped to attention in his saddle. "You, Caius, have Curan saddle a fast horse for you. You must go to Gloucester, tell my friend the earl that we are coming."

"Aye, my lord," said Kent.

"And Caius, see that my apprentice Drool comes to no harm," said I.

---

3. Perfidy—treachery, definitely not bosoms.

Kent nodded and went back across the drawbridge. The old king looked down to me.

"Oh, my pretty Black Fool, where from fatherly duty did I stray that such ingratitude should rise in Goneril like mad fever?"

"I am only a fool, my lord, but making a guess, I'd say the lady may have in her delicate youth required more discipline to shape her character."

"Speak plain, Pocket, I'll not hold harm against you."

"You needed to smack the bitch up when she was tender, my lord. Instead, now you hand your daughters the rod and pull down your own breeches."

"I'll have you flogged, fool."

"His word is like the dew," said the puppet Jones, "good only until put under light of day."

I laughed, simple fool that I am, no thought at all that Lear was becoming as inconstant as a butterfly. "I need to speak to Curan and find a horse for the journey, sirrah," said I. "I'll bring your cloak."

Lear sagged in the saddle now, spent now from his ranting. "Go, good Pocket. Have my knights prepare."

"So I shall," said I. "So I shall." I left the old man there alone outside the castle.

12.

A King's Road

Having set the course of events in motion, I wonder now if my training to be a nun, and my polished skills at telling jokes, juggling, and singing songs fully qualify me to start a war. I have so often been the instrument of the whims of others, not even a pawn at court, merely an accoutrement to the king or his daughters. An amusing ornament. A tiny reminder of conscience and humanity, tempered with enough humor so it can be dismissed, laughed off, ignored. Perhaps there is a reason that there is no fool piece on the chessboard. What action, a fool? What strategy, a fool? What use, a fool? Ah, but a fool resides in a deck of cards, a joker, sometimes two. Of no worth, of course. No real purpose. The appearance of a trump, but none of the power. Simply an instrument of chance. Only a dealer may give value to the joker. Make him wild, make him trump. Is the dealer Fate? God? The king? A ghost? Witches?

The anchoress spoke of the cards in the tarot, forbidden and pagan as they were. We had no cards, but she would describe them for me, and I drew their images on the stones of the antechamber in charcoal. "The fool's number is zero," she said, "but that's because he represents the infinite possibility of all things. He may become anything. See, he carries all of his possessions in a bundle on his back. He is ready for anything, to go anywhere, to become whatever he needs to be. Don't count out the fool, Pocket, simply because his number is zero."

Did she know where I was heading, or do her words only have meaning to me now, as I, the zero, the nothing, seek to move nations? War? I couldn't see the appeal.

Drunk, and dire of mood one night, Lear mused of war when I suggested that what he needed to cast off his dark aspect was a good wenching. "Oh, Pocket, I am too old, and the joy of a fuck withers with my limbs. Only a good killing can still boil lust in my blood. And one will not do, either. Kill me a hundred, a thousand, ten thousand on my command—rivers of blood running through the fields—that's what pumps fire into a man's lance."

"Oh," said I. "I was going to fetch Shanker Mary for you from the laundry, but ten thousand dead and rivers of blood might be a bit beyond her talents, majesty."

"No, thank you, good Pocket, I shall sit and slide slowly and sadly into oblivion."

"Or," said I, "I could put a bucket on Drool's head and beat him with a sack of beets until the floor is splattered crimson while Shanker Mary gives you a proper tug to accentuate the gore."

"No, fool, there is no pretending to war."

"What's Wales doing, majesty? We could invade the Welsh, perpetrate enough slaughter to raise your spirits, and have you back for tea and toast."

"Wales is ours now, lad."

"Oh bugger. What's your feeling on attacking North Kensington, then?"

"Kensington's not a mile away. Practically in our own bailey."

"Aye, nuncle, that's the beauty of it, they'd never see it coming. Like a hot blade through butter, we'd be. We could hear the widows and orphans wailing from the castle walls—like a horny lullaby for you."

"I should think not. I'm not attacking neighborhoods of London to amuse myself, Pocket. What kind of tyrant do you think me?"

"Oh, above average, sire. Well above bloody average."

"I'll have you speak no more of war, fool. You've too sweet a nature for such dastardly pursuits."

Too sweet? *Moi?* Methinks the art of war was made for fools, and fools for war. Kensington trembled that night.

On the road to Gloucester I let my anger wane and tried to comfort the old king as best I could by lending him a sympathetic ear and a gentle word when he needed it.

"You simple, sniveling old toss-beast! What did you expect to happen when you put the care of your half-rotted carcass in the talons of that carrion bird of a daughter?" (I may have had some residual anger.)

"But I gave her half my kingdom."

"And she gave you half the truth in return, when she told you she loved you all."

The old man hung his head and his white hair fell in his face. We sat on stones by the fire. A tent was set in the wood nearby for the king's comfort, as there was no manor house in this northern county for him to take refuge. The rest of us would sleep outside in the cold.

"Wait, fool, until we are under the roof of my second daughter," said Lear. "Regan was always the sweet one, she will not be so shabby in her gratitude."

I had no heart to chide the old man any more. Expecting kindness from Regan was hope sung in the key of madness. Always the sweet one? Regan? I think not.

My second week in the castle I found young Regan and Goneril in one of the king's solars, teasing little Cordelia, passing a kitten the little one had taken a fancy to over her head, taunting her.

"Oh, come get the kitty," said Regan. "Be careful, lest it fly out the window." Regan pretended she might throw the terrified little cat out the window, and as Cordelia ran, arms stretched out to grab the kitten, Regan reeled and tossed the kitten to Goneril, who swung the kitten toward another window.

"Oh, look, Cordy, she'll be drowned in the moat, just like your traitor mother," said Goneril.

"Nooooooo!" wailed Cordelia. She was nearly breathless from running sister to sister after the kitten.

I stood in the doorway, stunned at their cruelty. The chamberlain had told me that Cordelia's mother, Lear's third queen, had been accused of treason and banished three years before. No one knew exactly the circumstances of the crime, but there were rumors that she had been practicing the old religion, others that she had committed adultery. All the chamberlain knew for sure was that the queen had been taken from the tower in the dead of night, and from that time until my arrival at the castle, Cordelia had not uttered a coherent syllable.

"Drowned as a witch, she was," said Regan, snatching the kitten out of the air. But this time the little kitten's claws found royal flesh. "Ow! You little shit!" Regan tossed the kitten out the window. Cordelia loosed an ear-shattering scream.

Without thinking I dived through the window after the cat and caught the braided cord with my feet as I flew through. I caught the kitten about five feet below the window as the cord burned between my ankles. Not having thought the move completely through, I hadn't counted on how to catch myself, kitten in hand, when the cord slammed me into the tower wall. The cord tightened around my right ankle. I took the impact on that shoulder and bounced while I watched my coxcomb flutter like a wounded bird to the moat below.

I tucked the kitten into my doublet, then climbed back up the cord and in through the window. "Lovely day for a constitutional, don't you think, ladies?"

The three of them all stood with their mouths hanging open, the older sisters had backed against the walls of the solar. "You lot look like you could use some air," said I.

I took the kitten from my doublet and held it out to Cordelia. "Kitty's had quite an adventure. Perhaps you should take her to her mum for a nap." Cordelia took the kitten from me and ran out of the room.

"We can have you beheaded, fool," said Regan, shaking off her shock.

"Anytime we want," said Goneril, with less conviction than her sister.

"Shall I send in a maid to tie back the tapestry, mum?" I asked, with a grand wave to the tapestry I'd loosed from the wall when I leapt.

"Uh, yes, do that," commanded Regan. "This instant!"

"This instant," barked Goneril.

"Right away, mum." And with a grin and a bow, I was gone from the room.

I made my way down the spiral stairs clinging to the wall, lest my heart give out and send me tumbling. Cordelia stood at the bottom of the stairs, cradling the kitten, looking up at me as if I were Jesus, Zeus, and St. George all back from a smashing day of dragon slaying. Her eyes were unnaturally wide and she appeared to have stopped breathing. Bloody awe, I suppose.

"Stop staring like that, lamb, it's disturbing. People will think you've a chicken bone caught in your throat."

"Thank you," she said, with a great, shoulder-shaking sob.

I patted her head. "You're welcome, love. Now run along, Pocket has to fish his hat from the moat and then go to the kitchen and drink until his hands stop shaking or he drowns in his own sick, whichever comes first."

She backed away to let me pass, never taking her eyes from mine. It had been thus since the night I arrived at the tower—when her mind first crept out from whatever dark place it had been living before my arrival—those wide, crystal-blue eyes looking at me with unblinking wonder. The child could be right creepy.

"Do not make yourself a maid to surprise, nuncle," said I. I held the reins of my and the king's horse as they drank from an ice-laced stream some hundred miles north of Gloucester. "Regan is a treasure to be sure, but she may have the same mind as her sister. Although they will deny it, it's often been the case."

"I cannot think it so," said the king. "Regan will receive us with open arms." There was a racket behind us and the king turned. "Ah, what is this?"

A gaily painted wagon was coming out of the wood toward us. Several of the knights reached for swords or lances. Captain Curan waved for them to stand at ease.

"Mummers, sire," said the Captain.

"Aye," said Lear, "I forgot, the Yule is nearly on us. They'll be going to Gloucester as well, I'll wager, to play for the Yule feast. Pocket, go tell them that we grant them safe passage and they may follow our train under our protection."

The wagon creaked to a stop. Happening upon a train of fifty knights and attendants in the countryside would put any performer on guard. The man driving the wagon stood at the reins and waved. He wore a grand purple hat with a white plume in it.

I leapt the narrow stream, and made my way up the road. When the driver saw my motley he smiled. I, too, smiled, in relief—this was not the cruel master from my own days as a mummer.

"Hail, fool, what finds you so far from court and castle?"

"I carry my court with me and my castle lies ahead, sirrah."

"Carry your court? Then that white-haired old man is—"

"Aye, King Lear himself."

"Then you are the famous Black Fool."

"At your bloody service," said I, with a bow.

"You're smaller than in the stories," said the big-hatted weasel.

"Aye, and your hat is an ocean in which your wit wanders like a lost plague ship."

The mummer laughed. "You give me more than my due, sirrah. We trade not in wit like you, wily fool. We are thespians!"

With that, three young men and a girl stepped out from behind the wagon and bowed gracefully and with far too much flourish than was called for.

"Thesbians," said they, in chorus.

I tipped my coxcomb. "Well, I enjoy a lick of the lily from time to time myself," said I, "but it's hardly something you want to paint on the side of a wagon."

"Not *lesbians*," said the girl, "*thesbians*. We are actors."

"Oh," said I. "That's different."

"Aye," said big hat. "We've no need of wit—the play's the thing, you see. Not a word passes our lips that hasn't been chewed thrice and spat out by a scribe."

"Unburdened by originality are we," said an actor in a red waistcoat.

The girl said, "Although we do bear the cross of fabulously shiny hair—"

"Blank slates, we are," said another of the actors.

"We are mere appendages of the pen, so to speak," said big hat.

"Yeah, you're a bloody appendage, all right," I said under my breath. "Well, actors then. Smashing. The king has bade me tell you that he grants you safe passage to Gloucester and offers his protection."

"Oh my," said big hat. "We are only going as far as Birmingham, but I suppose we could double back from Gloucester if his majesty wishes us to perform."

"No," said I. "Please, do pass through and on to Birmingham. The king would never impede the progress of artists."

"You're certain?" said big hat. "We've been rehearsing a classic from antiquity, *Green Eggs and Hamlet*, the story of a young prince of Denmark who goes mad, drowns his girlfriend, and in his remorse, forces spoiled breakfast on all whom he meets. It was pieced together from fragments of an ancient Merican manuscript."

"No," said I. "I think it will be too esoteric for the king. He is old and nods off during long performances."

"Shame," said big hat. "A moving piece. Let me do a selection for you. *'Green eggs, or not green eggs? That is the question. Whether 'tis nobler in the mind to eat them in a box, with a fox—'"*

"Stop!" said I. "Go now, and quickly. War has come to the land and rumor has it that as soon as they've finished with the lawyers, they're going to kill all the actors."

"Really?"

"Aye," I nodded most sincerely. "Quick, on to Birmingham, before you are slaughtered."

"Everyone jump on," said big hat, and the actors did as directed. "Fare thee well, fool!" Then he snapped the reins and drove off, the wagon's wheels bouncing in the ruts of the road.

Lear's train parted and watched as the team pulled the wagon by at a gallop.

"What was that?" asked Lear when I returned.

"Wagonload of knobs," said I.

"Why do they hurry, so?"

"We commanded it so, nuncle. Half their troupe is ill with fever. We want them nowhere near your men."

"Oh, good show, then, lad. I thought you might be missing the life and were going to join their troupe."

I shuddered at the thought. It had been a cold December day like this when I'd first come to the White Tower with my mummer troupe. We were decidedly not thespians, but singers, jugglers, and acrobats, and I a special asset because I could do all three. Our master was a crooked Belgian named Belette, who bought me from Mother Basil for ten shillings and the promise to feed me. He spoke Dutch, French, and a very broken English, so I don't know how he managed to secure the White Tower for a performance that Christmas, but I was told later that the troupe that was supposed to have performed had suddenly taken ill with stomach cramps and I suspect that Belette poisoned them.

I had been with Belette for months, and except for the beatings and cold nights sleeping under a wagon, I had received little but my daily bread, the occasional cup of wine, and the skills of knife-throwing and sleight of hand as it could be applied to purse cutting.

We were led into the great hall at the tower, which was filled with nobles reveling and feasting on platters of food such as I had never seen. King Lear sat at the center of the main table, flanked by two beautiful girls about my age, who I would later find out were Regan and Goneril. Beside Regan sat Gloucester, his wife, and their son Edgar. The intrepid Kent sat on the other side next to Goneril. Under that table, at Lear's feet, a little girl was curled up, watching the celebration—wide-eyed, like a frightened animal, clinging to a rag doll. I must confess, I thought the child might be deaf or even simpleminded.

We performed for perhaps two hours, singing songs of the saints during dinner, then moving on to bawdier fare as the wine flowed and the guests loosened their hold on propriety. By late in the evening everyone was laughing, the guests were dancing with the performers, and even the commoners who lived in the castle had joined the party, but the little girl remained under the table, making not a sound. Not a smile, not an eyebrow raised in delight. There was light there behind those crystal-blue eyes—this was not a simpleton—but she seemed to be staring out of them from afar.

I crawled under the table and sat next to her. She barely acknowledged my presence. I leaned in close and nodded toward Belette, who stood by a column near the center of the hall, leering lecherously at the young girls who frolicked about him. I could see the little girl spied the scoundrel, too. Ever so softly, I sang a little song the anchoress had taught me, with the lyrics changed a bit to adapt to the situation.

"Belette was a rat, was a rat, was a rat, was a rat,
Belette was a rat, was a rat, was a rat, was a rat,
Belette was a rat who ate his tail."

And the little girl pulled back and looked at me, as if to see if I had really sung such a thing. And I sang on:

"Belette was a rat, was a rat, was a rat,
Belette was a rat, was a rat, was a rat,
Belette was a rat, who drowned in a pail."

And the little girl cackled—a broken, little-girl yodel of a laugh that rang of innocence and joy and delight.

I sang on, and ever so softly, she sang with me,

"Belette was a rat, was a rat, was a rat,
Belette was a rat—"

And we were no longer alone under the table. There was another pair of crystal-blue eyes, and behind them a white-haired king. The old king smiled and squeezed my biceps. And before the other guests noticed that the king was under the table, he sat back up on his throne, but he reached down and lay a hand across the little girl's shoulder and the other upon mine. It was a hand reached across a vast chasm of reality—from the highest position of ruler of the realm, to a lowborn orphan boy who slept in the mud under a wagon. I thought it must have been how a knight felt when the king's sword touched his shoulder, elevating him to nobility.

"Was a rat, was a rat, was a rat," we sang.

When the party died down and noble guests hung drunk over the tables, the servants piled onto the floor before the fire, Belette began to move among the revelers and tap each of his performers, calling them to gather by the door. I had fallen asleep under the table, and the little girl against my arm. He pulled me up by my hair. "You did nothing all night. I watched." I knew there was a beating in store for when we got back to the wagon, and I was prepared for it. At least I had eaten some supper at the feast.

But as Belette turned to drag me away he stopped, abruptly. I looked up to see the master frozen in space, a sword-point pressed into his cheek just below his eye. He let go of my hair.

"Good thought," said Kent, the old bull, pulling his sword back, but holding it steadily aimed, a hand's breadth from Belette's eye.

There was a sound of coin on the table and Belette couldn't help but look down, even at the peril of his life. A doeskin purse as big as a man's fist lay before him.

The chamberlain, a tall, severe chap who looked perpetually down his nose, stood beside Kent. He said, "Your payment, plus ten pounds, which you shall accept as payment for this boy."

"But—" said Belette.

"You are a word from your mortality, sirrah," said Lear. "Do go on." He sat straight and regal on his throne, one hand pressed to the cheek of the little girl, who had awakened and was clinging to his leg.

Belette took the purse, bowed deeply, and backed across the hall. The other mummers of my troupe bowed and followed him out.

"What is your name, boy?" asked Lear.

"Pocket, your majesty."

"Well, then, Pocket, do you see this child?"

"Yes, majesty."

"Her name is Cordelia. She is our youngest daughter, and henceforth shall be your mistress. You have one duty above all, Pocket. That is to make her happy."

"Yes, majesty."

"Take him to Bubble," said the king. "Have her feed and bathe him, then find him new clothes."

Back on the road to Gloucester, Lear said, "So, what is your will, Pocket? Would you be a traveling mummer again—trade the comfort of the castle for the adventure of the road?"

"Apparently, I have, nuncle," said I.

We camped at the stream, which froze over during the night. The old man sat shivering by the fire with his rich fur cloak wrapped around him; the garment so full and the man so slight that it appeared he was being consumed by a slow but well-groomed beast. Only his white beard and the hawk nose were visible outside the cloak—two stars of fire shone back in the cape creature, his eyes.

Snow fell around us in great wet orgies of flakes, and my own woolen cloak, which I'd pulled over my head, was sodden.

"Have I been so unfit as a father that my daughters would turn on me so?" asked Lear.

Why, now, did he choose to stare into the dark barrel of his soul, when he'd been content all these years to simply scoop out his desires and let the consequences wash over whomever they may? Bloody inopportune time for introspection, after you've given away the roof over your head. But I did not say so.

"What would I know of proper fathering, sire? I had no father nor mother. I was reared by the Church, and I'd not give a hot squirt of piss for the lot of them."

"Poor boy," said the king. "As long as I live, you shall have father and family."

I would have pointed out that he had himself declared his crawl to the grave commenced, and that given his performance with his daughters, I might do better to go forth an orphan, but the old man had rescued me from the life of a slave and wanderer, and given me a home in the palace, with friends and, I suppose, family of a sort. So I said, "Thank you, majesty."

The old man sighed heavily and said, "None of my three queens ever loved me."

"Oh, for fuck's sake, Lear, I'm a jester, not a bloody wizard. If you're going to keep diving into the muck of your regrets then I'll just hold your sword for you and you can see if you can get your ancient ass moving enough to fall on the pointy part so we can both get some bloody peace."

Lear laughed then—twisted old oak that he was— and patted my shoulder. "I could ask nothing more of a son than he give me laughter in my despair. I'm off to bed. Sleep in my tent, tonight, Pocket, out of the cold."

"Aye, sire." I was touched by the old man's kindness, I cannot deny it.

The old man tottered over to his tent. One of the pages had been carrying hot stones into the tent for an hour and I felt the heat rush out as the king ducked inside.

"I'll be in after I've had a wee," said I. I walked to the edge of the fire's light and beside a great bare elm was relieving myself when a blue light shimmered in the forest before me.

"Well, that's a woolly tuft of lamb wank," said a woman's voice, just as the girl ghost stepped out from behind the tree upon which I was weeing.

"God's balls, wisp, I've almost peed on you!"

"Careful, fool," said the ghost, looking frighteningly solid now—just a tad translucent—snowflakes were passing through her. But I was not frightened.

"Warm thy grateful heart,
In the king's family,
But for his royal crimes,
You'd not an orphan be."

"That's it?" I asked. "Rhymes and riddles? Still?"

"All you need for now," said the ghost.

"I saw the witches," said I. "They seemed to know you."

"Aye," said the ghost. "There's dark deeds afoot at Gloucester, fool. Don't lose sight."

"Sight of what?"

But she was gone, and I was standing in the woods, my willie in my hand, talking to a tree. On to Gloucester in the morning, and I'd see what I was not to lose sight of. Or some such nonsense.

Cornwall's and Regan's flags flew over the battlements alongside Gloucester's, showing they had already arrived. Castle Gloucester was a bundle of towers surrounded by a lake on three sides and by a wide moat at the front—no outer curtain wall like the White Tower or Albany, no bailey, just a small front courtyard and a gatehouse that protected the entrance. The city wall, on the land side of the castle, provided the outer defenses for stables and barracks.

As we approached, a trumpet sounded from the wall announcing us. Drool came running across the drawbridge, his arms held high. "Pocket, Pocket, where have you been? My friend! My friend!"

I was greatly relieved to see him alive, but the great, simple bear pulled me from my horse and hugged me until I could barely breathe, dancing me in a circle, my feet flying in the air as if I was a doll.

"Stop licking, Drool, you lout, you'll wear my hair off."

I clouted the oaf on the back with Jones and he yowled. "Ouch. Don't hit, Pocket." He dropped me and crouched, hugging himself as if he were his own comforting mother, which he may have been, for all I know. I saw red-brown stains on his shirt back, and so lifted it to see the cause.

"Oh, lad, what has happened to you?" My voice broke, tears tried to push out of my eyes, and I gasped. The muscular slab of Drool's back was nearly devoid of skin—his hide had been torn and scabbed over and torn again by a vicious lash.

"I've missed you most awful," said Drool.

"Aye, me too, but how happened these stripes?"

"Lord Edmund says I am an insult to nature and must be punished."

Edmund. Bastard.

13.
A Nest of Villains

Edmund. Edmund would have to be dealt with, forces turned on him, and I fought the urge to find the black-hearted fiend and thread one of my throwing daggers between his ribs, but a plan was already in place, or one of sorts, and I still held the purse with the two remaining puffballs the witches had given me. I swallowed my anger and led Drool into the castle.

"'Lo, Pocket! Is that you, lad?" A Welsh accent. "Is the king with you?"

I saw the top of a man's head sticking through the stocks set in the middle of the courtyard. His hair was dark and long and hung in his face. I approached and bent down to see who it was.

"Kent? You've found yourself a cruel collar."

"Call me Caius," said the old knight. "Is the king with you?"

The poor fellow couldn't even look up.

"Aye. On his way. The men are stabling their horses in the town. How came you to be in the stocks?"

"I tangled with that whoreson Oswald, Goneril's steward. Cornwall judged me the offender and had me thrown in the stocks. I've been here since last evening."

"Drool, fetch some water for this good knight," said I. The giant loped off to find a bucket. I walked around behind Kent, patted him lightly on his bottom.

"You know, Kent, er—Caius, you are a very attractive man."

"You rascal, Pocket, I'll not be buggered by you."

I smacked his bottom again, dust rose from his trousers. "No, no, no, not me. Not my cup of tea. But Drool, now he'd shag the night if he wasn't afraid of the dark. And hung like an ox, that one is. I suspect you'll extrude stools untapered for a fortnight once Drool's laid the bugger to ya. Supper'll dump through you like a cherry pit out a church bell."

Drool was returning now carrying a wooden bucket and a dipper across the courtyard.

"No! Stop!" shouted Kent. "Villainy! Violation! Stop these fiends!"

Guards were looking down from the walls. I scooped a dipper of water from the bucket and threw it in Kent's face to calm him. He sputtered and struggled against the stocks.

"Easy, good Kent, I was just having you on. We'll get you out of there as soon as the king arrives." I held the dipper for the knight and he drank deeply.

When he finished he gasped, "Christ's codpiece, Pocket, why'd you go on like that?"

"Pure evil incarnate, I reckon."

"Well, stop it. It doesn't suit you."

"I'm working on the fit," said I.

Lear came through the gatehouse seconds later, flanked by Captain Curan and another older knight. "What's this?" asked the king. "My messenger in stocks! How came this to be? Who put you here, man?"

"Your daughter and son-in-law, sire," said Kent.

"No. By Jupiter's beard, I say, no," said Lear.

"Aye, by St. Cardomon's scaly feet[1] I say, aye," said Kent.

"By the flapping foreskin of Freya, I say, bugger all!" said Jones.

---

1. "By St. Cardomon's scaly feet"—the legend goes that St. Cardomon was a monk from Italy to whom the Archangel Raziel appeared, asking for a drink of water. While looking for water, Cardomon accidentally wandered into a cave that led into hell. There he was lost for forty days and forty nights, and while his feet burned when he first arrived, he soon developed the green and scaly feet of a lizard, and was protected from the fires of hell. When he returned to the angel with a flagon of ice-water (which no one had seen before), he was granted the gift of scaly feet for all time and it is often said that a woman with feet so rough that they will tear the bedsheets are "blessed by St. Cardomon." Cardomon is the patron saint of combination skin, cold beverages, and necrophilia.

And they looked at the puppet, confident on his stick.

"Thought we was swearing by whatever we could come up with," said the puppet. "Do go on."

"I say no," continued Lear. "'Tis worse than murder, to treat a messenger of the king so. Where is my daughter?"

The old king stormed through the inner gate, followed by Captain Curan and a dozen other knights from his train who had come into the castle.

Drool sat down in the dirt, splay-legged, his face even with Kent's, and said, "So, how've you been?"

"I'm in the stocks," said Kent. "Locked like this overnight."

Drool nodded, starting a string of his namesake down his chin. "So, not so good, then?"

"Nay, lad," said Kent.

"Better now that Pocket is here to save us, innit?"

"Aye, I'm a rescue in progress. Didn't see any keys in there when you were getting the water?"

"No. No keys," said Drool. "They've a laundress with smashing knockers works by the well sometimes, but she won't have a laugh with you. I asked her. Five times."

"Drool, you mustn't just go asking that sort of thing without some prelude," said I.

"I said [please]," said Drool.

"Well done, then, glad you've kept your manners in the face of so much villainy."

"Thank you, kind sir," said Drool in Edmund the bastard's voice, pitch-perfect, dripping with evil.

"That's un-bloody-settling," said Kent. "Pocket, think you could see about liberating me? I lost feeling in my hands a good hour ago and it won't go well for holding a sword if they have to be cut off from gangrene."

"Aye, I'll see to it," said I. "Let Regan vent some venom on her father, then I'll go see her for the key. She quite fancies me, you know?"

"You've weed on yourself, ain't ya?" said Drool, back in his own voice, but with a bit of a Welsh accent, no doubt to comfort the disguised Kent.

"Hours ago, and twice since," said Kent.

"I does that sometime in the night, when it's cold or it's too far to the privy."

"I'm just old and my bladder's shrunk to the size of a walnut."

"I've started a war," said I, since we seemed to be sharing privacies.

Kent struggled in the stocks to look at me. "What's this? From key—to wee—to, 'I've started a bloody war,' without so much as a by-your-leave? I'm bewildered, Pocket."

"Aye, which concerns me, as you lot are my army."

"Smashing!" said Drool.

The Earl of Gloucester came himself to release Kent. "I'm sorry, good man. You know I would not have allowed this, but once Cornwall has set his mind . . ."

"I heard you try," said Kent. The two had been friends in a former life, but now, Kent, lean and dark-haired, looked younger and more than a measure dangerous, while the weeks had weighed like years on Gloucester. He was near feeble, and struggled with the heavy key to the stocks. I took it from him gently and worked the lock.

"And you, fool, I'll not have you chiding Edmund for his bastardy."

"He's no longer a bastard, then? You married his mother. Congratulations, good earl."

"No, his mother is long dead. His legitimacy comes from the treachery of my other son, Edgar, who betrayed me."

"How so?" I asked, knowing full well how.

"He planned to take my lands from me and hasten me to the grave."

This was not what I had written in the letter. Certainly, the lands would be forfeit, but there had been no mention of murder of the old man. This was Edmund's doing.

"What have you done to anger our father?" said Drool, pitch-perfect in Edmund's voice.

We all turned and stared at the great oaf, the wrong-sized voice coming from his cavernous mouth.

"I have done nothing," said Drool in another voice.

"Edgar?" said Gloucester.

Indeed, it was Edgar's voice. I tensed at what might come next.

"Arm yourself and hide," the bastard's voice said. "Father has it in his mind that you have committed some offense, and he has ordered guards to seize you."

"What?" said Gloucester. "What dodgy magic is this?"

Then the bastard's voice again: "I have consulted the constellations, and they foretell of our father going mad and hunting you—"

At that point I clamped my hand over Drool's mouth.

"It's nothing, my lord," said I. "The Natural is not right in his mind. Fever, methinks. He mimics voices but not intent. His thoughts are a jumble."

"But those were the very voices of my sons," said Gloucester.

"Aye, but only in sound. Only in sound. Like a jabbering bird is the great fool. If you have quarters where I might take him—"

"And the king's most favored fool, and abused servant," added Kent, rubbing at the rash on his wrists left from the stocks.

Gloucester considered a moment. "You, good fellow, have been wrongly punished. Goneril's steward Oswald is less than honorable. And while I find it a mystery, Lear does love his Black Fool. There's an unused solar in the north tower. It leaks, but it will be out of the wind and close to your master, who will have quarters in the same wing."

"Aye, thank you, good lord," said I. "The Natural needs tending. We'll wrap him in blankets then I'll run down to the chemist for a leech."

We hustled Drool into the tower and Kent closed the heavy door and bolted it. There was one cathedral window with cracked shutters and two arrow loops, all set in alcoves, with tapestries pulled aside and tied to allow in the little light. We could see our breath in the winter air.

"Drop those tapestries," said Kent.

"Well, go grab some candles first," said I. "It'll be dark as Nyx's[2] bunghole once we pull the tapestries."

---

2. Nyx—Greek goddess of the night.

Kent left the solar and returned a few minutes later with a heavy iron candelabra with three lit candles. "A chambermaid is bringing us a brazier of charcoal and some bread and ale," said the knight. "Old Gloucester's a good sod."

"And survivor enough not to speak his mind to the king about his daughters," said I.

"I've learned some," said Kent.

"Aye." I turned to the Natural, who was playing with the wax dripping off the thick candles. "Drool, what was it you were saying? That bit with Edmund and Edgar plotting."

"I don't know, Pocket. I just says it, I don't know what's said. But Lord Edmund beats me when I talk in his voice. I'm an insult to nature and should be punished, says he."

Kent shook his head like a great hound clearing his ears of water. "What sort of convoluted wickedness have you set in motion, Pocket?"

"Me? This isn't my doing, this villainy is authored by that blackguard Edmund. But it will work for our plan. The conversations between Edgar and Edmund lie on the shelves of Drool's mind like forgotten volumes in a library, we need only prompt the git to open them. Now, to it. Drool, say the words of Edgar when Edmund advises him to hide."

And so we pried events out of Drool's memory using cues like a cat's paw,[3] and by the time we had warmed ourselves over the brazier and eaten our bread, we saw the pieces of Edmund's treachery played out as in the voices of the original players.

"So Edmund wounded himself and claimed that Edgar did it," said Kent. "Why didn't he simply slay his brother?"

"He needs to assure his inheritance first, and a knife to the back would have been suspect," said I. "Besides, Edgar is a formidable fighter—I don't think Edmund would face him."

"A traitor *and* a coward," said Kent.

"And those are his assets," said I. "Or we shall use them thus." I patted Drool's shoulder softly. "Good lad, excellent fool-craft. Now, I need you to see if you can say what I say in the voice of the bastard."

"Aye, Pocket, I'll give it a go."

I said, "Oh, my sweet lady Regan, thou art more fair than moonlight, more radiant than the sun, more glorious than all the stars. I must have you or I shall surely die."

In a wink Drool repeated my words back to me in the voice of Edmund of Gloucester, the intonation and

3. Cat's paw—a small crowbar, often used by thieves to jimmy windows open.

desperation in the perfect key to unlock Regan's affections, or so I'd wager.

"Howzat?" asked the git.

"Excellent," said I.

"Uncanny," said Kent. "How is it that Edmund let the Natural live? He must know he bears witness to his treachery."

"That is an excellent question. Let's go ask him, shall we?"

It occurred to me, as we made our way to Edmund's quarters, that since I had seen the bastard, the power of my protection, being King Lear, had waned somewhat, while Edmund's influence, and therefore immunity, had expanded when he became heir to Gloucester. In short, the deterrents to keep the bastard from murdering me had all but evaporated. I had only Kent's sword and Edmund's fear of ghostly retribution to protect me. The witches' pouch of puffballs weighed heavily as a weapon, however.

A squire showed me to an antechamber off Castle Gloucester's great hall.

"His lordship will receive only you, fool," said the squire.

Kent looked ready to bully the boy but I held up a hand to stay him. "I'll see that the door is left unlatched, good Caius. If I should call, please enter and dispatch the bastard with lethal vigor."

I grinned at the spot-faced squire. "Unlikely," said I. "Edmund holds me in very high esteem and I him. There will be little time between compliments to discuss business." I breezed by the young knight and into the chamber where Edmund was alone, sitting at a writing desk.

I said, "Thou scaly scalawag of a corpse-gorged carrion worm, cease your feast on the bodies of your betters and receive the Black Fool before vengeful spirits come to wrench the twisted soul from your body and drag it into the darkest depths of hell for your treachery."

"Oh, well spoken, fool," said Edmund.

"You think so?"

"Oh yes, I'm cut to the quick. I may never recover."

"Completely impromptu," said I. "With time and polish—well, I could go out and return with a keener edge on it."

"Perish the thought," said the bastard. "Take a moment to catch your breath and revel in your rhetorical mastery and achievement." He gestured toward a high-backed chair across from him.

"Thank you, I will."

"Still tiny, though, I see," said the bastard.

"Well, yes, Nature being the recalcitrant twat that she is—"

"And still weak, I presume?"

"Not of will."

"Of course not, I referred simply to your willowy limbs."

"Oh yes, in that case, I'm a bit of a soggy kitten."

"Splendid. Here to be murdered then, are you?"

"Not immediately. Uh, Edmund, if you don't mind my saying, you're being off-puttingly pleasant today."

"Thank you. I've adopted a strategy of pleasantness. It turns out that one can perpetrate all manner of heinous villainy under a cloak of courtesy and good cheer." Edmund leaned over the desk now, as if to take me into his most intimate confidence. "It seems a man will forfeit all sensible self-interest if he finds you affable enough to share your company over a flagon of ale."

"So you're being pleasant?"

"Yes."

"It's unseemly."

"Of course."

"So, you've received the dispatch from Goneril?"

"Oswald gave it to me two days ago."

"And?" I asked.

"Evidently the lady fancies me."

"And how do you feel about that?"

"Well, who could blame her, really? Especially now that I'm both pleasant *and* handsome."

"I should have cut your throat when I had the chance," said I.

"Ah, well, water under the bridge, isn't it? Excellent plan, with the letter to discredit my brother Edgar, by the way. Went smashingly. Of course I embellished somewhat. Improvised, if you will."

"I know," said I. "Implied patricide and the odd self-inflicted wound." I nodded toward his bandaged sword arm.

"Oh yes, the Natural talks to you, doesn't he?"

"Curious, then. Why is that bloody great oaf still drawing breath, knowing what he does about your plans. Fear of ghosts, is it?"

For the first time Edmund let his pleasant and insincere grin falter. "Well, there is that, but also, I quite enjoy beating him. And when I'm not beating him, having him around makes me feel more clever."

"You simple bastard, Drool makes anvils feel more clever. How bloody common of you."

That did it. Pretense of pleasantness fell when it came to questions of class, evidently. Edmund's hand dropped below the table and came up with a long fighting dagger. But alas, I was already in the process of swinging down hard with Jones's stick end and struck the bastard on his bandaged forearm. The blade went spinning in such a way that I was able to kick the hilt as it hit the floor and flip it up into my own waiting weapon hand. (To be fair, that is right or left, whether it was the juggling or the pickpocket training of Belette, I am agile with either hand.)

I flipped the blade and held it ready for a throw. "Sit! You're exactly a half-turn from hell, Edmund. Do twitch. Please do." He'd seen me perform with my knives at court and knew my skill.

The bastard sat, cradling his hurt arm as he did so. Blood was seeping through the bandage.

He spat at me, and missed. "I'll have you—"

"Ah, ah, ah," said I, brandishing the blade. "Pleasant."

Edmund growled, but stopped as Kent stormed into the room, knocking the door back on its hinges. His sword was drawn and two young squires were drawing theirs as they followed him. Kent turned and smashed the lead squire in the forehead with the hilt of his own weapon, knocking the boy backward off his feet, quite unconscious. Then Kent spun and swept the feet out from under the other with the flat of his sword and the lad landed on his back with an explosion of breath.

The old knight drew back to thrust through the squire's heart.

"Hold!" said I. "Don't kill him!"

Kent held and looked up, assessing the situation for the first time.

"I heard a blade clang. I thought the villain was murdering you."

"No. He gave me this lovely dragon-hilted dagger as a peace offering."

"That is not true," said the bastard.

"So," said Kent, paying particular attention to my readied weapon, "you're murdering the bastard, then?"

"Merely testing the weapon's balance, good knight."

"Oh, sorry."

"No worries. Thank you. I'll call you if I need you. Take that unconscious one with you, would you?" I looked at the other, who trembled on the floor. "Edmund, do instruct your knights to be pleasant toward my ruffian. He *is* a favorite of the king."

"Let him alone," grumbled Edmund.

Kent and the conscious squire dragged the other one out of the chamber and closed the door.

"You're right, this being pleasant is the dog's bollocks, Edmund." I flipped the dagger and caught it by the hilt. When Edmund made as if to move, I flipped it again and caught it by the blade. I raised a suspicious eyebrow at him. "So, you were saying about how well my plan had worked."

"Edgar is branded a traitor. Even now my father's knights hunt him. I will be lord of Gloucester."

"But, really, Edmund, is that enough?"

"Exactly," said the bastard.

"Uh, exactly what?" Had he already set his sights on Albany's lands, not even having spoken with Goneril? Now I was doubly unsure of what to do. My own plan to pair the bastard with Goneril and undermine the kingdom was the only thing keeping me from sending the dagger to his throat, and when I thought of the lash marks on poor Drool's back my hand quivered, wanting to loose the knife to its mark. But what had he set his sights on?

"The spoils of war can be as great as a kingdom," said Edmund.

"War?" How knew he of war? My war.

"Aye, fool. War."

"Fuckstockings," said I. I let the knife fly and ran out of the room, bells jingling.

As I approached our tower, I heard what sounded like someone torturing an elk in a tempest. I thought that Edmund might have sent an assassin for Drool after all, so I came through the door low, with one of my daggers at the ready.

Drool lay on his back on a blanket, a golden-haired woman with a white gown spread around her hips was riding him as if competing in the nitwit steeplechase. I'd seen her before, but never so solid. The two were wailing in ecstasy.

"Drool, what are you doing?"

"Pretty," said Drool, a great joyous, goofy grin on him.

"Aye, she's a vision, lad, but you're knobbing a ghost."

"No." The dim giant paused in his upward thrusting, lifted her by her waist and looked closely at her as if he'd found a flea in his bed.

"Ghost?"

She nodded.

Drool tossed her aside and with a long shuddering scream ran to the window and dove through, shattering the shutters as he went. The scream trailed off and ended with a splash.

The ghost pulled her gown down, tossed her hair out of her face, and grinned. "Water in the moat," she said. "He'll be fine. Guess I'll be going away half-cocked, though."

"Well, yes, but jolly good of you to take time from chain rattling and delivering portents of bloody doom to shag the beef-brained boy."

"Not up for a spirity tumble yourself, then?" She made as if to lift her gown above her hips again.

"Piss off, wisp, I've got to go fish the git out of the moat. He can't swim."

"Not keen on flight, neither, evidently?"

No time for this. I sheathed my dagger, wheeled on my heel and started out the door.

"Not your war, fool," said the ghost.

I stopped. Drool was slow at most things, perhaps he would be so at drowning. "The bastard has his own war?"

"Aye." The ghost nodded, fading back to mist as she moved.

"A fool's best plan
Plays out to chance,
But a bastard's hope,
Arrives from France."

"Thou loquacious fog, thou nattering mist, thou serpent-tongued steam, for the love of truth, speak straight, and no sodding rhyme."

But in that moment she was gone.

"Who are you?" I shouted to the empty tower.

14.

On Tender Horns

I shagged a ghost," said Drool, wet, naked, and for-lorn, sitting in the laundry cauldron under Castle Gloucester.

"There's always a bloody ghost," said the laundress, who was scrubbing the lout's clothes, which had been most befouled in the moat. It had taken four of Lear's men, along with me, to pull the great git from the stinking soup.

"No excuse for it, really," said I. "You've the lake on three sides of the castle, you could open the moat to the lake and the offal and stink would be carried away with the current. I'll wager that one day they find that stagnant water leads to disease. Breeds hostile water sprites, I'll wager."

"Blimey, you're long-winded for such a wee fellow," said the laundress.

"Gifted," I explained, gesturing grandly with Jones. I, too, was naked, but for my hat and puppet stick, my own apparel having taken a glazing of oozy moat mess during the rescue as well.

"Sound the alarm!" Kent came storming down the steps into the laundry, sword unsheathed and followed closely by the two young squires he'd trounced not an hour before. "Bolt the door! To arms, fool!"

"Hello," said I.

"You're naked," said Kent, once again feeling the need to voice the obvious.

"Aye," said I.

"Find the fool's kit, lads, and get him into it. Wolves are loosed on the fold and we must defend."

"Stop!" said I. The squires stopped thrashing wildly around the laundry and stood at attention. "Excellent. Now, Caius, what are you on about?"

"I shagged a ghost," said Drool to the young squires. They pretended they couldn't hear him.

Kent shuffled forward, held back some by the alabaster grandeur of my nakedness. "Edmund was found with a dagger through his ear, pinned to a high-backed chair."

"Bloody careless eater he is, then."

"'Twas you who put him there, Pocket. And you know it."

"*Moi?* Look at me? I am small, weak, and common, I could never—"

"He's called for your head. He hunts the castle for you even now," said Kent. "I swear I saw steam coming out his nostrils."

"Not going to spoil the Yule celebration, is he?"

"Yule! Yule! Yule!" chanted Drool. "Pocket, can we go see Phyllis? Can we?"

"Aye, lad, if there's a pawnbroker in Gloucester, I'll take you soon as your kit is dry."

Kent raised a startled porcupine of an eyebrow. "What is he on about?"

"Every Yule I take Drool down to Phyllis Stein's Pawnshop in London and let him sing 'Happy Birthday' to Jesus, then blow the candles out on the menorah."

"But the Yule's a pagan holiday," said one of the squires.

"Shut up, you twat. Do you want to ruin the twit's fun? Why are you here, anyway? Aren't you Edmund's men? Shouldn't you be trying to put my head on a pike or something?"

"They've changed allegiance to me," said Kent. "After the thrashing I gave them."

"Aye," said squire one. "We've more to learn from this good knight."

"Aye," said squire two. "And we were Edgar's men, anyway. Lord Edmund is a scoundrel, if you don't mind me saying, sir."

"And, dear Caius," said I. "Do they know that you are a penniless commoner and can't really maintain a fighting force as if you were, say—oh, I don't know—the Earl of Kent?"

"Excellent point, Pocket," said Kent. "Good sirs, I must release you from your service."

"So we won't be paid, then?"

"My regrets, no."

"Oh, then we'll take our leave."

"Fare thee well, keep your guard up, lads," said Kent. "Fighting's done with the whole body, not only the sword."

The two squires left the laundry with a bow.

"Will they tell Edmund where we're hiding?" I asked.

"I think not, but you better get your kit on just the same."

"Laundress, how progresses my motley?"

"Steamin' by the fire, sir. Dry enough to wear indoors, I reckon. Did I hear it right that you put a dagger through Lord Edmund's ear?"

"What, a mere fool? No, silly girl. I'm harmless. A jab from the wit, a poke to the pride are the only injuries a fool inflicts."

"Shame," said the laundress. "He deserves that and worse for how he treats your dim friend—" She looked away. "—and others."

"Why *didn't* you just kill the scoundrel outright, Pocket?" asked Kent, kicking subtlety senseless and rolling it up in a rug.

"Well, just shout it out, will you, you great lummox."

"Aye, like you'd never do such a thing, 'Top of the morning; grim weather we're having; I've started a bloody war!'"

"Edmund has his own war."

"See, you did it again."

"I was coming to tell you when I found the girl ghost having a go at Drool. Then the lout leapt out the window and the rescue was on. The ghost implied that the bastard might be rescued by France. Maybe he's allied with bloody King Jeff to invade."

"Ghosts are notoriously unreliable," said Kent. "Did you ever consider that you might be mad and hallucinating the whole thing? Drool, did you see this ghost?"

"Aye, I had a half a laugh wif her before I got frightened," said Drool, sadly, contemplating his tackle through the steamy water. "I fink I gots deaf on me willie."

"Laundress, help the lad wash the death off his willie, would you?"

"Not bloody likely," said she.

I held the tip of my coxcomb to stay any jingling and bowed my head to show my sincerity. "Really, love, ask yourself, *What would Jesus do?*"

"If he had smashing knockers," added Drool.

"Don't help."

"Sor-ry."

"War? Murder? Treachery?" reminded Kent. "Our plan?"

"Aye, right," said I. "If Edmund has his own war it will completely bollocks up our plans for civil war between Albany and Cornwall."

"All well and good, but you didn't answer my question. Why didn't you just slay the bastard?"

"He moved."

"So you meant to kill him?"

"Well, I hadn't thought it through completely, but when I sent his dagger at his eye socket I believed that there might be a fatal outcome. And I must say, although I didn't stay to revel in the moment, it was very satisfying. Lear says that killing takes the place of bonking in the ancient. You've killed a multitude of chaps, Kent. Do you find that to be the case?"

"No, that's a disgusting thought."

"And yet, with Lear lies your loyalty."

"I'm beginning to wonder," said Kent, sitting down now on an overturned wooden tub. "Who do I serve? Why am I here?"

"You are here, because, in the expanding ethical ambiguity of our situation, you are steadfast in your righteousness. It is to you, my banished friend, that we all turn—a light amid the dark dealings of family and politics. You are the moral backbone on which the rest of us hang our bloody bits. Without you we are merely wiggly masses of desire writhing in our own devious bile."

"Really?" asked the old knight.

"Aye," said I.

"I'm not sure I want to keep company with you lot, then."

"Not like anyone else will have you, is it? I need to see Regan before my bastard ear piercing poisons our cause. Will you take her a message, Kent—er, Caius?"

"Will you put on your trousers, or at least your cod-piece?"

"Oh, I suppose. That had always been part of the plan."

"Then I will bear your message to the duchess."

"Tell her—no, ask her—if she still holds the candle she promised for Pocket. Then ask her if I may meet her somewhere private."

"I'm off, then. But try to manage not to get murdered while I'm gone, fool."

"Kitten!" said I.

"You poxy little vermin," said Regan, in glorious red. "What do you want?"

Kent had led me to a chamber far in the bowels of the castle. I couldn't believe that Gloucester would house royal guests in an abandoned dungeon. Regan must have somehow found her own way here. She had an affinity for such places.

"You received the letter from Goneril, then?" I asked.

"Yes. What is it to you, fool?"

"The lady confided in me," said I, bouncing my eyebrows and displaying a charming grin. "What is your thought?"

"Why would I want to dismiss father's knights, let alone take them into my service? We have a small army at Cornwall."

"Well, you're not at Cornwall, are you, love?"

"What are you saying, fool?"

"I'm saying that your sister bade you come to Gloucester to intercept Lear and his retinue, and thus stop him from going to Cornwall."

"And my lord and I came with great haste."

"And with a very small force, correct?"

"Yes, the message said it was urgent. We needed to move quickly."

"So, when Goneril and Albany arrive, you will be away from your castle and nearly defenseless."

"She wouldn't dare."

"Let me ask you, lady, where do you think the Earl of Gloucester's allegiance lies?"

"He is our ally. He has opened his castle to us."

"Gloucester, who was nearly usurped by his eldest son—you think he sides with you?"

"Well, with Father, then, which is the same thing."

"Unless Lear is aligned with Goneril against you."

"But she relieved him of his knights. He ranted about it for an hour after his arrival, called Goneril every foul name under the sun, and praised me for my sweetness and loyalty, even overlooking my throwing his messenger into the stocks."

I said nothing. I removed my coxcomb, scratched my head, and sat on some dusty instrument of torture to observe the lady by torchlight and watch her eyes as the rust ground off the twisted gears of her mind. She was simply lovely. I thought about what the anchoress had said about a wise man only expecting so much perfection in something as its nature allows. I thought that I might, indeed, be witnessing the perfect machine. Her eyes went wide when the realization hit.

"That bitch!"

"Aye," said I.

"They'll have it all, she and Father?"

"Aye," said I. I could tell her anger didn't arise from the betrayal, but from not having thought of it first.

"You need an ally, lady, and one with more influence than this humble fool can provide. Tell me, what do you think of Edmund the bastard?"

"He's fit enough, I suppose." She chewed a fingernail and concentrated. "I'd shag him if my lord wouldn't murder him—or come to think of it, maybe because he would."

"Perfect!" said I.

Oh Regan, patron saint of Priapus,[1] the most slippery of the sisters: in disposition preciously oily, in discourse, deliciously dry. My venomous virago, my sensuous charmer of serpents—thou art truly perfection.

Did I love her? Of course. For even though I have been accused of being an egregious horn-beast, my horns are tender, like the snail's—and never have I hoisted the horns of lust without I've taken a prod from Cupid's barb as well. I have loved them all, with all my heart, and have learned many of their names.

Regan. Perfect. Regan.

Oh yes, I loved her.

She was a beauty to be sure—there was none in the kingdom more fair; a face that could inspire poetry

---

1. Priapus—a Greek god whose lust was so strong he was cursed with a permanent erection that was so large he was unable to move. The medical condition priapism is named for him.

and a body that inspired lust, longing, larceny, treachery, perhaps even war. (I am not without hope.) Men had murdered each other in competition for her favors—it was a hobby with her husband, Cornwall. And to her credit, while she could smile as a bloke bled to death with her name on his lips, she was not tight-fisted with her charms. It only added to the tension around her that *someone* was going to be shagged silly in the near future, and how much more thrilling if his life hung by a thread as he did the deed. In fact, the promise of violent death might be to the princess Regan like the nectar of Aphrodite herself, now that I think of it.

Why else would she have called for my death all those years ago, when I had so diligently served her, after Goneril had left the White Tower to wed Albany. It had begun, it seems, with a bit of jealousy.

"Pocket," said Regan. She was perhaps eighteen or nineteen at the time, but unlike Goneril, had been exploring her womanly powers for years on various lads about the castle. "I find it offensive that you gave personal counsel to my sister, yet when I call you to my chambers I get nothing but tumbling and singing."

"Aye, but a song and a tumble seem all that's needed to lift the lady's spirits, if I may say so."

"You may not. Am I not fair?"

"Extremely so, lady. Shall I compose a rhyme to your beauty? *A ravishing tart from Nantucket* —"

"Am I not as fair as Goneril?"

"Next to you, she is less than invisible, just a shimmering envious vacuum, is she."

"But do *you*, Pocket, find me attractive—in a carnal way—the way you did my sister? Do you want me?"

"Ah, of course, lady, from the morning I wake, I have but one thought, one vision: of your deliciousness, under this humble and unworthy fool, writhing naked and making monkey noises."

"Really, that's all you think about?"

"Aye, and occasionally breakfast, but it's only seconds before I'm back to Regan, writhing, and monkey noises. Wouldn't you like to have a monkey? We should have one around the castle, don't you think?"

"So all you think of is this?" And with that, she shrugged off her gown, red as always, and there she stood, raven-haired and violet-eyed, snowy fair and finely fit, as if carved by the gods from a solid block of desire. She stepped out of the pool of bloodred velvet and said, "Drop your puppet stick, fool, and come here."

And I, ever the obedient fool, did.

And oh it led to many months of clandestine monkey noises: howling, grunting, screeching, yipping,

squishing, slapping, laughing, and no little bit of barking. (But there was no flinging of poo, as monkeys are
wont to do. Only the most decent, forthright monkey
sounds as are made from proper bonking.) I put my
heart into it, too; but the romance was soon crushed
beneath her cruel and delicate heel. I suppose I shall
never learn. It seems a fool is not so often taken as a
medicine for melancholy, as for ennui, incurable and
recurring among the privileged.

"You've been spending a lot of time with Cordelia of
late," said Regan, basking glorious in the gentle glow
of the afterbonk (your narrator in a sweaty puddle on
the bedside floor, having been summarily ejected after
rendering noble service). "I am jealous."

"She's a little girl," said I.

"But when she has you, I cannot. She's my junior.
It's not acceptable."

"But, lady, it's my duty to keep the little princess
smiling, your father has commanded it. Besides, if I
am otherwise engaged you can have that sturdy fellow
you fancy from the stable, or that young yeoman with
the pointy beard, or that Spanish duke or whatever he
is that's been about the castle for a month. Does that
bloke speak a word of English? I think he may be
lost."

"They are not the same."

I felt my heart warm at her words. Could it be real affection?

"Well, yes, what we share is—"

"They rut like goats—there's no art to it, and I weary of shouting instructions to them, especially the Spaniard—I don't think he speaks a word of English."

"I'm sorry, milady," said I. "But that said, I must away." I stood and gathered my jerkin from under the wardrobe, my leggings from the hearth, my codpiece from the chandelier. "I've promised to teach Cordelia about griffins and elves over tea with her dolls."

"You'll not," said Regan.

"I must," said I.

"I want you to stay."

"Alas, parting is such sweet sorrow," said I. And I kissed the downy dimple at the small of her back.

"Guard!" called Regan.

"Pardon?" I inquired.

"Guard!" The door to her solar opened and an alarmed yeoman looked in. "Seize this scoundrel. He hath ravaged your princess." She had conjured tears, in that short span of time. A bit of a wonder, she was.

"Fuckstockings," said I, as two stout yeomen took me by the arms and dragged me down to the great hall in Regan's wake, her dressing gown open and flowing out behind her as she wailed.

It seemed a familiar motif, yet I did not feel the confidence that comes with rehearsal. Perhaps it was that Lear was actually holding court before the people when we entered the great hall. A line of peasants, merchants, and minor noblemen waited as the king heard their cases and made judgments. Still in his Christian phase, he had been reading about the wisdom of Solomon, and had been experimenting with the rule of law, thinking it quaint.

"Father, I insist you hang this fool immediately!"

Lear was taken aback, not only by the shrillness of his daughter's demand, but by the fact that she stood frontally bare to all the petitioners and made no effort to close her red gown. (Tales would be told of that day, of how many a plaintiff, having seen the snowy-skinned princess in all her glory, did hold his grievance pitiful, indeed, his life worthless, and went home to beat his wife or drown himself in the mill pond.)

"Father, your fool hath violated me."

"That's a fluttering bottle of bat wank, sire," said I. "Begging your pardon."

"You speak rashly, daughter, and you appear frothing-dog mad. Calm yourself and state your grievance. How hath my fool offended?"

"He hath shagged me roughly, against my will, and finished too soon."

"By force? Pocket? He isn't eight stone on a feast day—he couldn't shag a cat by force."

"That's not true, sire," said I. "If the cat is distracted with a trout, then—well, uh, nevermind—"

"He violated my virtue and spoiled my virginity," said Regan. "I insist you hang him—hang him twice, the second time before he's finished choking from the first—that'll be fitting justice."

I said: "What has put vengeance in your blood, princess? I was just going to tea with Cordelia." Since the little one wasn't present, I hoped invoking her name might awaken the king to my cause, but it only seemed to incense Regan.

"Forced me down and used me like a common tart," said Regan, adding rather more pantomime than the petitioners in the hall could bear. Several began to beat their fists to their heads, others grabbed at their groins and sank to their knees.

"No!" said I. "I've had many a wench by stealth, a few by guile, a number by charm, a brace by mistake, the odd harlot for coin, and, when all else has failed, I've made do by begging, but by God's blood, none by force!"

"Enough!" said Lear. "I'll hear no more. Regan, close your robe. As I have decreed, we are a kingdom of laws. There shall be a trial, and if the rascal is found guilty, then I'll see him hanged twice myself. Make way for a trial."

"Now?" asked the scribe.

"Yes, now," said Lear. "What do we need? A couple of chaps to do the prosecuting and defending, grab a few of those peasants for witnesses, and with due process, *habeas corpus*, fair weather and whatnot, we'll have the fool dangling black-tongued before tea. Will that suit you, daughter?"

Regan closed her robe and turned away coyly. "I suppose."

"And you, fool?" Lear winked at me, none too subtly.

"Aye, majesty. A jury, perhaps, chosen from that same group as the witnesses." Well, one has to make an effort. From their reaction I would be acquitted, on a "who could blame" him basis: *justifiable shaggicide,* they'd call it. But no.

"No," said the king. "Bailiff read the charges."

The bailiff obviously hadn't written up charges, so he unrolled a scroll on which was written something entirely unconnected to my case, and faked it: "The Crown states that on this day, October fourteenth, year of Our Lord, one thousand, two hundred, and eighty-eight, the fool known as Pocket, did with forethought and malice, shag the virgin princess Regan."

There was cheering from the gallery, a little scoffing from the court.

"There was no malice," said I.

"Without malice, then," said the bailiff.

At this point, the magistrate, who normally functioned as a castle steward, whispered to the bailiff, who normally was the chamberlain. "The magistrate wishes to know how was that?"

"'Twas sweet, yet nasty, your honor."

"Note that the accused hath stated that it was [sweet and nasty], thereby admitting his guilt."

More cheering.

"Wait, I wasn't ready."

"Smell him," said Regan. "He reeks of sex, like fish and mushroom and sweat, doesn't he?"

One of the peasant witnesses ran forth and sniffed my bits mercilessly, then looked to the king, nodding.

"Aye, your honor," said I. "I'm sure I have an odor about me. I must confess, I was *sans* trou today in the kitchen, while awaiting my laundry, and Bubble had left a casserole out on the floor to cool, and it did trip me and I fell prick-deep in gravy and goo—but I was on my way to chapel at the time."

"You put your dick in my lunch?" said Lear. Then to the bailiff, "The fool put his dick in my lunch?"

"No, in your beloved daughter," said Regan.

"Quiet, girl!" barked the king. "Captain Curan, send a guard to watch the bread and cheese before the fool has his way with it."

It went on like that, with things looking rather grim for me as the evidence mounted against me, peasants taking the opportunity to describe the most lecherous acts they could imagine a wicked fool might perpetrate on an unsuspecting princess. I thought testimony of the sturdy stable boy particularly damning at first, but eventually it led to my acquittal.

"Read that back, so the king may hear the true heinous nature of the crime," said my prosecutor, who I believe butchered cattle for the castle as his normal vocation.

The scribe read the stable boy's words: "Yes, yes, yes, ride me, you crashing tree-cocked stallion."

"That's not what she said," said I.

"Yes, it is. It's what she always says," said the scribe.

"Aye," said the steward.

"Aye, it is," said the priest.

"*Sí,*" said the Spaniard.

"Well, she never says that to me," said I.

"Oh," said the stable boy. "Then it's 'Prance, you twig-dicked little pony,' is it?"

"Possibly," said I.

"She never says that to me," said the yeoman with the pointy beard.

Then there was a moment of silence, while all who had spoken looked around at one another, then furiously avoided eye contact and found spots on the floor of great interest.

"Well," said Regan, chewing a fingernail as she spoke, "there is a chance that, uh, I was having a dream."

"Then the fool did not take your virtue?" asked Lear.

"Sorry," said Regan sheepishly. "It was but a dream. No more wine at lunch for me."

"Release the fool!" said Lear.

The crowd booed.

I walked out of the hall side by side with Regan.

"He might have hung me," I whispered.

"I'd have shed a tear," said she with a smile. "Really."

"Woe to you, lady, should you leave that rosebud asterisk of a bum-hole unguarded on our next meeting. When a fool's surprise comes unbuttered, a Pocket's pleasure will a princess punish."

"Oooo, do tease, fool, shall I put a candle in it so you can find your way."

"Harpy!"

"Rascal!"

"Pocket, where have you been?" said Cordelia, who was coming down the corridor. "Your tea has gone cold."

"Defending big sister's honor, sweetness," said I.

"Oh bollocks," said Regan.

"Pocket dresses the fool, but he is ever our hero, isn't he, Regan?" said Cordelia.

"I think I'm going to be ill," said the elder princess.

"So, love," said I, rising from my perch on the torture machine and reaching into my jerkin. "I'm pleased you feel that way about Lord Edmund, for he has sent me with this letter."

I handed her the letter. The seal was dodgy, but she wasn't looking at the stationery.

"He's smitten with you, Regan. In fact, so smitten he tried to cut off his own ear to deliver with this missive, to show you the depth of his affection."

"Really? His ear."

"Say nothing at the Yule feast, tonight, lady, but you'll see the bandage. Mark it as a tribute of his love."

"You saw him cut his ear?"

"Yes, and stopped him before the deed was done."

"Was it painful, do you think?"

"Oh yes, lady. He has already suffered more than have others in months of knowing you."

"That's so sweet. Do you know what the letter says?"

"I was sworn not to look upon pain of death, but come close—"

She leaned close to me and I squeezed the witch's puffball under her nose. "I believe it speaks of a midnight rendezvous with Edmund of Gloucester."

15.

In a Lover's Eye

A warm wind blew in from the west, completely cocking up the Yule. Druids like snow round Stonehenge during the festival, and burning down the forest is all the more satisfying if there's a chill in the air. As it was, it looked like we'd have rain for the feast. The clouds rolling over the horizon looked like they'd been born of a summer storm.

"Them look like summer storm clouds," said Kent. We were hiding in the barbican above the gate, looking out over the walled village of Gloucester and the hills beyond. I'd been hiding since my encounter with Edmund. Evidently the bastard was somewhat put out with me.

We could see Goneril and her train entering the outer gates. She rode with a dozen soldiers and attendants, but noticeably, the Duke of Albany was not with her.

A sentry on the wall called out the approach of the Duchess of Albany. Gloucester and Edmund appeared in the courtyard, followed by Regan and Cornwall. Regan was working to keep her eyes off of Edmund's bandaged ear.

"This should be interesting," said I. "They swarm like vultures over a corpse."

"Britain's the corpse," said Kent. "And we baited her to be torn apart."

"Nonsense, Kent. Lear's the corpse. But ambitious scavengers do not wait for his death to begin their dining."

"You've a deeply wicked side, Pocket."

"Truth has a deeply wicked side, Kent."

"There's the king," said Kent. "No one attends him. I should go to him."

Lear shuffled into the courtyard wearing his heavy fur cape.

"Like looking down on a lubricious chess set, isn't it? The king moves in tiny steps, with no direction, like a drunkard trying to avoid the archer's bolt. The others work their strategies and wait for the old man to fall. He has no power, yet all power moves in his orbit and to his mad whim. Do you know that there's no fool piece on the chessboard, Kent?"

"Methinks the fool is the player, the mind above the moves."

"Well, that's a scratchy spot of cat wank." I turned to the old knight. "But bloody well said. Go to Lear, then. Edmund won't dare molest you, and Cornwall must pretend some contrition for throwing you into the stocks. The princesses will be burning bright for Edmund's eye, and Gloucester—well, Gloucester proffers hospitality before jackals, he is well occupied."

"What will you do?"

"I seem to have rendered myself undesirable, as impossible as that sounds. I need to find us a spy—someone more stealthy, devious, and underhanded than my own sweet nature allows."

"Good luck with that," said Kent.

"I loathe you, I despise you, I curse your existence and the foul demons that spawned you. You sicken me with anger and bilious hatred."

"Oswald," said I. "You're looking well." Drool and I had intercepted him in a corridor.

There is an unwritten edict, that when negotiating with an enemy, one does not reveal his knowledge of that enemy's agenda, even unto death. It's a point of honor, of sorts, but I see it as petty play-acting, and I had no intention of indulging in it with Oswald. Yet, I had need of his spidery talents, so some finesse was required.

"I would give an arm to see you hang, fool," said Oswald.

"Oh, an excellent starting point," said I. "Don't you think, Drool?"

"Aye, Pocket," said Drool, who loomed between Oswald and me, a thick table leg unsuccessfully concealed behind his back. Oswald might make as to draw his sword, but Drool would have beaten his brains into bloody marmalade before the blade cleared its scabbard. Unspoken, but understood. "Smashing good start," said the giant.

"So, Oswald, let us go from there. Say you get what you want. Say you lose an arm, and I am hanged, how then is life better for your fine self? Your quarters more comfortable? Wine taste better, will it?"

"It's unlikely, but let's explore the possibilities, shall we?"

"Very well," said I. "You first. Sever an arm and Drool here will hang me. You have my word."

"You have my word," said Drool, in my voice.

"Stop wasting my time, fool. My lady is arriving and I need to go to her."

"Ah, there's the rub, Oswald. What you want. What do you really want."

"You could never know."

"Your lady's approval?"

"I have that."

"Ah, that's right, your lady's love."

Oswald became still then, as if I had taken the breath from the corridor in which we stood. To prove such was not the case, I pressed on.

"You want your lady's love, her respect, her power, her submission, her bottom in the air before you, her begging for satisfaction and mercy—that about it?"

"I am not so base as you, fool."

"And yet the very reason you hate me is that I have been to that place."

"You have not. She has not loved you, nor respected you, nor given you power. You were an amusement at best."

"Yet I know the way there, my coal-hearted friend. I know the way a servant might find such favor."

"She could never. I am of common blood."

"Oh, I'm not saying I could make you duke, only that you would be her lord in body, heart, and mind. You know her weakness for scoundrels, Oswald. Did you yourself not pimp your lady to Edmund?"

"I did not. I only delivered a message. And Edmund is heir to an earldom."

"Just this bloody week he is. And don't act as if you don't know what was in that message. I have the power, Oswald, given me by three witches in the Great Birnam

Wood, to put a spell upon your lady so she will adore and desire you."

Oswald laughed, not something he did often. His face was not fit for it and he looked like he had something caught in his back teeth. "What kind of fool do you think me? Out of the way."

"And all you have to do is what your lady would have you do anyway, serve her desires," said I. I needed to make my case quickly. "She is bewitched already, you know? You were there."

Oswald had been backing away from Drool, off to find another route to the courtyard and Goneril, when he stopped.

"You were there, Oswald. At Albany. Goneril was having a grab at my tackle and you came in. You'd just come through the door, I heard it. I had this purse in my hand." I held up the silk pouch the witches had given me. "Remember?"

"I was there."

"And I handed your lady a letter and said it was from Edmund of Gloucester. Remember?"

"Aye. And she dumped you on your arse."

"Right you are. And sent you here, to deliver a message to Edmund. Had she ever made a note of the bastard before, Oswald? You are with her nearly every waking moment. Had she noted him before?"

"No. Not once. She gave some notice to Edgar, but not the bastard."

"Exactly. She is bewitched to love Edmund, and I can do the same for you. You'll die a frustrated toady any other way, Oswald. I've one more spell left."

Oswald took careful steps back to me, like he was walking a wire rather than the stone floor of a castle corridor. "Why wouldn't you use it for yourself?"

"Well, for one, you would know, and I presume you would not be slow to inform Lord Albany, who would quickly have me hanged. And second, I had three such spells, and I have used one for myself already."

"Not the Duchess of Cornwall?" I could tell Oswald was aghast at the idea, yet there was an excitement in his eye.

I showed him a sly grin and flicked the bells of my hat with Jones. "I've a rendezvous with her this very night after the Yule feast—midnight, in the abandoned North Tower."

"You dastardly little monster!"

"Oh sod off, Oswald. Would you have a princess of your own or not?"

"What do I have to do?"

"Almost nothing," said I. "But it will take some strength of character for you to see this through. First, you must counsel your lady to keep peace with her sister, and convince her to relieve Lear of the remainder of his force. Then, you must have your lady rendezvous with Edmund at the second bell of the watch."

"Two in the bloody morning?"

"Watch how she leaps at the chance. She's bewitched, remember. It is critical that she ally herself with the house of Gloucester, even if it is in secret. I know that will be difficult for you, but you must endure it. If you are going to have the lady and her power, someone will have to dispatch the Duke of Albany— someone who will be of no loss when hanged. The bastard Edmund is perfect for the part, is he not?"

Oswald nodded, his eyes getting larger with my every word. His whole life he had carried messages and run errands for Goneril, but at last he could see reward in sight for being intrigue's pawn. Fortunately, the possibility blinded him to reason. "When will the lady be mine?"

"When all is in placc, catch-fart, when all is in place. What do you know of a military force coming from France?"

"Why, nothing."

"Then skulk and eavesdrop. Edmund knows of such a force, or he has constructed a rumor. Find out what you can. Find out, but do not speak to Edmund of his rendezvous with your lady, he thinks it a secret."

Oswald stood to his full height (he'd been bending over to talk face-to-face with me). "What do you gain from this, fool?"

I had hoped he wouldn't ask. "Like you, even with love, there are those who would stand in the way of my happiness. I need you and those affected by your deeds to help them out of my way."

"You would kill the Duke of Cornwall?"

"He is one, but no matter who loves me, I am bound to Lear—I am his slave."

"So you would kill the king, too? No worries, fool, I can do that. You have a deal."

"Fuckstockings!" said I.

"Jolly good show, Pocket," said Kent. "Go looking for a messenger and end up setting a bloody assassin loose on the king. A born diplomat, you are."

"Sarcasm is very unattractive in the elderly, Kent. I couldn't very well call him off, my sincerity would have been questioned."

"You weren't being sincere."

"Well, conviction then. Just stay by Lear during the Yule feast and don't let him eat anything unless you've eaten it first. If I know Oswald, he'll try to slay the king using the most cowardly means."

"Or not at all."

"What?"

"What makes you think Oswald was telling you the truth any more than you were telling it to him?"

"I'm counting on his lying to a degree."

"But to what degree?"

I paced in a circle around our little tower room. "What a wimpled wagon of nun wank this is. I'd rather juggle fire blindfolded. I'm not built for these dark dealings—I'm better suited for laughter, children's birthdays, baby animals, and friendly bonking. The sodding witches got it wrong."

"And yet, you've set a civil war in motion and sent an assassin after the king," said Kent. "Grand ambition for a children's birthday clown, don't you think?"

"You've become bitter in your dotage, you know?"

"Well, perhaps my duties as food taster will end my bitterness."

"Just keep the old man alive, Kent. Since the Yule feast is still on, I take it dear Regan didn't tell Lear that she was taking his knights yet."

"The lady tried to make peace between Goneril and her father. She only served to calm the old man enough that he agreed to come to the feast."

"Good. No doubt she'll make her move on the morrow." I grinned. "If she's well enough."

"Wicked," said Kent.

"Justice," said I.

Regan came up the spiral stairs alone. The single candle she carried in a storm lantern cast her shadow tall up the stone wall like the very specter of a shaggable death. I stood outside the solar door, candelabra in one hand, the door latch in the other.

"Happy Christmas, kitten," said I.

"Well, that feast was complete crap, wasn't it? Bloody Gloucester, pagan twat, calling it the feast of St. Stephen instead of Christmas. There's no presents on the feast of bloody Stephen. Without presents I'd rather celebrate Yule for the winter solstice; at least then you get to sacrifice a pig and build a cracking huge fire."

"Gloucester was being deferential to your Christian beliefs as it was, love. The holiday is Saturnalia[1] for him and Edmund, proper orgy it is. So perhaps there's a present for you yet to be unwrapped."

She smiled then. "Perhaps. Edmund was so coy at the feast—barely looking my way. Fear of Cornwall, I suppose. But you were right, his ear was bandaged."

---

1. Saturnalia—the celebration of the winter solstice in the Roman pantheon, paying tribute to Saturn, the "sower of seeds." Celebration of Saturnalia involved much drunkenness and indiscriminate shagging. Observed in modern times by the ritual of the "office Christmas party."

"Aye, lady, and I'm to tell you that he's a bit modest about it. He may not wish to be fully seen."

"But I saw him at the feast."

"Aye, but he's hinted that there may have been other self-punishment performed in your honor and he's shy."

A joyous child at Christmas she suddenly was—visions of a bloke lashing himself dancing in her head.

"Oh, Pocket, do let me in."

And so I did. I opened the door, and slipped the storm lantern from her grasp as she passed. "Ah, ah, ah, love. No more light than that one candle. He's ever so shy."

I heard Edmund's voice say from behind the tapestry, "Oh, my sweet lady, Regan, thou art more fair than moonlight, more radiant than the sun, more glorious than all the stars. I must have you or I shall surely die."

I slowly closed and latched the door.

"No, my goddess, undress there," said Edmund's voice. "Let me watch you."

I'd been all evening coaching Drool on what to say and exactly how to say it. Next he would comment on her loveliness, then ask her to blow out the single candle on the table and join him behind the tapestry, at which point he was to unceremoniously snog her soggy and shag her silly.

It sounded rather like what I'd guess would be the auditory effect of a bull elk trying to balance a wildcat on a red-hot poker. There was no little bit of yowling, growling, squealing, and screeching going on by the time I saw the second light coming up the stairs. I could see by the shadow that the lantern bearer was leading with a drawn sword. Oswald had been true to his treacherous nature, just as I had calculated.

"Put down that blade, you git, you'll put someone's eye out."

The Duke of Cornwall rounded the stairs with blade lowered, a bewildered look on his face. "Fool?"

"What if a child was running down the stairs?" I said. "Awkward explaining to Gloucester why his beloved toddler grandson was wearing a yard of Sheffield steel through his gizzard."

"Gloucester doesn't have a grandson," said Cornwall, surprised, I think, that he was engaged in this discussion.

"That doesn't diminish the need for basic weapons safety."

"But I'm here to slay you."

"*Moi?*" said I, in perfect fucking French. "Whatever for?"

"Because you are shagging my lady."

There was a great bellow from the tower room, followed by a female feral screech. "Was that pain or pleasure, would you say?" I asked.

"Who is in there?" Cornwall raised his sword again.

"Well, it is your lady, and she is most certainly being shagged, by the bastard Edmund of Gloucester, but prudence would have you stay your blade." I laid Jones across the duke's wrist and pushed his sword hand down. "Unless you care nothing for being King of Britain."

"What are you on about, fool?" The duke very much wanted to do some killing, but his ambition was trumping his bloodlust.

"Oh ride me, you great, tree-cocked rhinoceros!" screamed Regan from the next room.

"She still says that?" I asked.

"Well, usually it's 'tree-cocked stallion,'" said Cornwall.

"She does get good wear out of a metaphor." I put my hand on his shoulder for comfort. "Aye, a sad surprise, for you, I'll wager. At least when a man, after looking into his soul, finally stoops to fuck a snake, he hopes at least not to see pairs of boots already lined up outside her burrow."

He shook me off. "I'll kill him!"

"Cornwall, you are about to be attacked. Even now Albany prepares to take all of Britain for his own. You'll need Edmund and the forces of Gloucester to prevail against him, and when you do, you'll be king. If you go in that room now, you will kill a horn-beast, but you will lose a kingdom."

"God's blood," said Cornwall. "Is this true?"

"Win the war, good sirrah. Then kill the bastard at your leisure, when you can take your time and do it right. Regan's honor is, well, malleable, is it not?"

"You're sure about this war?"

"Aye. It's why you need to take Lear's remaining knights and squires, just as Goneril and Albany took the others. And you mustn't let Goneril know you know. Even now your lady is assuring Gloucester's allegiance to your side."

"Really? That's why she's shagging Edmund?"

It hadn't occurred to me until I'd said it, but it really did work quite nicely. "Oh yes, my lord, her enthusiasm is inspired by her fierce loyalty to you."

"Of course," said Cornwall, sheathing his sword. "I should have seen it."

"That doesn't mean you can't kill Edmund when it's over," said I.

"Absolutely," said the duke.

When Cornwall was gone and some time after the first bell had rung for the watch, I knocked on the door and peeked my head in.

"Lord Edmund," said I. "There's a stirring in the duke's tower. Perhaps you should say your farewells."

I held Regan's storm lantern at the crack of the door so she could find her way out, and a few moments later she stumbled out of the solar with her gown on backward, her hair in knots, and a slick of drool running in a river between and over her breasts. Overall, in fact, she looked quite slippery.

She was dazed and limping in a way that seemed she couldn't quite figure which side to favor, and she was dragging one shoe by its strap around her ankle.

"Lady, shall I get your other shoe?"

"Sod it," she said, waving drunkenly, or what seemed like drunkenly, almost falling down the stairs. I steadied her, helped her get her gown turned around, swabbed her down a bit with her skirt, then took her arm and helped her down the stairs.

"He's quite a bit larger close up than he appears across the room."

"That so?"

"I shan't sit down for a fortnight."

"Ah, sweet romance. Can you make it to your quarters, kitten?"

"I think so. You're clever, Pocket—start thinking of excuses for Edmund if I'm not able to get out of bed tomorrow."

"My pleasure, kitten. Sleep well."

I made my way back upstairs where Drool was standing trouserless by the candle, still sporting enough of an erection to bludgeon a calf senseless.

"Sorry, I came out, Pocket, it were dark."

"No worries, lad. Good show."

"She were fit."

"Aye. Quite."

"What's a rhinoceros?"

"It's like a unicorn with armored bollocks. It's a good thing. Chew these mint leaves and let's get you wiped down. Practice your Edmund lines while I look for a towel."

When the watch rang the second bell, the scene was set. Another storm lantern illuminated the stairs and cast a buxom shadow up the wall.

"Pumpkin!"

"What are you doing here, worm?"

"Just keeping watch. Go in, but leave your lantern with me. Edmund is shy about the injury he has inflicted on himself in your honor."

Goneril grinned at the prospect of the bastard's pain and went in.

A few minutes passed before Oswald crept up the stairs.

"Fool? You're still alive?"

"Aye." I held my hand up to my ear. "But listen to the children of the night—what music they make."

"Sounds like a moose trying to shit a family of hedgehogs," said the scoundrel.

"Oh, that's good. I was thinking more of moo cow being beaten with a flaming goose, but you may have it. Ah, who's to say? We should leave, good Oswald, and give the lovers their privacy."

"Did you not meet with Princess Regan?"

"Oh, we changed the rendezvous to the fourth bell of the watch, why?"

16.
A Storm Rising

The storm blew in during the night. I was eating my breakfast in the kitchen when a row erupted in the courtyard. I heard Lear bellow and left to attend him, leaving my porridge with Drool. Kent intercepted me in the corridor.

"So the old man lived through the night?" said I.

"I slept at his door," said Kent. "Where were you?"

"Trying to see two princesses ruthlessly shagged and starting a civil war, thank you, and with no proper supper, neither."

"Fine feast," said Kent. "Ate till I nearly burst just to see the king went unpoisoned. Who is bloody St. Stephen, anyway?"

Then I saw Oswald coming down the corridor.

"Good Kent, go see that the daughters don't kill the king, and that Cornwall doesn't kill Edmund, and that the sisters don't kill each other, and if you can help it, don't kill anyone. It's too early for killing."

Kent hurried off as Oswald reached me.

"So," said Oswald, "you lived through the night?"

"Of course, why wouldn't I?" I asked.

"Well, because I told Cornwall of your rendezvous with Regan and I expected him to slay you."

"Oh for fuck's sake, Oswald, show a little guile, would you? The state of villainy in this castle is rubbish, what with Edmund being pleasant and you being straightforward. What's next, Cornwall starts feeding orphans while bloody bluebirds fly out of his bum? Now, let's try it again, see if you can at least keep up a pretense of evil. Go."

"So, you lived through the night?" said Oswald.

"Of course, why wouldn't I?" I asked.

"Oh, no reason, I was worried about you."

I clouted Oswald on the ear with Jones. "No, you nitwit, I'd never believe you're concerned for my welfare—you're a right weasel, aren't you?"

He made to reach for his sword and I hit his wrist a vicious blow with Jones's stick end. The villain leapt back and rubbed his bruised wrist.

"Despite your incompetence, our agreement stands. I need you to consult with Edmund. Give him this letter from Regan." I handed him the letter I'd written at first light. Regan's hand was easy to duplicate. She dotted her i's with hearts. "Don't break the seal, it professes her devotion for him, but instructs him to show no outward affection for her. You must also caution him against showing any deference to your lady Goneril in front of Regan. And because I know the intrigue confuses you, let me map out your interest here. Edmund will dispatch your Lord Albany, thus releasing your lady to other affections, only then will we reveal to Cornwall that Edmund has cuckolded him with Regan, and the duke will dispatch the bastard, at which time, I will cast the love spell on Goneril, sending her into your own ferrety arms."

"You could be lying. I tried to have you killed. Why would you help me?"

"Excellent question. First, I, unlike you, am not a villain, therefore I can be expected to proceed with a modicum of integrity. And, second, I wish to visit revenge on Goneril for how she has treated me, her younger sister, Cordelia, and King Lear. I can think of no better punishment for her than pairing her with the man-shaped tower of excrement that is yourself."

"Oh, that's reasonable," said Oswald.

"Off you go, then. See that Edmund doesn't show deference."

"I might slay him myself, for violating my lady."

"No, you won't, you're a coward. Or had you forgotten?"

Oswald started to quiver then with anger, but he did
not try to reach for his sword.

"Run along, mate, Pocket's got a bumload of foolin'
yet to do."

A randy hand of wind groped the courtyard, sending the sisters' skirts tossing and snapping their hair
in their faces. Kent crouched and clung to his great
broad-brimmed hat to keep it from being carried
away. The old king held his fur cape tight around
him and squinted against the dust, while the Duke
of Cornwall and Earl of Gloucester stood by the great
gate for shelter—the duke content, it seemed, to let
his duchess do the talking. I was relieved to see that
Edmund was not in attendance, so I danced into the
courtyard, bells a-jingle, song in heart.

"Hi ho!" said I. "Everyone get a proper bonking for
the Saturnalia, did they?"

The two sisters looked at me blankly, as if I might
have been speaking Chinese or dog, and they had
not, overnight, each received rousing repeated bon-
kings from an enormous donkey-donged nitwit.
Gloucester looked down, embarrassed, I suppose,
over abandoning his own pantheon for St. Stephen,
and a wholly bollocks holy holiday feast. Cornwall
sneered.

"Ah," said I. "Then a crispy biscuit baby Jesus cornu-bloody-copia of Christmas cheer, was it? Silent night, camels and wise men—frankenstein, gold, and myrrh all around then?"

"Sodding Christian harpies want to take away my knights," said Lear. "I've already lost half my train to you, Goneril, I'll not lose the rest."

"Oh, yes, sire," said I. "Christianity is their fault. I forgot that the wind blew out of a pagan sky for you today."

Regan stepped forward then, and yes, she was walking a bit bow-legged. "Why do you need to keep fifty men, Father? We've plenty of servants to tend to you."

"And," said Goneril, "they will be under our charge, so there will be no discord within the walls of our homes."

"I'm of my sister's mind on this," said Regan.

"You're always of your sister's mind," said Lear. "An original thought would crack your feeble skull like a thunderbolt, you craven vulture."

"That's the spirit, sire," said I. "Treat them like bins of used nappies and watch them come around. A wonder they've turned out so delightful with fathering of that quality."

"Take them, then, you flesh-tearing harpies! Would that I could drag your mother from her tomb and accuse her of most grievous adultery, for you cannot be issue from my loins and treat me so."

I nodded and lay my head on Goneril's shoulder. "Evidently the adultery comes from Mum's side of the family, pumpkin—the bitterness and stunning bosoms are from Papa."

She pushed me aside, despite my wisdom.

Lear was losing all control now, trembling as he shouted impotently at his daughters, looking weaker and more slight with every word. "Hear me, gods! If it be you that stir these daughters' hearts against their father, then touch me with noble anger, and stain not my man's cheeks with women's weapons, the water drops."

"Those aren't tears on your cheeks, nuncle," said I. "It's raining."

Gloucester and Cornwall looked away, embarrassed for the old man. Kent had his hands on the king's shoulders and was trying to lead him gently out of the rain. Lear shrugged him off and stormed up to his daughters.

"You unnatural hags! I will have such revenges on you both that the world—er, I will do such things that I don't even know yet, but they will be horrible—the very terrors of the earth! But I'll not weep! I'll not. Even if my heart shall break into a hundred thousand shards, I shall not weep. O fool, I shall go mad!"

"Aye, nuncle, smashing good start you're off to."
I tried to put an arm around Lear's shoulders, but he
elbowed me away.

"Rescind your orders, harpies, or I shall leave this
house." He made for the great gate.

"It is for your own good, Father," said Goneril.
"Now, cease this ranting and come inside."

"I gave you all!" screeched Lear, waving a palsied
claw at Regan.

"And you took your bloody time giving it, too, you
senile old fuck," said Regan.

"She came up with that one all on her own, nuncle,"
said I, looking on the bright side.

"I will go," threatened Lear, another step toward
the gate. "I'm not having you on. I'll head right out
that door."

"Pity," said Goneril.

"Shame, really," said Regan.

"Here I go. Right out that gate. Never to return. All
alone."

"Ta," said Goneril.

"*Au revoir*," said Regan, in nearly perfect fucking
French.

"I mean it." The old man was actually through the
gate now.

"Close it," said Regan.

"But, lady, it's not fit for man nor beast out there," said Gloucester.

"Fucking close it!" said Goneril. She ran forward and pushed the great iron lever by the gatehouse with all her might. The heavy, iron-clad portcullis slammed down, the points just missing the old king as they set in the ports a foot deep in the stone.

"I'll go," said Lear, through the grate. "Don't think I won't."

The sisters left the courtyard for the shelter of the castle. Cornwall followed them and called for Gloucester to come along.

"But this storm," said Gloucester, watching his old friend through the bars. "No one should be out in this storm."

"He brought it on himself," said Cornwall. "Now, come along, good Gloucester."

Gloucester pulled himself away from the grate and followed Cornwall into the castle, leaving just Kent and me standing in the rain in only our woolen cloaks. Kent looked tortured over the old man's fate.

"He's alone, Pocket. It's not even noon and the sky is as dark as midnight. Lear is outside and alone."

"Oh buggering bugger," said I. I looked at the chains leading up to the top of the gatehouse, the beams that protruded from the walls, the crenellations at the top to protect the archers. Damn the anchoress and Belette for my monkey-training as an acrobat. "I'll go with him. But you have to hide Drool from Edmund. Talk to the laundress with the smashing knockers, she'll help. She fancies the lad, no matter what she says."

"I'll go get help to crank up the gate," said Kent.

"Not to worry. You look after the Natural, and watch your back for Edmund and Oswald. I'll return with the old man when I can." And with that I shoved Jones down the back of my jerkin, ran and leapt onto the massive chain, spidered up it hand over hand, swung up onto one of the beams that protruded from the stone above, then hopped from beam to beam until I could find a handhold in the stone—and scurried up another story to the top of the wall. "Sorry sodding fortress," I shouted to Kent with a wave. In a wink I was over the wall and down the drawbridge chains on the other side to the ground below.

The old man was already at the gates of the walled village, nearly disappearing amid the rain, tottering out onto the heath in his fur cape, looking like an ancient sodden rat.

ACT III

Jesters do oft prove prophets.

—*King Lear*, Act V, Scene 3, Regan

17.

Reigning Fools, Hailing Nutters

B low, wind, crack your cheeks! Rage! Blow!" thundered Lear.

The old man had perched himself on the top of a hill outside Gloucester and was shouting into the wind like a bloody lunatic, even as lightning raked the sky with white-hot claws and thunder shook me to my ribs.

"Come in from there, you bloody decrepit old looney!" said I, huddled under a holly bush nearby; drenched and cold and at the end of my patience with the old man. "Come back to Gloucester and ask shelter from your daughters."

"Oh, ye heartless gods! Send your oak-cleaving thunderbolts down on me!

Burn me with your sulfurous and life-ending fires!

Singe my white head and reduce me to a pillar of ash!

Strike me dead! Let your wrath take fiery form and smite me!

Take me, spare no violence!

I do not blame thee, thou art not my daughters!

I've given you nothing and expect no quarter!

Do your horrible pleasure direct,

To a poor, infirm, despised old man!

Crack the sky! Strike me dead!"

The old man paused as a thunderbolt split a tree on the heath with blinding fire and a noise that would send statues to shitting themselves. I ran out from under my bush to the king's side.

"Come in, nuncle. Take some shelter under a shrub, if only to take the sting out of the rain."

"I need no shelter. Let nature take her naked revenge."

"Fine, then," said I. "Then you won't be needing this." I took the old man's heavy fur cape, tossed him my sodden woolen cloak, and retreated to my shrubbery and the relative shelter of the heavy animal skin.

"Hey?" said Lear, bewildered.

"Go on," said I. "*Crack the sky, fry your old head, mash your balls, et cetera, et cetera.* I'll prompt you if you lose your place."

And off he went again:

"Mighty Thor, send your thunderbolts to cease this weary heart!

Neptune's waves, beat these limbs from their joints!
Hecate's claws, tear my liver and sup upon my soul!
Baal, blast my bowels from their unhealthy home!
Jupiter, strew the land with my shredded muscle!"

The old man stopped his tirade for a moment and
the madness went out of his eyes. He looked to me.
"It's really fucking cold out here."

"Like being struck by a bolt of the bloody obvious
on the road to Damascus, innit, nuncle?" I held open
the great fur cloak and nodded for the old man to join
me in it under my shrubbery. He crept down the hill,
careful not to slip in the rivulets of mud and water that
cascaded by, and ducked under the cover with me."

The old man shuddered and put his skeletal arm
around my shoulders. "Rather closer than we're accus-
tomed to, eh, boy?"

"Aye, nuncle, did I ever tell you that you are a very
attractive man?" said Jones, poking his puppety head
out of the cloak.

And the old man began to laugh, and he laughed
until his shoulders shook and the laughter broke into
a jarring cough, and that continued until I thought
he might expectorate vital organs. I caught some
freezing rain in my cupped hand and held it for him
to sip.

"Don't make me laugh, boy. I'm mad with grief and
rage and I've no stomach for jests. You should stand

clear, lest a thunderbolt scorch you when the gods heed my challenge."

"Nuncle, begging pardon, but, you arrogant old tosser! The gods aren't going to strike you down with a thunderbolt simply because you asked them. Why would they accommodate you with a thunderbolt? More likely a carbuncle, festered and gone fatal, or perhaps a thankless child or two, being how the gods love their irony."

"The cheek!" said Lear.

"Oh yes, cheeky gods they are," said I. "And you named off a bushel of them, too. Now if you are struck down we won't even know who to blame unless lightning brands a signature in your old hide. You should have dared one, then waited an hour perhaps before calling fire down from the whole lot at a go."

The king wiped rain out of his eyes. "I've set a thousand monks and nuns to pray for my forgiveness and the pagans slaughter goats by the herd for my salvation, but I fear it is not enough. Not once did I act in the interest of my people, not once did I act in the interest of my wives or my daughters' mothers—I have served myself as god and I find I am little forgiving. Be kind, Pocket, lest you one day face the darkness as I do. Or, in absence of kindness, be drunk."

"But, nuncle," said I. "I do not need to be cautious for the day when I become frail. I am frail now. And on the bright side, there may be no God at all, and the evil deeds you've done will be their own reward."

"Perhaps I don't even rate a righteous slaughtering," sobbed Lear. "The gods have sent these daughters to suck out my life blood. It is punishment for how I treated my own father. Do you know how I became king?"

"Pulled a sword out of a stone and slayed a dragon with it, didn't you?"

"No, that never happened."

"Sodding convent education. Buggered if I know then, nuncle. How *did* Lear become king?"

"My own father, I murdered him. I do not deserve a noble death."

I was speechless. I had been in service of the king over a decade and never had I heard of this. The story went that old King Bladud had handed the kingdom over to Lear and went to Athens, where he learned to be a necromancer, then returned to Britain and died from the plague in service of the goddess Minerva at the temple at Bath. But before I could gather my wits for a reply, lightning cracked the sky, illuminating a hulking creature that was making its way across the hillside toward us.

"What's that?" I asked.

"A demon," said the old man. "The gods have sent a monster to take their revenge on me."

The thing was covered in slime, and walking as if it had just been constructed from the very earth over which it slogged. I felt for the daggers at the small of my back and pulled one from its sheath. There'd be no knife throwing in this downpour—I wasn't even sure I could hold the blade steady for a thrust.

"Your sword, Lear," said I. "Draw and defend." I stood and stepped out of the shelter of the shrubbery. I spun Jones so his stick end was at the ready, and drew a flourish in the air with my dagger.

"Come hither, demon! Pocket's got a coach ride back to the underworld for thee."

I crouched, thinking to leap aside as the thing lunged. Although it described the shape of a man, I could see long slimy tendrils dragging from it, and mud oozing off of it. Once it stumbled I'd leap on its back and see if I could cause it to fall and slide down the hillside, away from the old king.

"No, let it take me," said Lear. Suddenly the old man shrugged off his fur cloak and charged at the monster, his arms wide, as if offering his very heart to the beast. "Slay me, ye merciless god—rend this black heart from Britain's chest!"

I could not stop him and the old man fell into the beast's arms. But to my surprise, there was no tearing of limbs or bashing of brains. The thing caught the old man and lowered him gently to the ground.

I lowered my blade and inched forward. "Leave him, beast."

The thing was kneeling over Lear, whose eyes were rolled back in his head even as he twitched as if in a fit. The beast looked at me and I saw streaks of pink through the mud, the whites of its eyes.

"Help me," it said. "Help me get him to shelter."

I stepped forth and wiped the mud away from the thing's face. It was a man, covered with mud so thick it even ran out of his mouth and coated his teeth, but a man just the same, vines or rags, I couldn't tell which, trailed off his arms. "Help poor Tom bring him out of the cold," said he.

I sheathed my dagger, retrieved the old man's cape, and helped the muddy, naked bloke carry King Lear into the wood.

It was a tiny cabin, barely enough room to stand in, but the fire was warm and the old woman stirred a pot that smelled of boiling meat and onions, like breath of the Muses it was, on this dank night. Lear stirred, now hours since we brought him in from the rain. The king reclined on a pallet of straw and skins. His fur cloak still steamed by the fire.

"Am I dead?" asked the old man.

"Nay, nuncle, but ye were close enough to lick death's salty taint," said I.

"Back, foul fiend!" said the naked fellow, waving at the very air before his eyes. I had helped him wash away much of the mud, so now he was merely filthy and mad, but no longer misshapen.

"Oh, poor Tom is cold! So cold."

"Aye, we can tell that," said I. "Unless you're just a crashingly large bloke what was born with a willie the size of a raisin."

"The fiend makes Tom eat the swimming frog, the tadpole, lizards, and ditch-water—I eat cow dung for salads and swallow rats and bits of dead dogs. I drink pond scum, and in every village I am beaten and thrown into stocks. Away, fiend! Leave poor, cold Tom alone!"

"Blimey," said I. "The loonies are in full bloom tonight."

"I offered him some stewed mutton," said the old woman by the fire, without turning, "but no, he had to have his frogs and cow pies. Right fussy eater for a naked nutter."

"Pocket," said Lear, clawing at my arm. "Who is that large, naked chap?"

"He calls himself Tom, nuncle. Says he's pursued by the devil."

"He must have daughters. See here, Tom, did you give all to your daughters? Is that what drove you mad and poor even until you are naked?"

Tom crawled across the floor until he was at Lear's side.

"I was a vain and selfish servant," said the nutter. "I slept with my mistress every night and woke thinking of putting it to her again in the morning. I drank and caroused and made merry, even while my half brother fought a crusade for a Church for which he held no faith. I took all without thought for those who had nothing. Now I have nothing—not a stitch, not a crumb, not a coin, and the devil dogs me to the ends of the earth for my selfishness."

"You see," said Lear, "only a man's cruel daughters could drive him to such a state."

"He didn't say that, you daft geezer. He said he was a selfish libertine and the devil took his kit."

The old woman turned now. "Aye, the fool's right. The younger nutter has no daughters, 'tis his own unkindness that curses him." She crossed the cabin with two steaming bowls of stew and set them before us on the floor. "And it's your own evil hounds you, Lear, not your daughters."

The old woman, I'd seen her before. She was one of the crones from the Great Birnam Wood. Different togs and somewhat less green, but this was surely Rosemary, the cat-toed witch.

Lear slid to the floor and grabbed poor Tom's hand. "I have been selfish. I have thought nothing of the weight of my deeds. My own father I imprisoned in the temple at Bath because he was a leper, and later had him killed. My own brother I did murder when I suspected him of bedding my queen. No trial, not even the honor of a challenge. I had him murdered in his sleep without proof. And my queen is dead, too, for my jealousy. My kingdom is the fruit of treachery, and treachery have I reaped. I do not deserve to even wear clothes on my back. You are true, Tom, that you have nothing. I, too, shall have nothing, as is my just reward!"

The old man began to tear off his clothes, ripping at the collar of his shirt, tearing more of his parchment-like skin than the linen. I stayed his hand, held his wrists and tried to catch his eye with my own, to pull him back from madness.

"Oh, I have wronged my sweet Cordelia!" the old man wailed. "The only one who loved me and I have wronged her! My one true daughter! Gods, tear these clothes from my back, tear the meat from my bones!"

Then I felt claws clamp on my own wrists and I was pulled away from Lear as if I had been drawn by heavy iron shackles. "Let him suffer," hissed the witch in my ear.

"But I have made this pain," said I.

"Lear's pain is of his own making, fool," she said. With that I felt the room spinning and I heard the voice of the girl ghost telling me to sleep. "Sleep, sweet Pocket."

"Who's the muddy naked bloke snogging the king's noggin?" asked Kent.

I awoke to see the old knight standing in the doorway with the Earl of Gloucester. The storm still raged outside, but by firelight I could see the naked nutter Tom O'Bedlam had wrapped himself around Lear and was kissing the king's bald head as if blessing a newborn babe.

"Oh majesty," said Gloucester, "can't you find better company than this? Who is this rough beast?"

"He is a philosopher," said Lear. "I will talk with him."

"Poor Tom O'Bedlam, is he," said Tom. "Eater of tadpoles, cursed and damned by demons."

Kent looked to me and I shrugged. "Both mad as cat herds," said I. I looked around for the old woman as a witness, but she was gone.

"Well, snap to, majesty, I bring news from France," said Kent.

"Hollandaise sauce, excellent on eggs?" I inquired.

"No," said Kent. "More urgent."

"Wine and cheese complement one another nicely?" I further queried.

"No, you rasp-tongued rascal, France has landed an army at Dover, and there's rumor they've forces hidden in other cities around the British coast, ready to strike."

"Oh, well, that does trump the wine and cheese news, then, doesn't it?"

Gloucester was trying to pry Tom off King Lear, but having a hard time doing so while keeping mud off his cloak. "I've sent word to the French camp at Dover that Lear is here," said Gloucester. "I've made the case to the king's daughters to let me bring him in from the storm, but they will not relent. Even in my own home my power has been usurped by the Duke of Cornwall. Regan and Cornwall have taken command of Lear's knights, and with them, my castle."

"We come to bring you to a hovel at the city wall," said Kent. "When the storm breaks, Gloucester will send a cart to take Lear to the French camp at Dover."

"No," said Lear. "Let me talk to my philosopher friend in private." He pawed at mad Tom. "He knows much of how life should be lived. Tell me, friend, why is there thunder?"

Kent turned to Gloucester and shrugged. "He's not in his right mind."

"Who can blame him?" said Gloucester. "After what his daughters have done—his very flesh rising up against him. I had a beloved son who conspired to murder me, and just the thought of that nearly drove me mad."

"Do you nobles have any reaction to hardship besides going bloody barking and running off to eat dirt?" said I. "Hitch up your bollocks and get on with it, would you? Caius, what of Drool?"

"I left him hidden in the laundry, but Edmund will find him when his mind turns full to the task. Right now he is distracted by trying to avoid the sisters and conspiring with Cornwall."

"My son, Edmund, he is still true," said Gloucester.

"Yes, right, milord," said I. "And mind you don't trip on the honeysuckle sprouting from his bum when you next see him. Do you have means to get me into the castle without Edmund knowing I'm there?"

"I suppose. But I take no commands from you, fool. You are but a slave, and an impudent one at that."

"You're still angry over my jesting about your dead wife, aren't you?"

"Do the fool's will!" boomed Lear. "His word is as mine."

A slight breeze then would have knocked me off my feet, so shocked was I. Oh, there was still madness glowing in the old man's eyes, but so was the fire of his authority. A feeble, babbling wretch one moment, the next a dragon deep inside the old man barked fire.

"Yes, your majesty," said Gloucester.

"He's a good lad," said Kent, by way of easing the bite of Lear's command.

"Nuncle, bring your naked madman and let us go with Gloucester, to this hovel by the city wall. I'll retrieve my nitwit apprentice from the castle and off we'll be to meet up with the bloody frog King Jeff at Dover."

Kent rubbed my shoulder. "A sword in support then?"

"No, thank you," said I. "You stay with the old man, get him to Dover." I pulled Kent over by the fire and bade him bend down so I could whisper in his ear. "Did you know that Lear murdered his brother?"

The old knight's eyes went wide, then narrowed as if he were in pain. "He gave the order."

"Oh, Kent. Thou loyal old fool."

18.

Kitten's Claws

We entered Castle Gloucester in stealth, which does not suit me, as you might guess. I am better suited to entering a room with a series of somersaults, a clack-stick, rude noise, and a *"top o' the mornin' to ye, tossers!"* I'm fitted out in bells and puppets, for fuck's sake. All this sneaking and subterfuge was wearing on me. I followed the Earl of Gloucester through a secret hatch in the stable and into a tunnel that passed under the moat. We waded through a foot of cold water in the dark, making for a slosh in my step as well as a jingle. I'd never fit Drool through the narrow passage, even if I could chase the dark with a torch. The tunnel opened through another hatch in the floor of the dungeon. The earl took his leave in the very torture chamber where I had met Regan.

"I'm off to arrange the passage for your master to Dover, fool. I still have a few servants who are true to me."

I felt indebted to the old man for helping me into the castle, especially given his former bitterness toward me. "Steer clear of the bastard, your grace. I know he is your favored son, but not rightly so. He's a villain."

"Don't disparage Edmund, fool. I know your conniving ways. Only last evening he stood with me in protest against Cornwall's treatment of the king."

I could tell Gloucester about the letter I'd forged in Edgar's hand, about the bastard's plan to usurp his brother, but what could he do? Likely he'd storm into Edmund's quarters and the bastard would murder him on the spot.

"Right, then," said I. "Be careful, my lord. Cornwall and Regan are a four-fanged viper, and if they should turn their venom on Edmund, you must let him go. Do not come to his aid, lest you, too, are scratched with poisonous pricks."

"My last true son. Shame on you, fool," said the earl. He scoffed and hurried out of the dungeon and up the stairs.

I thought to prevail upon one god or another to protect the old man, but if the gods were working in my favor, they would continue unbidden, and if they opposed, there was no need to alert them to my cause. It pained me, but I took off my shoes and hat and tucked them into my jerkin to still the bells. Jones had remained back at the hovel with Lear.

The laundry lay in the lower levels of the castle, so I made my way there first. The laundress with the aforementioned knockers of the smashing persuasion was hanging a basketload of shirts by the fire when I entered.

"Where's Drool, love?" I asked.

"Hidden," she said.

"I know he's bloody hidden, otherwise asking would have been superfluous, wouldn't it?"

"Just want me to give him up, then? How do I know you're not out to kill him? That old knight who brought him here said not to let anyone know where he was."

"But I'm here to get him out of the castle. Rescue him, as it were."

"Aye, you say that, but—"

"Listen, you bloody tart, give up the git!"

"Emma," said the laundress.

I sat down on the hearth and rested my head in my hands. "Love, I've spent the night in a storm with a witch and two raving nutters. I've a brace of wars to see to, as well as the summary violation of two princesses and consequent cuckolding of a pair of dukes.

I'm heartbroken, aggrieved for the loss of a friend, and the great drooling lummox that is my apprentice is evidently wandering the castle in search of a mortal chest wound. Pity a fool, love—another non sequitur may dash my brittle sanity to splinters."

"My name is Emma," said the laundress.

"I'm right here, Pocket," said Drool, standing up in the great cauldron. A pile of laundry on his head had been concealing his great empty melon as he lurked in the water. "Knockers hided me. She's a love."

"You see," said Emma. "He keeps calling me Knockers."

"It's a compliment, love."

"It's disrespectful," she said. "My name's Emma."

I will never understand women. The laundress, it would seem, dressed in a manner that accentuated, indeed, celebrated her bosoms—a tightly cinched waist pushing bits up until they bloomed out of a swooping neckline—yet a chap notices and the lady takes offense. I will never understand it.

"You know he's a complete nitwit, don't you, Emma?"

"Just the same."

"Fine. Drool, apologize to Emma for saying how smashing her knockers are."

"Sorry about your knockers," said Drool, bowing his head so his laundry hat dropped back into the drink.

"Satisfied, Emma?" I asked.

"I suppose."

"Good. Now, do you know where Captain Curan, the commander of King Lear's knights might be?"

"Oh yes," said Emma. "Lord Edmund and the duke consulted me this morning on all the military matters, as they are wont to do—me being a laundress and having access to all the best bloody tactics and strategies and the lot."

"Sarcasm will make your tits fall off," said I.

"Will not," said she, her arm going to a support position.

"It's a known fact," I said, nodding earnestly, then looking to Drool, who also nodded earnestly and said, "It's a known fact," note for note in my voice.

"That's bloody spooky." Emma shuddered. "You lot can get out of my laundry."

"Very well, then," said I. I motioned for Drool to climb out of the cauldron. "I thank you for looking after the Natural, Emma. I wish there were something I could—"

"Kill Edmund," she said.

"Pardon?"

"The son of a guild builder were going to marry me before I came to work here. A respected man. Edmund took me against my will and bragged about it in the village. My lad wouldn't have me then. No one worth his

salt will have me, except the bastard, and him whenever he wants. 'Tis Edmund who commanded that I
wear this low frock. Says he'll set me out with the pigs
if I don't give him service. Kill him for me."

"But lass, I'm just a fool. A clown. A small one at
that."

"There's more to you than that, you black-hatted
rascal. I've seen them wicked daggers at your back, and
I can see who's pulling the strings round this castle,
and it ain't the duke or the old king. Kill the bastard."

"Edmund beated me," said Drool. "And she do have
smashing knockers."

"Drool!"

"Well, she do."

"All right, then," said I, taking the laundress's hand.
"But in time. We've things to accomplish first." I
bowed over her hand, kissed it, then turned on my heel
and padded barefoot out of the laundry to set history.

"Heinous fuckery," Drool whispered to the laundress with a wink.

I hid Drool in the gatehouse among the heavy chains
that I had used for my escape when I pursued Lear
into the storm. Getting the lummox up on the wall and
to the gatehouse undetected was no small task, and he
left a dripping trail on the stones until we gained the

castle exterior, but the guard was light in the tempest, so most of the way we went across the top of the walls unseen. My feet felt as if they'd been set in ice by the time I came back in to a fire, but there was no other way. Drool in the tight space of the secret tunnel, with his fear of the dark was not something I would wish on an enemy. I found a woolen blanket and wrapped the lout in it to await my return.

"Guard my shoes and my satchel, Drool."

I made my way, dodging from nook to cranny, through the kitchen, to the servants' entrance into the great hall, hoping I might get a moment with Regan there. The hall's massive fireplace would be an enticement for the princess on such a frigid day, for as much as she took to the activities of a dungeon, she was drawn to heat like a cat.

Because Castle Gloucester had no curtain wall, even the great hall was fitted with arrow loops, so the edifice might be defended at all levels from an attack by water. The arrow loops, while shuttered, were notoriously drafty, so arrases[1] were hung over the alcoves against the wind—the perfect place for a fool to watch, warm himself, and find his moment.

---

1. Arrases—tapestries and carpets hung across alcoves to cut down on drafts or preserve privacy. In *Hamlet*, Polonius is stabbed while hiding behind an arras.

I slipped into the room behind a brace of serving girls and into the alcove nearest the fireplace. She was there, by the fire, in a heavy, hooded, black fur robe, only her face revealed to the world.

I pulled the tapestry aside and was about to call to her when the latch was thrown on the hall's main doors and the Duke of Cornwall entered, wearing his usual finery with the red lion crest on his chest, but more pointedly, Lear's crown—the one the old man had thrown on the table that fateful night at the White Tower. Even Regan seemed startled to see it on the head of her husband.

"My lord, is it prudent to wear the crown of Britain when our sister is still in the castle?"

"Right, right, we must keep up appearances as if we don't know that Albany raises an army against us." Cornwall took the crown off and hid it under a cushion by the hearth. "I am to meet Edmund here and lay a plan for the duke's undoing. One hopes that your sister can be kept out of harm's way."

Regan shrugged. "If she throws herself under destiny's hooves, who are we to save her brains from being pulped?"

Cornwall took her in his arms and kissed her passionately.

Oh lady, thought I, *push him away lest you debase your lovely lips with villainy.* Then it occurred to me, and perhaps rather later than it should have, that she would no more taste villainy than a garlic eater will taste the stinking rose on another. The lady had evil on her breath already.

Even as the duke held her tight and professed his adoration of her, she wiped her mouth on her sleeve behind his back. She pushed the duke away when the bastard Edmund entered the hall.

"My lord," said Edmund, only nodding to Regan. "Our plans for Albany must be delayed. Look at this letter."

The duke took the parchment from Edmund.

"What?" said Regan. "What, what, what?"

"France has landed forces. He knows of unrest between ourselves and Albany and has hidden forces in coastal cities all over Britain."

Regan snatched the parchment out of Cornwall's hand and read it for herself. "This is addressed to Gloucester."

Edmund bowed in false contrition. "Aye, milady, I found it in his closet and brought it here as soon as I saw its contents."

"Guard!" called Cornwall. The great doors opened and a soldier looked in. "Bring me the Earl of Gloucester. Give no deference to his title, he is a traitor."

I looked for a way back to the kitchen, to perhaps find Gloucester and warn him of the bastard's treachery, but Edmund faced the alcove where I was hiding and there was no getting out undiscovered. I opened the shutter to the arrow loop. Even if I could manage to wiggle through it, the wall was a sheer drop to the lake below. I palmed the shutter closed and latched it.

The latch on the main doors clanked again and I returned to the gap between the wall and the tapestry, from which I saw Goneril enter, trailed by two soldiers who held Gloucester by the arms. The old man looked as if he had given up already and hung between the soldiers like a drowned man.

"Hang him," said Regan, turning to warm her hands by the fire.

"What is this?" said Goneril.

Cornwall handed her the letter and stood looking over her shoulder while she read.

"Pluck out his eyes," she said, making an effort not to look at Gloucester.

Cornwall took the letter gently from her hand and put his hand on her shoulder in brotherly support. "Leave him to our displeasure, sister. Edmund, keep our sister company and see her safely home. Lady, tell your duke we must unite against this foreign force. We'll send dispatches quickly between us. Go now, Earl of Gloucester, you do not want to see the dealings with this traitor."

Edmund couldn't conceal a smile upon being addressed by the title he had lusted after for so many years. "I will," said Edmund. He offered his arm to Goneril, who took it. They started out of the hall.

"No!" said Regan.

Everyone stopped. Cornwall stepped between Regan and her sister. "Lady, now is the time when we must all be united against the foreign power."

Regan gritted her teeth and turned back to the fire, waving them away. "Go."

Edmund and Goneril left the hall.

"Bind him to that chair, then leave us," Cornwall commanded his soldiers.

They tied the old earl to a heavy chair and stood back.

"You are my guests," said Gloucester. "Do me no foul play."

"Filthy traitor," said Regan. She took the letter from her husband and threw it in the old man's face. She grabbed a pinch of Gloucester's beard and yanked it out. The earl yowled.

"So white, and such a traitor," she said.

"I am no traitor. I am loyal to my king."

She pulled another pinch from his beard. "What letters do you have late from France? What is their plan?"

Gloucester looked at the parchment on the floor. "I have only that."

Cornwall charged up to Gloucester and pulled the old man's head back by the back of his hair. "Speak now, to whose hands have you sent the lunatic king? We know you've sent him aid."

"To Dover. I sent him to Dover. Only a few hours ago."

"Why Dover?" said Regan.

"Because I would not see your cruel nails pluck out his old eyes or your sister tear his flesh with her boarish fangs. Because there are those who would care for him there. Not put him out in the storm."

"He lies," said Regan. "There's a smashing torture chamber in the dungeon, shall we?"

But Cornwall would not wait. In a second he was sitting astraddle the old man and was digging his thumb into Gloucester's eye socket. Gloucester screamed until his voice broke and there was a sickening pop.

I reached for one of my throwing daggers.

The main door to the hall cracked and heads popped up in the stairwell from the kitchen.

"Why Dover?" said Regan.

"Thou carrion bird!" said Gloucester with a cough. "Thou she-devil, I'll not say."

"Then you'll not see light again," said Cornwall, and he was on the old man again.

I would not have it. I drew back my dagger to cast it, but before I could, a band like ice encircled my wrist and I looked to see the girl ghost right beside me, staying my throw, in fact, paralyzing me. I could move only my eyes to look back on the horror playing out in the great hall.

Suddenly a boy brandishing a long butcher knife ran out of the kitchen stairwell and leapt on the duke. Cornwall stood and tried to draw his sword, but could not get it clear of the scabbard before the boy was on him, plunging the knife into his side. As the lad pulled back to stab again Regan drew a dagger from the sleeve of her robe and plunged it into the boy's neck, then stepped back from the spray of blood. The boy clawed at his neck and fell.

"Away!" Regan shrieked, waving the dagger at the servants in the kitchen stairwell and the main door and they all disappeared like frightened mice.

Cornwall climbed unsteadily to his feet and plunged his sword into the boy's heart. Then he sheathed his sword and felt his side. His hand came away bloody.

"Serves you right, you scurvy vermin," said Gloucester.

With that Cornwall was on him again. "Out, foul jelly!" he shouted, digging his thumb into the earl's good eye, but in that instant Regan's dagger snapped down and took the eye. "Don't trouble yourself, my lord."

Gloucester passed out then from the pain and hung limp in his bonds. Cornwall stood and kicked the old man's chest, knocking him over backward. The duke looked on Regan with adoring eyes, filled with the warmth and affection that can only come from watching your wife dirk another man's eye out on your behalf, evidently.

"Your wound?" said Regan.

Cornwall held his arm out to his wife and she walked into his embrace. "It glanced across my ribs. I'll bleed some and it pains me, but if bound, it'll not be mortal."

"Pity," said Regan, and she plunged her dagger under his sternum and held it as his heart's blood poured over her snowy-white hand.

The duke seemed somewhat surprised.

"Bugger," he said, then he fell. Regan wiped her dagger and her hands on his tunic. She sheathed the blade in her sleeve, then went to the cushion where Cornwall had hidden her father's crown, pulled back her hood, and fitted it on her head.

"Well, Pocket," said the Duchess, without turning to the alcove where I was hidden. "How does it fit?"

I was somewhat surprised (although somewhat less so than the duke).

The ghost released me then, and I stood behind the tapestry, my knife still poised for the throw.

"You'll grow into it, kitten," said I.

She looked to my alcove and grinned. "Yes, I will, won't I? Did you want something?"

"Let the old man go," I said. "King Jeff of France has landed his army at Dover, that's why Gloucester sent Lear there. You'd be wise to set a camp farther south. Rally your forces, with Edmund's and Albany's at the White Tower, perhaps."

The great doors creaked and a head peeked in, a helmeted soldier.

"Send for a physician," Regan called, trying to sound distressed. "My lord has been wounded. Throw his attacker on the dung heap and cast this traitor out the front gate. He can smell his way to Dover and his decrepit king."

In a moment the chamber was filled with soldiers and servants and Regan walked out, casting one last look and a sly smile to my hiding place. I have no idea why she left me alive. I suspect it's because she still fancied me.

I slipped out through the kitchen and made my way back to the gatehouse.

The ghost stood over Drool, who was cowering under his blanket in the corner. "Come on, you lovely brute, give us a proper snog."

"Leave him be, wisp!" said I, although she was nearly as solid as a mortal woman.

"Balls up[2] your jaunty murdering for the day, did I, fool?"

2. Balls up—slang, to ruin, to fuck up, also "bollocks up" and "cock up."

"I might have saved the old man's second eye."

"You wouldn't have."

"I might have sent Regan to join her duke in whatever hell he inhabits."

"No, you wouldn't have." Then she held up a ghostly finger, cleared her throat, and rhymed:

"When a second sibling's base derision,
Proffers lies that cloud the vision,
And severs ties that families bind,
Shall a madman rise to lead the blind."

"You've said that one, already."

"I know. Bit prematurely, too. Sorry. I think you'll find it much more relevant now. Even a slow git like yourself can solve the riddle now, I reckon."

"Or you could just fucking tell me what it means," said I.

"Sorry, can't do it. Ghostly mystery and whatnot. Ta." And with that she faded away through the stone wall.

"I dinna shag the ghost, Pocket," wailed Drool. "I dinna shag her."

"I know, lad. She's gone. Get up now, we've got to monkey down the drawbridge chains and find the blind earl."

19.

Shall a Madman Rise

Gloucester was wandering around outside the castle, just beyond the drawbridge, coming dangerously close to tumbling into the moat. The storm was still raging and bloody rain streamed down the earl's face from his empty eye sockets.

Drool caught the old man by the back of his cloak and lifted him like he was a kitten. Gloucester struggled and waved about in horror, as if he'd been snatched up by some great bird of prey instead of an enormous nitwit.

"There, there," said Drool, trying to calm the old man the way one might try to settle a frightened horse. "I gots you."

"Bring him away from the edge and set him down, Drool," said I. "Lord Gloucester, this is Pocket, Lear's fool. We're going to take you to shelter and bandage your wounds. King Lear will be there, too. Just take Drool's hand."

"Get away," said the earl. "Your comforts are in vain. I am lost. My sons are scoundrels, my estate is forfeit. Let me fall in the moat and drown."

Drool set the old man down and pointed him toward the moat. "Go on, then, milord."

"Grab him, Drool, you wooden-headed ninny!"

"But he told me to let him drown, and he's an earl with a castle and the lot, and you're only a fool, Pocket, so I got to do what he says."

I strode forth, grabbed Gloucester and led him away from the edge. "He's not an earl anymore, lad. He has nothing but his cloak to protect him from the rain, like us."

"He's got nothing?" said Drool. "Can I teach him to juggle so he can be a fool?"

"Let's get him to shelter and see that he doesn't bleed to death first, then you can give him fool lessons."

"We're going to make a fool of ye," said Drool, clapping the old man on the back. "That'll be the dog's bollocks, won't it, milord?"

"Drown me," said Gloucester.

"Being a fool is ever so much better than being an earl," said Drool, far too cheery for a cold-dismal day of post-maiming. "You don't get a castle but you make people laugh and they give you apples and sometimes one of the wenches or the sheeps will have a laugh with you. It's the mutt's nuts,[1] it is."

I stopped and looked at my apprentice. "You've been having a laugh with sheep?"

Drool rolled his eyes toward the slate sky. "No, I—we have pie sometimes, too, when Bubble makes it. You'll like Bubble. She's smashing."

Gloucester seemed to lose all his will then, and let me lead him through the walled town, taking weak, halting steps. As we passed a long, half-timbered building I took to be barracks I heard someone call my name. I looked to see Curan, Lear's captain, standing under an awning. He waved us over and we stood with our backs hard to the wall to try to escape the rain.

"Is that the Earl of Gloucester?" asked Curan.

"Aye," said I. I told Curan what had transpired inside the castle and out on the heath since I'd last seen him.

"God's blood, two wars. Cornwall dead. Who is master of our force, now?"

"Mistress," said I. "Stay with Regan. The plan is as before."

"No, it's not. We don't even know who her enemy is, Albany or France."

---

1. The mutt's nuts—informal for the dog's bollocks.

"Aye, but your action should be the same."

"I'd give a month's wages to be behind the blade that slays that bastard Edmund."

At the mention of his son, Gloucester started wailing again. "Drown me! I will suffer no more! Give me your sword that I may run upon it and end my shame and misery!"

"Sorry," I said to Curan. "He's been a bit of a weepy little Nancy to be around since they ripped his eyes out."

"Well, you might bandage him up. Bring him in. Hunter's still with us. He's right handy with a cauterizing iron."

"Let me end this suffering," wailed Gloucester. "I can no longer endure the slings and arrows—"

"My lord Gloucester, would you please, by the fire-charred balls of St. George, shut the fuck up!"

"Bit harsh, innit?" said Curan.

"What, I said 'please.'"

"Still."

"Sorry, Gloucester, old chap. Most excellent hat."

"He's not wearing a hat," said Curan.

"Well, he's blind, isn't he? If you hadn't said anything he might have enjoyed his bloody hat, mightn't he?"

The earl started wailing again. "My sons are villains and I have no hat." He made to go on, but Drool clamped his great paw over the old man's mouth.

"Thanks, lad. Curan, do you have any food?"

"Aye, Pocket, we can spare as much bread and cheese as you can carry, and one of the men can scare up a flask of wine, too, I'll wager. His lordship has been most generous in providing us with fare," Curan said for the benefit of Gloucester. The old man began struggling against Drool's grip.

"Oh, Curan, you've set him off again. Hurry, if you please. We've got to find Lear and head to Dover."

"Dover it is, then? You'll join with France?"

"Aye, bloody King Jeff, great froggy, monkey-named, woman-stealing ponce that he is."

"You're fond of him, then?"

"Oh do piss off, captain. Just see to it that whatever force Regan might send after us doesn't catch us. Don't mutiny, just make your way to Dover east, then south. I'll take Lear south, then east."

"Let me come with you, Pocket. The king needs more protection than two fools and a blind man."

"The old knight Caius is with the king. You will serve the king best by serving his plan here." Not strictly true, but would he have done his duty if he thought his commander a fool? I think not.

"Aye, then, I'll get your food," said Curan.

When we arrived at the hovel, Tom O'Bedlam stood outside, naked in the rain, barking.

"That barking bloke is naked," said Drool, for once not singing praise to St. Obvious, as we were actually traveling with a blind fellow.

"Aye, but the question is, is he naked because he's barking, or is he barking because he's naked?" I asked.

"I'm hungry," said Drool, his mind overchallenged.

"Poor Tom is cold and cursed," said Tom between barking fits, and for the first time seeing him in daylight and mostly clean, I was taken aback. Without the coat of mud, Tom looked familiar. Very familiar. Tom O'Bedlam was, in fact, Edgar of Gloucester, the earl's legitimate son.

"Tom, why are you out here?"

"Poor Tom, that old knight Caius said he had to stand in the rain until he was clean and didn't stink anymore."

"And did he tell you to bark and talk about yourself in the third person?"

"No, I thought up that bit on my own."

"Come inside, Tom. Help Drool with this old fellow."

Tom looked at Gloucester for the first time and his eyes went wide and he sank to his knees. "By the cruelty of the gods," said he. "He's blind."

I put my hand on his shoulder and whispered, "Be steadfast, Edgar, your father needs your help." In that moment a light came into his eye like a spark of sanity returning and he nodded and stood up, taking the earl's arm. *Shall a madman rise to lead the blind.*

"Come, good sir," said Edgar. "Tom is mad, but he is not beyond aiding a stranger in distress."

"Just let me die!" said Gloucester, trying to push Edgar away. "Give me a rope so I may stretch my neck until my breath is gone."

"He does that a lot," I said.

I opened the door, expecting to see Lear and Kent inside, but the hovel was empty, and the fire had died down to embers. "Tom, where is the king?"

"He and his knight set out for Dover."

"Without me?"

"The king was mad to be back in the storm. 'Twas the old knight said to tell you they were headed for Dover."

"Here, here, bring the earl inside." I stood aside and let Edgar coax his father into the cabin. "Drool, throw some wood on the fire. We can stay only long enough to eat and dry out. We must be after the king."

Drool ducked through the door and spotted Jones sitting on a bench by the fire where I had left him. "Jones! My friend," said the dolt. He picked up the puppet stick and hugged it. Drool is somewhat unclear on the art of ventriloquism, and although I have explained to him that Jones speaks only through me, he has developed an attachment to the puppet.

"Hello, Drool, you great sawdust-brained buffoon. Put me down and stoke the fire," said Jones.

Drool tucked the puppet stick in his belt and began breaking up kindling with a hatchet by the hearth while I portioned out the bread and cheese that Curan had given us. Edgar did his best to bandage Gloucester's eyes and the old man settled down enough to eat some cheese and drink a little wine. Unfortunately, the wine and the blood loss, no doubt, took the earl from inconsolable wailing grief to a soul-smothering, sable-colored melancholy.

"My wife died thinking me a whoremonger, my father thought me damned for not following his faith, and my sons are both villains. I thought for a turn that Edmund might have redeemed his bastardy by being good and true, by fighting infidels in the Crusade, but he is more of a traitor than his legitimate brother."

"Edgar is no traitor," I said to the old man. Even as I said it Edgar held a finger to his lips and signaled for me to speak no further. I nodded to show I knew his will and would not give his identity away. He could be Tom as long as he wished, or for as long as he needed, for all I cared, as long as he put on some bloody trousers. "Edgar was always true to you, my lord. His treachery was all devised for your eyes by the bastard Edmund. It was two sons' worth of evil done by one. Edgar may not be the sharpest arrow in the quiver, but he is no traitor."

Edgar raised an eyebrow to me in question. "You'll make no case for your intelligence sitting there naked and shivering when there's a fire and blankets you can fashion into warm robes, good Tom," said I.

He rose from his father's side and went over to the fire.

"Then it is I who have betrayed Edgar," said Gloucester. "Oh, the gods have seen fit to rain misery down on me for my unsteady heart. I have sent a good son into exile with hounds at his heels and left only the worms as heirs to my only estate: this withered blind body. Oh, we are but soft and squishy bags of mortality rolling in a bin of sharp circumstance, leaking life until we collapse, flaccid, into our own despair." The old man began to wave his arms and beat at his brow, whipping himself into a frenzy, causing his bandages to unravel. Drool came over to the old man and wrapped his arms around him to hold him steady.

"It's all right, milord," said Drool. "You ain't leakin' hardly at all."

"Let me send this broken house to ruin and rot in death's eternal cold. Let me shuffle off this mortal coil—my sons betrayed, my king usurped, my estates seized—let me end this torture!"

He really was making a very good argument.

Then the earl grabbed Jones and tore him out of Drool's belt. "Give me your sword, good knight!"

Edgar made to stop his father and I threw out an arm to hold him back—a toss of my head stopped Drool from interceding.

The old man stood, put the stick end of Jones under his rib cage, then fell forward onto the dirt floor. The breath shot from his body and he wheezed in pain. My cup of wine had been warming by the fire and I threw it on Gloucester's chest.

"I am slain," croaked the earl, fighting for breath. "The lifeblood runs from me even now. Bury my body on the hill looking down upon Castle Gloucester. And beg forgiveness of my son Edgar. I have wronged him."

Edgar again tried to go to his father and I held him back. Drool was covering his mouth, trying not to laugh.

"I grow cold, cold, but at least I take my wrong-doings to my grave."

"You know, milord," I said. "The evil that men do lives after them, the good is oft interred with their bones, or so I've heard."

"Edgar, my boy, wherever you are, forgive me, forgive me!" The old man rolled on the floor, and seemed somewhat surprised when the sword on which he thought himself impaled fell away. "Lear, forgive me that I did not serve you better!"

"Look at that," said I. "You can see his black soul rising from his body."

"Where?" said Drool.

A frantic finger to my lips silenced the Natural. "Oh, great carrion birds are rending poor Gloucester's soul to tatters! Oh, Fate's revenge is upon him, he suffers!"

"I suffer!" said Gloucester.

"He is bound to the darkest depths of Hades! Never to rise again."

"Down the abyss I go. Forever a stranger to light and warmth."

"Oh, cold and lonely death has taken him," said I. "And a right shit he was in life, likely he'll be buggered by a billion barb-dicked devils now."

"Cold and lonely Death has me," said the earl.

"No, it hasn't," said I.

"What?"

"You're not dead."

"Soon, then. I've fallen on this cruel blade and my life runs wet and sticky between my fingers."

"You've fallen on a puppet," said I.

"No, I haven't. It's a sword. I took it from that soldier."

"You took my puppet stick from my apprentice. You've thrown yourself on a puppet."

"You knave, Pocket, you're not trustworthy and would jest at a man even as his life drains. Where is that naked madman who was helping me?"

"You threw yourself on a puppet," said Edgar.

"So I'm not dead?"

"Correct," said I.

"I threw myself on a puppet?"

"That is what I've been saying."

"You are a wicked little man, Pocket."

"So, milord, how do you feel, now that you've returned from the dead."

The old man stood up and tasted the wine on his fingers. "Better," said he.

"Good. Then let me present Edgar of Gloucester, the erstwhile naked nutter, who shall see you to Dover and your king."

"Hello, Father," said Edgar.

They embraced. There was crying and begging for forgiveness and filial snogging and overall the whole business was somewhat nauseating. A moment of quiet sobbing by the two men passed before the earl resumed his wailing.

"Oh, Edgar, I have wronged thee and no forgiveness from you can undo my wretchedness."

"Oh for fuck's sake," said I. "Come, Drool, let us go find Lear and on to Dover and the sanctuary of the bloody fucking French."

"But the storm still rages," said Edgar.

"I've been wandering in this storm for days. I'm as wet and cold as I know how to get, and no doubt a fever will descend any hour now and crush my delicate form with heavy heat, but by the rug-munching balls of Sappho, I'll not spend another hour listening to a blind old nutter wail on about his wrong-doings when there's a stack of wrongs yet to be done. *Carpe diem*, Edgar. *Carpe diem*."

"Fish of the day?" said the rightful heir to the earldom of Gloucester.

"Yes, that's it. I'm invoking the fish of the bloody day, you git. I liked you better when you were eating frogs and seeing demons and the lot. Drool, leave them half the food and wrap yourself as warm as you can. We're off to find the king. We'll see you lot in Dover."

ACT IV

As flies to wanton boys, are we to the gods.
They kill us for their sport.

—*King Lear*, Act IV, Scene 1, Gloucester

20.

A Pretty Little Thing

Drool and I slogged through the cold rain for a day, across hill and dale, over unpaved heath and roads that were little more than muddy wheel ruts. Drool affected a jaunty aspect, remarkable considering the dark doings he had just escaped, but a light spirit is the blessing of the idiot. He took to singing and splashing gaily through puddles as we traveled. I was deeply burdened by wit and awareness, so I found sulking and grumbling better suited my mood. I regretted that I hadn't stolen horses, acquired oilskin cloaks, found a fire-making kit, and murdered Edmund before we left. The latter, among many reasons, because I could not ride upon Drool's shoulders, as his back was still raw from Edmund's beatings. Bastard.

I should say here, that after some days in the elements, the first I'd spent there since my time with

Belette and the traveling mummer troupe many years ago, I determined that I am an indoor fool. My lean form does not fend off cold well, and it seems no better at shedding water. I fear I am too absorbent to be an outdoor fool. My singing voice turns raspy in the cold, my japes and jokes lose their subtlety when cast against the wind, and when my muscles are slowed by an unkind chill, even my juggling is shit. I am untempered for the tempest, unsuited for a storm—better fit for fireplace and featherbed. Oh, warm wine, warm heart, warm tart, where art thou? Poor, cold Pocket, a drowned and wretched rat is he.

We traveled in the dark for miles before we smelled meat-smoke on the wind and spotted the orange light of an oil-skinned window in the distance.

"Look, Pocket, a house," said Drool. "We can sit by the fire and maybe have a warm supper."

"We've no money, lad, and nothing to trade them."

"We trade 'em a jest for our supper, like we done before."

"I can think of nothing amusing to do, Drool. Tumbling is out of the question, my fingers are too stiff to work Jones's talk string, and I'm too weary even for the simple telling of a tale."

"We could just ask them. They might be kind."

"That's a blustery bag of tempest toss, innit?"

"They might," insisted the oaf. "Bubble once give me a pie without I ever jested a thing. Just give it to me, out of the kindness of her heart."

"Fine. Fine. We shall prevail upon their kindness, but should that fail, prepare yourself to bash in their brains and take their supper by force."

"What if there's a lot of 'em? Ain't you going to help?"

I shrugged and gestured to my fair form: "Small and weary, lad. Small and weary. If I'm too weak to perform a puppet show, I think the brain-bashing duties will, by necessity, fall upon you. Find a sturdy stick of firewood. There, there's a woodpile over there."

"I don't want to bash no brains," said the stubborn nitwit.

"Fine, here, take one of my daggers." I handed him a knife. "Give a good dirking to anyone who requires it."

At that point the door opened and a wizened form stepped into the doorway and raised a storm lantern. "Who goes there?"

"Beggin' pardon, sirrah," said Drool. "We was wondering if you required a good dirking this evening?"

"Give that to me." I snatched the dagger away from the git and fitted it into the sheath at my back.

"Sorry, sir, the Natural jests out of turn. We are looking for some shelter from the storm and perhaps a hot meal. We've only bread and a little cheese, but we will share it for the shelter."

"We are fools," said Drool.

"Shut up, Drool, he can see that by my kit and your empty gaze."

"Come in, Pocket of Dog Snogging," said the bent figure. "Mind your head on the doorjamb, Drool."

"We're buggered," said I, pushing Drool through the door ahead of me.

Witches three. Parsley, Sage, and Rosemary. Oh no, not in the Great Birnam Wood where they are generally kept, where one might fairly expect to encounter them, but here in a warm cabin off the road between the Gloucestershire villages of Tossing Sod and Bongwater Crash? A flying house, perhaps? It's rumored that witches are afraid of such structures.

"I thought you was an old man but you is an old woman," said Drool to the hag who had let us in. "Sorry."

"No proof, please," said I, afraid that one of the hags might confirm her gender by lifting her skirts. "The lad's suffered enough of late."

"Some stew," said the crone Sage, the warty one. A small pot hung over the fire.

"I've seen what you put in your stew."

"Stew, stew, true and blue," said the tall witch, Parsley.

"Yes, please," said Drool.

"It's not stew," said I. "They call it stew because it rhymes with bloody *blue,* but it's not stew."

"No, it's stew," said Rosemary. "Beef and carrots and the lot."

"Afraid it is," said Sage.

"Not bits of bat wing, eye of lecher, sweetbreads of newt, and the lot, then?"

"A few onions," said Parsley.

"That's it? No magical powers? No apparitions? No curse? You appear out here in the middle of nowhere— nay, on the very fringe of the tick's knickers that sucks the ass of nowhere—and you've no agenda except to feed the Natural and me and give us a chance to chase the chill?"

"Aye, that's about it," said Rosemary.

"Why?"

"Couldn't think of nothin' that rhymes with onions," said Sage.

"Aye, we were right fucked for spell casting once the onions went in," said Parsley.

"Truth be told, *beef* put us against the wall, didn't it?" said Rosemary.

"Yeah, *fief*, I suppose," mused Sage, rolling her good eye toward the ceiling. "And *teef*, although strictly speaking, that ain't a proper rhyme."

"Right," said Parsley. "No telling what kind of dodgy apparition you'll conjure you cock up the rhyme like that. *Fief. Teeth.* Pathetic, really."

"Stew, please," said Drool.

I let the crones feed us. The stew was hot and rich and mercifully devoid of amphibian and corpse bits. We broke out the last of the bread Curan had given us and shared it with the witches, who produced a jug of fortified wine and poured it for all. I warmed both inside and out, and for the first time in what seemed days, my clothes and shoes were dry.

"So, it's going well, then?" asked Sage, after we'd each had a couple of cups of wine.

I counted out calamities on my digits: "Lear stripped of his knights, civil war between his daughters, France has invaded, Duke of Cornwall murdered, Earl of Gloucester blinded, but reunited with his son, who is a raving loony, the sisters enchanted and in love with the bastard Edmund—"

"I shagged 'em proper," added Drool.

"Yes, Drool boffed them until both walked unsteady, and, let's see, Lear wanders across the moors to find sanctuary with the French at Dover." Handfuls of happenings.

"Lear suffers, then?" asked Parsley.

"Greatly," said I. "He's nothing left. A great height from which to fall, being king of the realm reduced to a wandering beggar, gnawed from the inside by regret for deeds he did long ago."

"You feel for him, then, Pocket?" asked Rosemary, the greenish, cat-toed witch.

"He rescued me from a cruel master and brought me to live in his castle. It's hard to hold hatred with a full stomach and a warm hearth."

"Just so," said Rosemary. "Have some more wine."

She poured some dark liquid into my cup. I sipped it. It tasted stronger, warmer than before.

"We've a gift for you, Pocket." Rosemary brought out a small leather box from behind her back and opened it. Inside were four tiny stone vials, two red and two black. "You'll be needing these."

"What are they?" My vision began to blur then. I could hear the witches' voices, and Drool snoring, but they seemed distant, as if down a tunnel.

"Poison," said the witch.

That was the last I heard from her. The room was gone, and I found myself sitting in a tree near a quiet river and a stone bridge. It was autumn, I could tell, as the leaves were turning. Below me a girl of perhaps sixteen was washing clothes in a bucket on the river-bank. She was a tiny thing, and I would have thought her a child by her size, but her figure was quite womanly—perfectly proportioned, just a size smaller in scale than most.

The girl looked up, as if she heard something. I followed her gaze down the road to a column of soldiers on horseback. Two knights rode at the head of the train, followed by perhaps a dozen others. They rode under my oak tree and paused their horses on the bridge.

"Look at that," said the heavier of the two knights, nodding toward the girl. I heard his voice as if it were in my own head. "Pretty little thing."

"Have her," said the other. I knew the voice immediately, and with it I saw the face for who it was. Lear, younger, stronger, not nearly so grey, but Lear as sure as I'd ever seen him. The hawk nose, the crystal-blue eyes. It was him.

"No," said the younger man. "We need to make York by nightfall. We've no time to find an inn."

"Come here, girl," called Lear.

The girl came up the bank to the road, keeping her eyes to the ground.

"Here!" barked Lear. The girl hurried across the bridge until she stood only a few feet from him.

"Do you know who I am, girl?"

"A gentleman, sir."

"A gentleman? I am your king, girl. I am Lear."

The girl fell to her knees and stopped breathing.

"This is Canus, Duke of York, Prince of Wales, son of King Bladud, brother to King Lear, and he would have you."

"No, Lear," said the brother. "This is madness."

The girl was trembling now.

"You are brother to the king and you may have whom you want, when you want," said Lear. He climbed off his horse. "Stand up, girl."

The girl did, but stiffly, as if she were bracing for a blow. Lear took her chin in his hand and lifted it. "You are a pretty thing. She's a pretty thing, Canus, and she is mine. I give her to you."

The king's brother's eyes were wide and there was hunger there, but he said, "No, we haven't time—"

"Now!" boomed Lear. "You'll have her now!"

With that Lear grabbed the front of the girl's frock and ripped it, exposing her breasts. When she tried to cover up he pulled her arms away. Then he held her and barked commands while his brother raped her on the wide stone rail of the bridge. When Canus had finished and fell breathless between her legs, Lear shouldered him aside then lifted the girl by the waist and threw her over the rail into the river.

"Clean yourself!" he shouted. Then he patted his brother's shoulder. "There, she'll not haunt your dreams tonight. All subjects are property of the king, and mine to give, Canus. You may have any woman you want except one."

They mounted their horses and rode away. Lear hadn't even looked to see if she could swim.

I couldn't move, I couldn't cry out. All during the attack on the girl I felt as if I'd been lashed to the tree. Now I watched her crawl naked from the river, her clothes in tatters behind her, and she curled into a ball on the riverbank and sobbed.

Suddenly I was whisked out of the tree, like a feather on an errant wind, and I settled on the roof of a two-story house in a village. It was market day, and everyone was out, going from cart to cart, table to table, bargaining for meat and vegetables, pottery and tools.

A girl stumbled down the street, a pretty little thing, perhaps sixteen or seventeen, with a tiny babe in arms. She stopped at every booth and showed them the babe, then the villagers would reward her with rude laughter and send her to the next booth.

"He's a prince," she said. "His father was a prince."

"Go away, girl. You're mad. No wonder no one will have you, tart."

"But he's a prince."

"He looks to be a drowned puppy, lass. You'll be lucky if he lives the week out."

From one end of the village to the other she was laughed at and scorned. One woman, who must have been the girl's mother, simply turned away and hid her face in shame.

I floated overhead as the girl ran to the edge of town, across the bridge where she'd been raped, and up to a compound of stone buildings, one with a great soaring steeple. A church. She made her way to the wide double door, and there, she lay her baby on the steps. I recognized those doors, I'd seen them a thousand times. This was the entrance to the abbey at Dog Snogging. The girl ran away and I watched, as a few minutes later, the doors opened and a broad-shouldered nun bent and picked up the tiny, squalling baby. Mother Basil had found him.

Suddenly I was at the river again, and the girl, that pretty little thing, stood on the wide stone rail of the bridge, crossed herself, and leapt in. She did not swim. The green water settled over her.

My mother.

When I awoke the witches were gathered around me like I was a sumptuous pie just out of the oven and they were ravenous pie whores.

"So, you're a bastard then," said Parsley.

"And an orphan," said Sage.

"Both at once," said Rosemary.

"Surprised, then?" said Parsley.

"Lear not quite the kind old codger you thought him, eh?"

"A royal bastard, you are."

I gagged a bit, in response to the crones' collective breath, and sat up. "Would you back off you disgusting old cadavers!"

"Well, strictly speakin', only Rosemary's a cadaver," said the tall witch, Parsley.

"You drugged me, put that nightmare vision in my head."

"Aye, we did drug you. But you was just looking through a window to the past. There was no vision except what happened."

"Got to see your dear mum, didn't you?" said Rosemary. "How lovely for you."

"I had to watch her raped and driven to suicide, you mad hag."

"You needed to know, little Pocket, before you went on to Dover."

"Dover? I'm not going to Dover. I have no desire to see Lear." Even as I said it I felt fear run down my spine like the tip of a spike. Without Lear, I was no longer a fool. I had no purpose. I had no home. Still, after what he had done, I would have to find some other means to make my way. "I can rent out Drool for plowing fields and hoisting bales of wool and such. We'll make our way."

"Maybe he wants to go on to Dover."

I looked over to Drool, who I thought to still be asleep by the fire, but he was sitting there, staring at me wide-eyed, as if someone had frightened him and he'd forgotten how to talk.

"You didn't give him the same potion you gave me, did you?"

"It was in the wine," said Sage.

I went to the Natural and put my arm around his shoulder, or, as far around as I could reach, anyway. "Drool, lad, you're fine, lad." I knew how horrified I had been, with my superior mind and understanding of the world. Poor Drool must have been terrified. "What did you wicked hags show him?"

"He had a window on the past just like you."

The great oaf looked up at me then. "I was raised by wolfs," said he.

"Nothing can be done now, lad. Don't be sad. We've all things in our past we were better not remembering." I glared at the witches.

"I ain't sad," Drool said, standing up. He had to stoop to avoid hitting his head on the roof beams. "My brother nipped at me 'cause I didn't have no fur, but he didn't have no hands, so I throwed him against a tree and he didn't get up."

"You're but a pathetic dimwit," said I. "You can't be blamed."

"My mum only had eight teats, but after that there was only seven of us, so I got two. It were lovely."

He didn't really seem that bothered by the whole experience. "Tell me, Drool, have you always known you were raised by wolves?"

"Aye. I want to go outside and have a wee on a tree, now, Pocket. You want to come?"

"No, you go, love, I'm going to stay here and shout at the old ladies." Once the Natural was gone I turned on them again. "I'm finished doing your bidding. Whatever politics you want to engineer I'll have no more part of it."

The crones laughed at me in chorus, then coughed until finally Rosemary, the greenish witch, calmed her breath with a sip of wine. "No, lad, nothing so sordid as politics, we're about vengeance pure and simple. We don't give a weasel's twat about politics and succession."

"But you're evil incarnate and in triplicate, aren't you?" said I, respectfully. One must give due.

"Aye, evil is our trade, but not so deep a darkness as politics. Better business to dash a suckling babe's brains upon the bricks than to boil in that tawdry cauldron."

"Aye," said Sage. "Breakfast, anyone?" She was stirring something in the cauldron, I assumed it was the leftover hallucination wine from the night before.

"Well, revenge, then. I've no taste left for it."

"Not even for revenge on the bastard Edmund?"

Edmund? What a storm of suffering that blackguard had loosed upon the world, but still, if I never had to see him again, couldn't I forget about his damage?

"Edmund will find his just reward," said I, not believing it for a second.

"And Lear?"

I was angry with the old man, but what revenge would I have on him now? He had lost all. And I had always known him to be cruel, but so long as his cruelty didn't extend to me, I was blind to it. "No, not even Lear."

"Fine, then, where will you go?" asked Sage. She pulled a ladle of steaming liquid from the pot and blew on it.

"I'll take the Natural into Wales. We can call at castles until someone takes us in."

"Then you'll miss the Queen of France at Dover?"

"Cordelia? I thought bloody fucking froggy King Jeff was at Dover. Cordelia is with him?"

The hags cackled. "Oh no, King Jeff is in Burgundy. Queen Cordelia commands the French forces at Dover."

"Oh bugger," said I.

"You'll want to take them poisons we fixed for you," said Rosemary. "Keep them on you at all times. A need for them will present itself."

21.

At the White Cliffs

P ocket," said Cordelia, "have you ever heard of this warrior queen named Boudicca?" Cordelia was about fifteen at the time, and she had sent for me because she wished to discuss politics. She lay on her bed with a large leather volume open before her.

"No, lamb, who was she queen of?"

"Why, of the pagan Britons. Of us." Lear had recently shifted back to the pagan beliefs, thus opening a whole new world of learning for Cordelia.

"Ah, that explains it. Educated in a nunnery, love, I've a very shallow knowledge of pagan ways, although I have to say, their festivals are smashing. Rampant drunken shagging while wearing flower wreaths seems far superior to midnight mass and self-flagellation, but then, I'm a fool."

"Well, it says here that she kicked nine colors of shit out of the Roman legions when they invaded."

"Really, that's what it says, *nine colors of shit?*"

"I'm paraphrasing. Why do you think we've no warrior queens anymore?"

"Well, lamb, war requires swift and resolute action."

"And you're saying that a woman can't move with swift resolve?"

"I'm saying no such thing. She may move with swiftness and resolve, but only after choosing the correct outfit and shoes, and therein lies the undoing of any potential warrior queen, I suspect."

"Oh bollocks!"

"I'll wager your Boudicca lived before they invented clothing. Easy days then for a warrior queen. Just hitch up your tits and start taking heads, it was. Now, well, I daresay erosion would take down a country before most women could pick out their invading kit."

"Most women. But not me?"

"Of course not you, lamb. Them. I meant only weak-willed tarts like your sisters."

"Pocket, I think I shall be a warrior queen."

"Of what, the royal petting zoo at Boffingshire?"

"You'll see, Pocket. The whole of the sky will darken with the smoke from my army's fires, the ground will tremble under their horses' hooves, and kings will kneel outside their city walls, crowns in hand, begging to surrender rather than feel the wrath of Queen Cordelia fall upon their people. But I shall be merciful."

"Goes without saying, doesn't it?"

"And you, fool, will no longer be able to behave like the right shit that you are."

"Fear and trembling, love, that's all you'll get from me. Fear and bloody trembling."

"As long as we understand each other."

"So, it sounds as if you're thinking of conquering more than just the petting zoo?"

"Europe," said the princess, as if stating the unadorned truth.

"Europe?" said I.

"To start," said Cordelia.

"Well, then you had better get moving, hadn't you?"

"Yes, I suppose," said Cordelia, with a great silly grin. "Dear Pocket, would you help me pick an outfit?"

"She's already taken Normandy, Brittany, and the Aquitaine," said Edgar, "and Belgium soils itself at the mention of her name."

"Cordelia can be a bundle of rumpus when she sets her mind to something," said I. I smiled at the thought of her barking orders to the troops, all fury and fire from her lips, but those crystal-blue eyes hinting laughter at every turn. I missed her.

"Oh, I did betray her love and flay her sweet heart with stubborn pride," said Lear, looking madder and weaker than when I'd seen him last.

"Where is Kent?" I asked Edgar, ignoring the old king. Drool and I had found them above a cliff at Dover. They all sat with their backs to a great chalk boulder: Gloucester, Edgar, and Lear. Gloucester snored softly, his head on Edgar's shoulder. We could see smoke from the French camp not two miles away in the distance.

"He's gone to Cordelia, to ask her to accept her father into her camp."

"Why didn't you go yourself?" I asked Lear.

"I am afraid," said the old man. He hid his head under his arm, like a bird trying to escape the daylight beneath its wing.

It was wrong. I wanted him strong, I wanted him stubborn, I wanted him full of arrogance and cruelty. I wanted to see those parts of him I knew were thriving when he'd thrown my mother on the stones so many years ago. I wanted to scream at him, humiliate him, hurt him in eleven places and watch him crawl in his own shit, dragging his bloody pride and guts behind him in the dirt. There was no revenge to be satisfied on this trembling shell of Lear.

I wanted no part of it.

"I'm going to go nap behind those rocks," said I. "Drool, keep watch. Wake me when Kent returns."

"Aye, Pocket." The Natural went to the far side of Edgar's boulder, sat, and stared out over the sea. If we were attacked by a ship, he'd be Johnny-on-the-spot.

I lay down and slept perhaps an hour before there was shouting behind me and I looked over my boulders to see Edgar holding his father's head, steadying him as the old man stood on a rock, perhaps a foot above the ground.

"Are we at the edge?"

"Aye, there are fishermen on the beach below that look like mice. The dogs look like ants."

"What do the horses look like?" asked Gloucester.

"There aren't any horses. Just fishermen and dogs. Don't you hear the sea crashing below?"

"Yes. Yes, I do. Farewell, Edgar, my son. I am sorry. Gods, do your will!" With that the old man leaped off the rock, expecting to plummet hundreds of feet to his death, I reckon, so he was somewhat surprised when he met the ground in an instant.

"Oh my lord! Oh my lord!" said Edgar, trying to use a different voice and failing completely. "Sir, you have duly fallen from the cliffs above."

"I have?" said Gloucester.

"Aye, sir, can you not see?"

"Well, no, you git, my eyes are bandaged and bloody. Can *you* not see?"

"Sorry. What I saw was you fall from a great height and land as softly as if you were a feather floating down."

"I am dead, then," said Gloucester. He sank to his knees and seemed to lose his breath. "I am dead, yet I still suffer, my grief is manifest, my eyes ache even though they are not there."

"That's because he's fucking with you," said I.

"What?" said Gloucester.

"Shhhh," said Edgar. "'Tis a mad beggar, pay him no heed, good sir."

"Fine, you're dead. Enjoy," said I. I lay back on the ground, out of the wind, and pulled my coxcomb over my eyes.

"Come, come sit with me," said Lear. I sat up and watched Lear lead the blind man to his nest beneath the great boulders. "Let the cruelties of the world slide off our bent backs, friend." Lear put his arm around Gloucester and held him while he spoke to the sky.

"My king," said Gloucester. "I am safe in your mercy. My king."

"Aye, king. But I have no soldiers, no lands, no subject quakes before me, no servants wait, and even your bastard son hath treated you better than my own daughters."

"Oh, for fuck's sake," said I. But I could see that the old blind man was smiling, and for all his suffering, he found comfort in his friend the king, no doubt having been blinded to his scoundrel nature long before Cornwall and Regan took his eyes. Blinded by loyalty. Blinded by title. Blinded by shoddy patriotism and false righteousness. He loved his mad, murdering king. I lay back down to listen.

"Let me kiss your hand," said Gloucester.

"Let me wipe it first," said Lear. "It smells of mortality."

"I smell nothing, and see nothing evermore. I am not worthy."

"Art thou mad? See with your ears, Gloucester. Have you never seen a farmer's dog bark at a beggar, and thus chase him off? Is that dog the voice of authority? Is he better than the many for denying the man's hunger? Is a sheriff righteous who whips the whore, when it is for his own lust he punishes her? See, Gloucester. See who is worthy? Now we are stripped of finery, see. Small vices show through tattered clothes, when all is hidden beneath fur and fine robes. Plate sin with gold and the strong lance of justice breaks on decoration. Blessed are you, that you cannot see—for you cannot see me for what I am: wretched."

"No," said Edgar. "Your impertinence comes from madness. Do not weep, good king."

"Do not weep? We weep when we first smell the air. When we are born, we cry, that we come to this great stage of fools."

"No, all shall be well again, and—"

And there was a thump, followed by another, and a yowl.

"Die, thou blind mole!" came a familiar voice.

I sat up in time to see Oswald standing over Gloucester, a bloodied stone in one hand, his sword driven down through the old earl's chest. "You'll not poison my lady's cause further." He twisted the blade, and blood bubbled up out of the old man, but no sound did he make. He was quite dead. Oswald yanked his blade free and kicked Gloucester's body across Lear's lap, as the king cowered against the boulder. Edgar lay unconscious at Oswald's feet. The vermin drew back as if to drive his sword into Edgar's spine.

"Oswald!" I shouted. I stood behind my boulders as I drew a throwing knife from the sheath at my back. The worm turned to me, and pulled his blade up. He dropped the bloody stone he'd used to brain Edgar. "We have an arrangement," said I. "And further slaughter of my cohorts will cause me to doubt your sincerity."

"Sod off, fool. We've no arrangement. You're a lying cur."

"*Moi?*" said I, in perfect fucking French. "I can give you your lady's heart, and not in the unpleasant, eviscerated, no-shagging-except-the-corpse way."

"You have no such power. You've not bewitched Regan's heart, neither. 'Tis she who sent me here to kill this blind traitor who turns minds against our forces. And to deliver this." He pulled a sealed letter from his jerkin.

"A letter of mark, giving you permission in the name of the Duchess of Cornwall to be a total twat-goblin?"

"Your wit is dull, fool. It is a love letter to Edmund of Gloucester. He set out for here with a scouting party to assess the French forces."

"My wit is dull? My wit is dull?"

"Yes. Dull," said Oswald. "Now, *en garde*," said he in barely passable fucking French.

"Yes," said I, with an exaggerated nod. "Yes."

And with that, Oswald found himself seized by the throat and dashed several times against the boulders, which relieved him of his sword, his dagger, the love letter, and his coin purse. Drool then held the steward up and squeezed his throat, slowly but sternly, causing wet gurgling noises to bubble from his foul gullet.

I said,

"While unscathed by my rapier wit
You're choked to death by a giant git
By this gentle jester, is argument won
I'll leave you two to have your fun."

Oswald seemed somewhat surprised by the turn of events, so much so, that both his eyes and tongue protruded from his face in a wholly unhealthy way. He then began to surrender his various fluids and Drool had to hold him away to keep from being fouled by them.

"Drop him," said Lear, who still cowered by the boulders.

Drool looked to me and I shook my head, ever so slightly.

"Die, thou badger-shagging spunk monkey," said I.

When Oswald stopped kicking and simply hung limp and dripping, I nodded to my apprentice, who tossed the steward's body over the cliff as easily as if it were an apple core.

Drool went down on one knee over Gloucester's body. "I were going to teach him to be a fool."

"Aye, lad, I know you were." I stood by my boulders, resisting the urge to comfort the great murderous git with a pat on the shoulder. There was a rustling from over the top of the hill and I thought I heard the sound of metal on metal through the wind.

"Now he's blind *and* dead," said the Natural.

"Bugger," said I, under my breath. Then to Drool, "Hide, and don't fight, and don't call for me."

I fell flat to the ground as the first soldier topped the hill. *Bugger! Bugger! Bugger! Bloody bollocksing buggering bugger!* I reflected serenely.

Then I heard the voice of the bastard Edmund. "Look, my fool. And what's this? The king? What good fortune! You'll make a fine hostage to stay the hand of the Queen of France and her forces."

"Have you no heart?" said Lear, petting the head of his dead friend Gloucester.

I peeked out between my rocks. Edmund was looking at his dead father with the expression of someone who has just encountered rat scat in his toast for tea. "Yes, well, tragic I suppose, but with succession of his title determined and his sight gone, a timely exit was only polite. Who's this other deader?" Edmund kicked his unconscious half brother in the shoulder.

"A beggar," said Drool. "He were trying to protect the old man."

"This is not the sword of a beggar. Neither is this purse." Edmund picked up Oswald's purse. "These belong to Goneril's man, Oswald."

"Aye, milord," said Drool.

"Well, where is he?"

"On the beach."

"On the beach? He climbed down and left his purse and sword here?"

"He was a tosser," said Drool. "So I tossed him over. He kilt your old da."

"Oh, quite right. Well done, then." Edmund threw the purse to Drool. "Use it to bribe your jailer for a bread crust. Take them." The bastard motioned for his men to seize Drool and Lear. When the old man had trouble standing, Drool lifted him to his feet and steadied him.

"What about the bodies?" asked Edmund's captain.

"Let the French bury them. Quickly, to the White Tower. I've seen enough."

Lear coughed then, a dry, feeble cough like the creaking of Death's door hinges, until I thought he might collapse into a pile of blue. One of Edmund's men gave the old man a sip of water, which seemed to quell the coughing, but he couldn't stand or support his weight. Drool hoisted him up on one shoulder and carried him up the hill—the old man's bony bottom bouncing on the great git's shoulder as if it was the cushion of a sedan chair.

When they were gone I scrambled out of my hiding place and over to Edgar's prostrate body. The wound on his scalp wasn't deep, but it had bled copiously, as scalp wounds are wont to do. The resulting puddle of gore had probably saved Edgar's life. I got him propped against the boulder and brought him around with some gentle smacking and a stout splashing from his water skin.

"What?" Edgar looked around, and shook his head to clear his vision, a motion he clearly regretted immediately. Then he spotted his father's corpse and wailed.

"I'm sorry, Edgar," said I. "'Twas Goneril's steward, Oswald, knocked you out and killed him. Drool strangled the scurvy dog and tossed him over the cliff."

"Where is Drool? And the king?"

"Taken, by your bastard brother's men. Listen, Edgar, I need to follow them. You go to the French camp. Take them a message."

Edgar's eyes rolled and I thought he might pass out again, so I threw some more water in his face. "Look at me. Edgar, you must go to the French camp. Tell Cordelia that she should attack the White Tower directly. Tell her to send ships up the Thames and bring a force through London over land as well. Kent will know the plan. Have her sound the trumpet three times before they attack the keep. Do you understand?"

"Three times, the White Tower?"

I tore the back off of the dead earl's shirt, wadded it up, and gave it to Edgar. "Here, hold this on your noggin to staunch the blood."

"And tell Cordelia not to hold for fear for her father's life. I'll see to it that it's not an issue."

"Aye," said Edgar. "She'll not save the king by holding the attack."

22.

At the White Tower

"Tosser!" cried the raven.

No help was he in my stealthy entry to the White Tower. I'd packed my bells with clay, and darkened my face with the same, but no amount of camouflage would help if the raven raised an alarm. I should have had a guard bring him down with a crossbow bolt long before I left the Tower.

I lay in a shallow, flat-bottomed skiff I'd borrowed from a ferryman, covered with rags and branches so I might appear just another mass of jetsam floating in the Thames. I paddled with my right hand, and the cold water felt like needles until my arm went numb. Sheets of ice drifted in the water around me. Another good cold night and I might have walked into the Traitor's Gate, rather than paddled. The river fed the moat, and the moat led under a low arch and through the gate where English nobility had been bringing their family members for hundreds of years on the way to the chopping block.

Two iron-clad gates fit together at the center of the arch, chained in the middle below the waterline, and they moved ever-so-slightly in the current. There was a gap there, at the top, where the gates met. Not so wide that a soldier with weapons could fit through, but a cat, a rat, or a spry and nimble fool on the slim side might easily pass over. And so I did.

There were no guards at the stone steps inside, but twelve feet of water separated me from them, and my skiff would not fit through the gap at the top of the gate where I was perched. A fool was getting wet, there was no way around it. But it seemed to me that the water was shallow, only a foot or two deep. Perhaps I could keep my shoes dry. I took them off and tucked them into my jerkin, then slid down the gate into the cold water.

Great dog-buggering bollocks it was cold. Only to my knees, but cold. And I would have made it undiscovered, methinks, if I hadn't let slip a rather emphatic whisper of, "Great dog-buggering bollocks, that's cold!" I was met at the top of the stairs by the pointy part of a halberd, leveled malevolently at my chest.

"For fuck's sake," said I. "Do your worst, but get it done and drag my body inside where it's warm."

"Pocket?" said the yeoman at the other end of the spear. "Sir?"

"Aye," said I.

"I haven't seen you for months. What's that all over your face?"

"It's clay. I'm in disguise."

"Oh right. Why don't you come in and warm up. Must be dreadful cold in your wet stocking feet there."

"Good thought, lad," said I. It was the young, spot-faced yeoman whom I'd chastised on the wall when Regan and Goneril were first arriving to gain their inheritance. "Shouldn't you stay at your post, though? Duty and all that?"

He led me across the cobbled courtyard, into a servants' entrance to the main castle and down the stairs into the kitchen.

"Nah, it's the Traitor's Gate, innit? Lock on it as big as your head. Ain't no one coming through there. Not all bad. It's out of the wind. Not like up on the wall. Y'know the Duchess Regan is living here at the Tower now? I took your advice about not talking about her boffnacity,[1] even with the duke dead and all, can't be

1. Boffnacity—an expression of shagnatiousness, fit. From the Latin *boffus-natious.*

too careful. Although, I caught sight of her in a dressing gown one day she was up on the parapet outside her solar. Fine flanks on that princess, despite the danger of death and all for sayin' so, sir."

"Aye, the lady is fair, and her gadonk as fine as frog fur, lad, but even your steadfast silence will get you hung if you don't cease with the thinking aloud."

"Pocket, you scroungy flea-bitten plague rat!"

"Bubble! Love!" said I. "Thou dragon-breathed wart farm, how art thou?"

The ox-bottomed cook tried to hide her joy by casting an onion at me, but there was a grin there. "You've not eaten one full plate since you were last in my kitchen, have you?"

"We heard you was dead," said Squeak, a crescent of a smile for me beneath her freckles.

"Feed the pest," said Bubble. "And clean that mess off his face. Rutting with the pigs again, were you, Pocket?"

"Jealous?"

"Not bloody likely," said Bubble.

Squeak sat me down on a stool by the fire and while I warmed my feet she scrubbed the clay from my face and out of my hair, mercilessly battering me with her bosoms as she worked.

Ah, home sweet home.

"So, has anyone seen Drool?"

"In the dungeon with the king," said Squeak. "Although the guard ain't supposed to know it." She eyed the young yeoman who stood by.

"I knew that," he said.

"What of the king's men, his knights and guards? In the barracks?"

"Nah," said the yeoman. "Castle guard was a dog's breakfast until Captain Curan came down from Gloucester. He's got a noble-born knight as captain of every watch and the old guard man for man with any new ones. Crashing huge camps of soldiers outside the walls, forces of Cornwall to the west and Albany on the north. They say the Duke of Albany is staying with his men at camp. Won't come to the Tower."

"Wise choice, with so many vipers about the castle. What of the princesses?" I asked Bubble. Although she seemed never to leave her kitchen, she knew what was going on in every corner of the fortress.

"They ain't talking," said Bubble. "Taking meals in their old quarters they had when they was girls. Goneril in the east tower of the main keep. Regan in her solar on the outer wall on the south. They'll come together for the midday meal, but only if that bastard Gloucester is there."

"Can you get me to them, Bubble. Unseen?"

"I could sew you up in a suckling pig and send it over."

"Yes, lovely, but I did hope to return undiscovered, and trailing gravy might draw the attention of the castle's cats and dogs. Regrettably, I've had experience with such things."

"We can dress you as one of the serving lads, then," said Squeak. "Regan had us bring in boys instead of our usual maids. She likes to taunt and threaten them until they cry."

I regarded Bubble with steely recrimination. "Why didn't *you* suggest that?"

"I wanted to see you sewed up in a suckling pig, you oily rascal."

Bubble has struggled with her deep affection for me for years.

"Very well, then," said I. "A serving boy it is."

"You know, Pocket," said Cordelia, age sixteen. "Goneril and Regan say that my mother was a sorceress."

"Yes, I'd heard that, love."

"If that's so, then I'm proud of it. It means she didn't need some mangy man for her power. She had her own."

"Banished then, wasn't she?"

"Well, yes, that or drowned, no one will really say. Father forbids me to ask about it. But my point is that a woman should come to her power on her own. Did you know that the wizard Merlin gave up his powers to Vivian in exchange for her favors, and she became a great sorceress and queen, and put Merlin to sleep in a cave for a hundred years for his trouble?"

"Men are like that, lamb. You give them your favors and next thing you know they're snoring away like a bear in a cave. Way of the world, it is."

"You didn't do that when my sisters gave you their favors."

"They did no such thing."

"They did, too. Many times. Everyone in the castle knows it."

"Vicious rumors."

"Fine, then. When you have enjoyed the favors of women, who shall remain nameless, did you fall asleep afterward?"

"Well, no. But neither did I give up my magical powers or my kingdom."

"But you would have, wouldn't you?"

"Say, enough talk of sorcerers and such. What say we go down to the chapel and convert back to Christianity? Drool drank all the communion wine and ate all the leftover host when the bishop was ousted, so

I'll wager he's blessed enough to bring us into the fold without clergy. Burped the body of Christ for a week, he did."

"You're trying to change the subject."

"Curses! Discovered!" exclaimed the puppet Jones. "That'll teach you, you sooty-souled snake. Have him whipped, princess."

Cordelia laughed, liberated Jones from my grasp, and clouted me on the chest with him. Even when she was grown she bore a weakness for puppety conspiracy and Punch-and-Judy justice.

"Now, fool, speak truth—if the truth in you hasn't died starving from your neglect. Would you give up your powers and your kingdom for a lady's favor?"

"That would depend on the lady, wouldn't it?"

"Say me, for example?"

"*Vous?*" said I, my eyebrows raised in the manner of the perfectly fucking French.

"*Oui,*" said she, in the language of love.

"Not a chance," said I. "I'd be snoring before you had time to declare me your personal deity, which you would, of course. It's a burden I bear. Deep sleep of the innocent, I'd have. (Or, you know, the deep sleep of the deeply shagged innocent.) I suspect, come morning, you'd have to remind me of your name."

"You didn't sleep after my sisters had you, I know it."

"Well, threat of violent, post-coital death will keep you on the alert, won't it?"

She crawled across the rug until she was close then. "You are a dreadful liar."

"What was your name?"

She clouted me on the head with Jones and kissed me—quickly, but with feeling. That was the only time.

"I'd have your power *and* your kingdom, fool."

"Give me back my puppet, thou nameless tart."

Regan's solar was bigger than I remembered it. A fairly grand, round room, with a fireplace and a dining table. Six of us brought in her supper and set it out on the table. She was all in red, as usual, snowy shoulders and raven hair warmed to the eye by orange firelight.

"Wouldn't you rather lurk behind the tapestry, Pocket?"

She waved the others out of the room and closed the door.

"I kept my head down. How did you know it was me?"

"You didn't cry when I shouted at you."

"Blast, I should have known."

"And you were the only serving boy wearing a codpiece."

"Can't hide one's light under a bushel, can one?" She was infuriating. Did nothing surprise her? She spoke as if I'd been sent for and she'd been expecting me at any moment. Rather took the joy out of all the stealth and disguise. I was tempted to tell her she'd been duped and Drool-shagged just to see her reaction, but alas, there were still guards who were loyal to her, and I wasn't sure she wouldn't have me killed as it was. (I'd left my knives with Bubble in the kitchen, not that they'd help against a platoon of yeomen.) "So, lady, how goes the mourning?"

"Surprisingly well. Grief suits me, I think. Grief or war, I'm not sure which. But I've had good appetite and my complexion's been rosy." She picked up a hand mirror and regarded herself, then caught my reflection and turned. "But, Pocket, what *are* you doing here?"

"Oh, loyalty to the cause and all. With the French at our bloody doors, thought I'd come back to help defend home and hearth." It was probably best we not pursue the reasons why I was there, so I pressed on. "How goes the war, then?"

"Complicated. Affairs of state are complicated, Pocket. I wouldn't expect a fool to understand."

"But I'm a royal, now, kitten. Didn't you know?"

She put down her mirror and looked as if she might burst out laughing. "Silly fool. If you could catch nobility by touch you'd have been a knight years ago, wouldn't you? But alas, you're still common as cat shit."

"Ha! Yes, once. But now, cousin, blue blood runs in my veins. In fact, I've a mind to start a war and shag some relatives, which I believe are the prime pastimes of royalty."

"Nonsense. And don't call me cousin."

"Shag the country and kill some relatives, then? I've been noble less than a week, I don't have all the protocol memorized yet. Oh, and we *are* cousins, kitten. Our fathers were brothers."

"Impossible." Regan nibbled at some dried fruit Bubble had laid out on the tray.

"Lear's brother Canus raped my mother on a bridge in Yorkshire while Lear held her down. I am the issue of that unpleasant union. Your cousin." I bowed. *At your bloody service.*

"A bastard. I might have known."

"Oh, but bastards are vessels of promise, are they not? Or didn't I watch you slay your lord the duke, to run to the arms of a bastard—who is, I believe, now the Earl of Gloucester. By the way, how goes the romance? Torrid and unsavory, I trust."

She sat down then and ran her fingernails through her jet hair as if raking thoughts out of her scalp. "Oh,

I fancy him fine—although he's been a bit disappointing since that first time. But the intrigue is bloody exhausting, what with Goneril trying to bed Edmund, and he not being able to show me deference for fear of losing Albany's support, and bloody France invading in the midst of it all. If I'd known all that my husband had to tend to I'd have waited a while before killing him."

"There, there, kitten." I moved around behind her and rubbed her shoulders. "Your complexion is rosy and your appetite good, and you are, as always, a veritable feast of shagability. Once you're queen you can have everyone beheaded and take a long nap."

"That's just it. It's not like I can just put on the crown and go sovereigning merrily along—God, St. George, and the whole rotting mess into history. I have to defeat the fucking French, then I've got to kill Albany, Goneril, and I suppose I'll have to find Father and have something heavy fall on him or the people will never accept me."

"Good news on that, love. Lear's in the dungeon. Mad as a hatter, but alive."

"He is?"

"Aye. Edmund just returned from Dover with him. You didn't know?"

"Edmund is back?"

"Not three hours ago. I followed him back."

"Bastard! He hasn't even sent word that he's returned. I sent a letter to him in Dover."

"This letter?" I took the letter that Oswald had dropped. I'd broken the seal, of course, but she recognized it and snatched it out of my hand.

"How did you get that? I sent that with Goneril's man, Oswald, to give to Edmund personally."

"Yes, well, I sent Oswald to vermin Valhalla before delivery was secured."

"You killed him?"

"I told you, kitten, I'm nobility now—a murderous little cunt like the rest of you. Just as well, too, that letter's a flitty bit o' butterfly toss, innit? Don't you have any advisers to help you with that sort of thing? A chancellor or a chamberlain, a bloody bishop or someone?"

"I've no one. Everyone is at the castle in Cornwall."

"Oh, love, let your cousin Pocket help."

"Would you?"

"Of course. First, let's see to sister." I took two of the vials from the purse at my belt. "This red one is deadly poison. But the blue one is only *like* a poison, giving the same signs as if one is dead, but they will but sleep one day for each drop they drink. You could put two drops of this in your sister's wine—say, when you are ready to attack the French—and for two days she would sleep the sleep of the dead while you and Edmund did your will, and without losing the support of Albany in the war."

"And the poison?"

"Well, kitten, the poison may not be needed. You could defeat France, take Edmund for your own, and come to an agreement with your sister and Albany."

"I have an agreement with them now. The kingdom is divided as father decreed."

"I'm only saying that you may fight the French, have Edmund, and not have to slay your sister."

"And what if we don't defeat France?"

"Well, then, you have the poison, don't you?"

"Well, that's bollocks counseling," said Regan.

"Wait, cousin, I haven't told you the part where you make me Duke of Buckingham yet. I'd like that dodgy old palace, Hyde Park. St. James's Park, and a monkey."

"You're daft!"

"Named Jeff."

"Get out!"

I palmed the love letter from the table as I exited.

Quickly through the corridors, across the courtyard, and back to the kitchen where I traded my codpiece for a pair of waiter's breeches. It was one thing to leave Jones and my coxcomb with the ferryman, another to secret my blades away with Bubble, but giving up my codpiece was like losing my spirit.

"I was nearly undone by its enormity," said I to Squeak, to whom I handed the portable den of my manly inequity.

"Aye, a family of squirrels could nest in the extra space," Squeak observed, dropping a handful of the walnuts she'd been shelling into the empty prick pouch.

"Wonder you didn't rattle like a dried gourd when you walked," said Bubble.

"Fine. Cast aspersions on my manhood if you will, but I'll not protect you when the French arrive. They're unnaturally fond of public snogging and they smell of snails and cheese. I will laugh—ha!—as you both are mercilessly cheese-snogged by froggy marauders."

"Don't really sound that bad to me," said Squeak.

"Pocket, you'd better be off, lad," said Bubble. "Goneril's supper is going up now."

"*Adieu*," said I, a preview of the Frenchy future of my former friends and soon to be frog-snogged traitorous tarts. "*Adieu*." I bowed. I feigned fainting with a great wrist-to-brow flourish, and I left.

(I admit it, one does like to lubricate his recurrent entrances and exits with a bit of melodrama. Performance is all to the fool.)

Goneril's quarters were less spacious than Regan's, but luxurious, and there was a fire going. I hadn't set foot here since she'd left the castle to marry Albany, but upon returning I found I was simultaneously aroused and filled with dread—memories simmering under the lid of consciousness, I suppose. She wore cobalt with gold trim, daringly cut. She must have known Edmund was back.

"Pumpkin!"

"Pocket? What are you doing here?" She waved the other servers and a young lady who had been braiding her hair out of the room. "And why are you dressed in that absurd outfit?"

"I know," said I. "Poncy breeches. Without my codpiece I feel defenseless."

"I think they make you look taller," she said.

A dilemma. Taller in breeches or stunningly virile in a cod? Both illusions. Each with its advantage. "Which do you think makes a better impression on the fairer sex, love, tall or hung?"

"Isn't your apprentice both?"

"But he's—oh—"

"Yes." She bit into a winter plum.

"I see," said I. "So, what is it with Edmund? All the black kit?" What it was, was she was bewitched, was what it was.

"Edmund." She sighed. "I don't think Edmund loves me."

And I sat down, with all of Goneril's luncheon repast set before me, and considered cooling my forehead in the tureen of broth. Love? Sodding, bloody, tossing, bloody, sodding, bloody love? Irrelevant, superfluous, bloody, ruddy, rotten, sodding love? What ho? Wherefore? What the fuck? Love?

"Love?" said I.

"No one has ever loved me," said Goneril.

"What about your mother? Surely your mother?"

"I don't remember her. Lear had her executed when we were little."

"I didn't know."

"It was not to be spoken of."

"Jesus, then? Comfort in Christ?"

"What comfort? I'm a duchess, Pocket, a princess, perhaps a queen. You can't rule in Christ. Are you daft? You have to ask Christ to leave the room. Your very first war or execution and you're right fucked for forgiveness, aren't you? There's Jesusy disapproval and scowling at least and you have to act like you don't see it."

"He's infinite in his forgiveness," said I. "It says so somewhere."

"As should we all be, it also says. But I don't believe it. I've never forgiven our father for killing our mother and I never shall. I don't believe, Pocket. There's no comfort or love there. I don't believe."

"Me, either, lady. So, sod Jesus. Surely Edmund will fall in love with you when you become closer and he's had a chance to murder your husband. Love needs room to grow, like a rose." Or a tumor.

"He's passionate enough, although never so enthusiastic as that first night in the tower."

"Have you introduced him to your—well—special tastes?"

"Those will not win his heart."

"Nonsense, love, a black-hearted prince like Edmund verily starves to have his bum smacked by a fair damsel like yourself. Probably what he's craving, just too shy to ask."

"I think another has caught his eye. I think he fancies my sister."

No, that's his father's eye she caught, well, speared, really, I thought, but then I thought better. "Perhaps I can help you resolve the conflict, pumpkin." And at that, I produced the red and blue vials from my purse. I explained how one was for death-like sleep, and the other afforded more permanent rest. And as I did so, I cradled the silk purse that still held the last puffball the witches had given me.

What if I were to use it on Goneril? Bewitch her to love her own husband? Surely Albany would forgive her. He was a noble chap, despite being a noble. And with that, Regan could have that villain Edmund for herself, the conflict between the sisters would be settled, Edmund would be satisfied with his new role as Duke of Cornwall and Earl of Gloucester, and all would be well. Of course there were the issues of France attacking, Lear in the dungeon, and a wise and comely fool whose fate was uncertain . . .

"Pumpkin," said I, "perhaps if you and Regan came to an understanding. Perhaps if she were put to sleep until her army had done its duty against France. Perhaps mercy—"

And that was as far as I got, as the bastard Edmund came through the door at that moment.

"What is this?" demanded the bastard.

"Don't you fucking knock?" said I. "Bloody common bastard!" You'd have thought, now that I, too, was a half-noble bastard, that my disdain for Edmund might have diminished. Strangely, no.

"Guard. Take this worm to the dungeon until I have time to deal with him."

Four guards, not of the old Tower force, came in and chased me around the solar several times before I was tripped up by the constrained step of my waiter breeches. The lad they'd been made for must have been smaller even than I. They pinned my arms behind me and dragged me out of the room. As I went backward through the door, I called, "Goneril!"

She held up her hand and they stopped there and held me.

"You have been loved," said I.

"Oh, take him out and beat him," said Goneril.

"She jests," said I. "The lady jests."

23.

Deep in the Dungeon

My fool," said Lear, as the guards dragged me into the dungeon. "Bring him here, and unhand him." The old man looked stronger, more alert, aware. Barking orders again. But with the command he commenced a coughing fit that ended with a spot of blood on his white beard. Drool held a water skin for the old man while he drank.

"We've a beating to deliver, first," said one of the guards. "Then you'll have your fool, well striped as well as checkered."

"Not if you want any of these buns and ale," said Bubble. She'd come down another stairway and was carrying a basket covered with cloth and steaming the most delectable aroma of freshly baked bread. A flask of ale was slung over her shoulder and a bundle of clothes tucked under her free arm.

"Or we'll beat the fool and take your buns as well," said the younger of the two guards, one of Edmund's men and obviously not aware of the pecking order at the White Tower. Bugger God, St. George, and the white-bearded king if you must, but woe unto you if you crossed the cantankerous cook called Bubble, for there'd be grit and grubs baked into all you'd ever eat until the poison finally took you.

"You'll not want to press that bargain, mate," said I.

"The fool's wearing the kit of one of my servers," said Bubble, "and the boy's shivering naked in my kitchen." Bubble threw a bundle of black clothing through the bars into the cell with Drool and Lear. "Here's the fool's motley. Now strip, you rascal, and let me get back to my business."

The guards were laughing now. "Well, go on, little one, get your kit off," said the older guard. "We've hot buns and ale waiting."

I undressed in front of the lot of them, old Lear protesting from time to time, like anyone gave a hot bootful of piss what he had to say anymore. When I was radiant naked, the guards unlocked the door and I crept over to the bundle. Yes! My knives where there, secreted in with the rest. With a bit of sleight o' hand and a distraction from Bubble handing out buns and ale, I was able to secure them inside my jerkin when I dressed.

Two other guards joined the two outside of our cell and shared the bread and ale. Bubble waddled back up the stairs, shooting me a wink as she went.

"The king are melancholy, Pocket," said Drool. "We should sing him a song and cheer him up."

"Sod the sodding king," said I, looking directly into Lear's hawk eye.

"Watch yourself, boy," said Lear.

"Or what? You'll hold my mother down while she's raped, then throw her in the river? Have my father killed later, then? Oh, wait. Those threats are no longer valid, are they, uncle? You've carried them out already."

"What are you on about, boy?" The old man looked fearsome, as if he'd forgotten he'd been treated like so much chattel and thrown in a cage full of clowns, but instead faced a fresh affront.

"You. Lear. Do you remember? A stone bridge in Yorkshire, some twenty-seven years ago? You called a farm girl up from the riverbank, a pretty little thing, and held her down while you commanded your brother to rape her. Do you remember, Lear, or have you done so much evil that it all blends into a great black swath in your memory?"

His eyes went wide then, I could tell he remembered.

"Canus—"

"Aye, your poxy brother sired me then, Lear. And when no one would believe my mother that her son was the bastard of a prince, she drowned herself in that same river where you threw her that day. All this time I have called you nuncle—who would have thought it true?"

"It is not true," he said, his voice quivering.

"It is true! And you know it, you decrepit old poke[1] of bones. A warp of villainy and a woof of greed are all that hold you together, thou desiccated dragon."

The four guards had gathered at the bars and peered in as if they were the ones who were imprisoned.

"Blimey," said one of the guards.

"Cheeky little tosser," said another.

"No song, then?" asked Drool.

Lear shook his finger at me then, so angry was he that I could see blood moving in the veins of his forehead. "You shall not speak to me in this way. You are less than nothing. I plucked you from the gutter, and your blood will run in the gutter on my word before sundown."

1. Poke—a sack, bag; a pig in a poke was usually a cat, which is why you don't buy one, being as cats are not good eating.

"Will it, nuncle? My blood may run but it will not be on your word. On your word your brother may have died. On your word your father may have died. On your word your queens may have died. But not this princely bastard, Lear. Your word is but wind to me."

"My daughters will—"

"Your daughters are upstairs, fighting over the bones of your kingdom. They are your captors, you ancient nutter."

"No, they—"

"You sealed this cell when you killed their mother. They've both just told me as much." ·

"You've seen them?" He seemed strangely hopeful, as if I might have forgotten to bring the good news from his traitorous daughters.

"Seen them? I've shagged them." Silly, really, that it should matter, after all his dark deeds, all his slights and cruelties, that a fool should shag his daughters, but it did matter, and it was a way to unleash a little of the fury I felt toward him.

"You have not," said Lear.

"You have?" asked one of the guards.

I stood then, and strutted a bit for my audience, plus it was a better position for grinding my heel into Lear's soul. All I could see was the water closing over my mother's head, all I could hear was her screams as Lear held her. "I shagged them both, repeatedly, and with relish. Until they screamed, and begged and whimpered. I shagged them on the parapets overlooking the Thames, in the towers, under the table in the great hall, and once, I shagged Regan on a platter of pork in front of Muslims. I shagged Goneril in your own bed, in the chapel, and on your throne—which was her idea, by the way. I shagged them while servants watched and in case you were wondering, because they asked, and as any princess should be shagged, for the pure sweet nasty of it. And they—they did it because they hate you."

Lear had been wailing while I ranted, trying to drown me out. Now he growled, "They do not. They love me all. They have said."

"You murdered their mother, you decrepit loony! They've put you in a cell in your own dungeon. What do you need, a written decree? I tried to shag the hate out of them, nuncle, but some cures lie beyond a jester's talents."

"I wanted a son. Their mother would give me none."

"I'm sure if they had known that they wouldn't have despised you so deeply and done me so well."

"My daughters wouldn't have you. You didn't have them."

"Oh, I did, on my black heart's blood, I did. And when it first started, each of them would shout *Father* when she came. I wonder why. Oh yes, nuncle, I did indeed. And they wanted you to know—that's why they accused me before you. Oh yes, I bonked them both."

"No," wailed Lear.

"Me, too," said Drool, with a great juicy grin. "Beggin' your pardon," he quickly added.

"But not today?" asked one of the guards. "Right?"

"No, not today, you bloody nitwit. Today I killed them."

The French marched overland from the southeast and sailed ships up the Thames from the east. The lords of Surrey on the south showed no resistance and since Dover lay in the County of Kent, the forces of the banished earl not only offered no resistance, but joined the French in the assault on London. They'd marched and sailed across England without firing a single bolt or losing a single man. From the White Tower the guards could see the fires of the French drawing a great orange crescent in the night that illuminated the sky to the east and south.

When the captain made the call to arms at the castle, one of Lear's old knights or squires, under the command of Captain Curan, put a blade to the throat of any of Edmund's or Regan's men, demanding they yield or die. The personal guard forces within the castle had all been drugged by the kitchen staff with some mysterious non-lethal poison that mimicked the symptoms of death.

Captain Curan sent a message to the Duke of Albany from the French queen that if he stood down, in fact, stood with her, that he could return to Albany with his forces, his lands, and his title intact. Goneril's forces from Cornwall, and Edmund's from Gloucester, camped on the west side of the Tower, found they were flanked on the south and east by the French, and on the north by Albany. Archers and crossbowmen were dispatched to the Tower walls above the Cornwall army and a herald fought his way through the panicked forces to a commander, carrying the message that the forces of Cornwall were to lay down their weapons on the spot or death would rain down upon them such as they could not imagine.

No one was willing to die for the cause of Edmund, bastard of Gloucester, or the dead Duke of Cornwall. They laid down their weapons and marched three leagues to the west as instructed.

In two hours it was all over. Out of nearly thirty thousand men who took the field at the White Tower, barely a dozen were killed—all of those, Edmund's castle guards who refused to yield.

The four guards lay spread about the dungeon in various awkward positions, looking quite dead.

"Dodgy sodding poison," said I. "Drool, see if you can reach the one with the keys."

The Natural stretched through the bars, but the guard was too far away.

"I hope Curan knows we're down here."

Lear looked around wild-eyed again, as if his madness had returned. "What is this? Captain Curan is here? My knights?"

"Of course Curan is here. From the sound of the trumpets I'd say he's taken the castle, as was the plan."

"All your theater was misdirection, then?" said the king. "You're not angry?"

"Burning, you old twat, but I was growing weary with keeping the tirade up while the bloody poison took hold. You're no less a turd in the milk of human kindness than I have said."

"No," said the old man, as if my anger actually mattered to him. He began coughing again and caught a handful of blood for his effort. Drool propped him up and wiped his face. "I am king. I will not be judged by you, fool."

"Not just a fool, nuncle. Your brother's son. Did you have Kent murder him? The only decent bloke in your service and you turned him into an assassin, eh?"

"No, not Kent. It was another, not even a knight. A cutpurse who had come before the magistrate. It was he who Kent killed. I sent Kent after the assassin."

"He is vexed by it still, Lear. Did you have a cutpurse kill your father as well?"

"My father was a leper and necromancer. I could not bear his misshapen form ruling Britain."

"In your place, you mean?"

"Yes, in my place. Yes. But I did not send an assassin. He was in a cell at the temple at Bath. Out of the way, where no one might ever see him. But I could not take the throne until his death. I did not kill him, though. The priests there simply walled him up. Was time that killed my father."

"You walled him up? Alive?" I was shaking now, I thought I might have forgiven the old man, seeing him suffer, but now I could hear my blood in my ears.

The sound of boots on stone echoed in the dungeon and I looked up to see the bastard Edmund walk into the torchlight.

He kicked one of the unconscious guards and looked at them like he'd just discovered monkey come in his

Weetabix.[2] "Well, that's a spot of bother, isn't it?" he said. "I suppose I'll have to kill you myself, then." He stooped and took a crossbow from one of the guards' back, fit his foot in the stirrup, and cocked the string.

INTERMISSION

(Backstage with the Players)

"Pocket, you rascal, you've trapped me in a comedy."

"Well, for some, it is, yes."

"When I saw the ghost I thought tragedy was assured."

"Aye, there's always a bloody ghost in a tragedy."

"But the mistaken identity, the vulgarity, the lightness of theme and paucity of ideas, surely it's a comedy. I'm not dressed for comedy, I'm all in black."

"As am I, yet here we are."

"So it is a comedy."

"A black comedy—"

"I knew it."

"For me, anyway."

---

2. Weetabix—a British cereal biscuit whose taste and texture are generally thought to be improved by the addition of monkey come.

"Tragedy, then?"

"Bloody ghost *is* foreshadowing, innit?"

"But all the gratuitous shagging and tossing?"

"Brilliant misdirection."

"You're having me on."

"Sorry, no, it's pikeman's surprise for you in the next scene."

"I'm slain then?"

"To the great satisfaction of the audience."

"Oh bugger!"

"But there's good news, too."

"Yes?"

"It remains a comedy for me."

"God, you're an annoying little git."

"Hate the play, not the player, mate. Here, let me hold the curtain for you. Do you have any plans for that silver dagger? After you're gone, I mean."

"A bloody comedy—"

"Tragedies always end with tragedy, Edmund, but life goes on, doesn't it? The winter of our discontent turns inevitably to the spring of a new adventure. Again, not for you."

"I've never killed a king," said Edmund. "Do you think I'll be famous because of it?"

"You'll not garner favor with your duchesses by killing their father," said I.

"Oh, those two. Like these guards, quite dead, I'm afraid. They were sharing some wine over maps as they planned strategy for the battle and fell down foaming. Pity."

"These guards aren't dead. Merely drugged. They'll come around in a day or so."

He lowered the crossbow. "Then my ladies are only sleeping?"

"Oh no, they're quite dead. I gave them each two vials. One with poison, the other with brandy. Bubble used the knockout poison on the guards, so brandy was our non-lethal substitute. If either of them had decided to show mercy for the other, at least one would be alive. But, as you said, pity."

"Oh, well played, fool. But, that said, I'll have to throw myself on Queen Cordelia's mercy, let her know that I was brought into this horrid conspiracy against my will. Perhaps I'll retain the Gloucester title and lands."

"My daughters? Dead?" said Lear.

"Oh shut up, old man," said Edmund.

"They was fit," said Drool sadly.

"But when Cordelia hears of what you've really done?" I asked.

"Which brings us to our apex, doesn't it? You won't be able to tell Cordelia what has transpired."

"Cordelia, my one true daughter," wailed Lear.

"Shut the fuck up," said Edmund. He raised the crossbow, sighted through the bars at Lear, then stepped back and seemed to lose his aim, as one of my throwing daggers sprouted out of his chest with a thud.

He lowered the crossbow and looked at the hilt of the knife. "But you said pikeman's surprise?"

"Surprise," said I.

"Bastard!" snarled the bastard. He pulled the crossbow up to fire, this time at me, and I sent the second dagger into his right eye. The crossbow twanged and the heavy bolt rattled off the stone ceiling as Edmund spun and fell onto the pile of guards.

"That were smashing," said Drool.

"You'll be rewarded, fool," said Lear, his voice rattling with blood. He coughed.

"Nothing, Lear," said I. "Nothing."

Then there was a woman's voice in the chamber: "Ravens cry pork from the battlements, there's dead Edmund on the wind and bird beaks water at his scoundrel scent!"

The ghost. She stood over Edmund's body outside our cell, rather more ethereal and less solid than she'd been when last I'd seen her. She looked up from the

dead bastard and grinned. Drool whimpered and tried
to hide his head behind Lear's white mane.

Lear tried to wave her away, but the ghost floated
to the bars in front of him. "Ah, Lear, walled up your
father, did you? And?"

"Go away, spirit, do not vex me."

"Walled up your daughter's mother, didn't you?"
said the ghost.

"She was unfaithful!" cried the old man.

"No," said the ghost. "She was not."

I sat down on the cell floor, feeling light-headed
now. Killing Edmund had made me queasy, but this.
"The anchoress at Dog Snogging was your queen?" I
asked, my voice sounding faraway in my own ears.

"She was a sorceress," said Lear. "And she consorted
with my brother. I did not kill her. I could not bear it. I
had her imprisoned at the abbey in Yorkshire."

"Well you damn well killed her when you had her
walled up!" I shouted.

Lear cowered at my veracity. "She was unfaithful,
having dalliance with one of the local boys. I could not
bear the thought of her with another."

"So you ordered her walled up."

"Yes! Yes! And the boy was hanged. Yes!"

"You heinous monster!"

"She did not give me a son, either. I wanted a son."

"She gave you Cordelia, your favorite."

"And she was true to you," said the ghost. "Up to the time you sent her away."

"No!" The old king tried to wave the ghost away again.

"Oh yes. And you had your son, Lear. For years you had your son."

"I had no son."

"Another farm girl you took near another battlefield, this one in Iberia."

"A bastard? I have a bastard son?"

I saw hope rise in Lear's cold hawk eye and I wanted to strike it out the way that Regan had taken Gloucester's. I unsheathed the last of my throwing daggers.

"Yes," said the ghost. "You had a son, these many years, and you lie in his arms now."

"What?"

"The Natural is your son," said the ghost.

"Drool?" said I.

"Drool?" said Lear.

"Drool," said the ghost.

"Da!" said Drool. And he gave his newfound father a great, arm-rippling hug. "Oh Da!" There was a cracking of bones and the sickly sound of air escaping wet, crushed lungs. Lear's eyes bulged out of his head and his parchment-dry skin began to go blue as Drool gave him a lifetime of son's love all in a moment.

When the whistling sounds stopped coming out of the old man I went to Drool and pried his arms off, then lowered Lear's head to the floor. "Let loose, lad. Let him go."

"Da?" said Drool.

I closed the old man's crystal-blue eyes. "He's dead, Drool."

"Tosser!" said the ghost. She spat, a tiny gob of ghost spit that came out as a moth and fluttered away.

I stood then and spun on the ghost. "Who are you? What injustice has been done that can be undone so your spirit may rest, or will at least make you go away, thou ether-limbed irritation?"

"The injustice has been undone," said the ghost. "At last."

"Who are you?"

"Who am I? Who am I? Your answer is in a knock, good Pocket. Knock upon your coxcomb, and ask that trifling machine of thought wherefrom comes his art. Knock upon your cod, and ask the small occupant who wakes him in the night. Knock upon your heart, and ask the spirit there who woke it to the warmth of its home fire—ask that tender ghost who is this ghost before you."

"Thalia," said I, for I could, at last see her. I fell to my knees before her.

"Aye, lad. Aye." She put her hand on my head. "Arise, Sir Pocket of Dog Snogging."

"But, why? Why did you never say you were a queen? Why?"

"He had my daughter, my sweet Cordelia."

"And you always knew of my mother?"

"I heard stories, but I didn't know who your father was, not while I lived."

"Why didn't you tell me of my mother?"

"You were a little boy. That's not the sort of story for a little boy."

"Not so little you wouldn't have me off through an arrow loop."

"That was later. I was going to tell you, but he had me walled up."

"Because we were caught?"

The ghost nodded. "He always had a problem with the purity of others. Never his own."

"Was it horrible?" I had tried not to think of her, alone in the dark, dying of hunger and thirst.

"It was lonely. I was always lonely, except for you, Pocket."

"I'm sorry."

"You're a love, Pocket. Good-bye." She reached through the bars and touched my cheek, like the slightest brush of silk it was. "Care for her."

"What?"

She started to float toward the far wall where the body of Edmund lay.

She said:

"After grave offense to daughters three,
Soon the king a fool shall be."

"Nooooooo," wailed Drool. "My old da is dead."

"No he isn't," said Thalia. "Lear wasn't your father. I was having you on."

She faded away and I started to laugh and she was gone.

"Don't laugh, Pocket," said Drool. "I are an orphan."

"And she didn't even hand us the bloody keys," said I.

Heavy footsteps fell on the stairs and Captain Curan appeared in the passage with two knights. "Pocket! We've been looking for you. The day is ours and Queen Cordelia approaches from the south. What of the king?"

"Dead," said I. "The king is dead."

24.

Boudicca Rising

All my years as an orphan, only to find that I had a mother, but she killed herself over cruelty from the king, the only father I had ever known . . .

To find I had a father, but he, too, was murdered by order of the king . . .

To find the best friend I'd ever known was the mother of the woman I adored, and she was murdered, horribly, by order of the king, because of what I had done . . .

To go from being an orphan clown to a bastard prince to a cutthroat avenger for ghosts and witches in less than a week, and from upstart crow to strategist general in a matter of months . . .

To go from telling bawdy stories for the pleasure of an imprisoned holy woman to planning the overthrow of a kingdom . . .

It was bloody disorienting, and not a little tiring. And I'd built quite an appetite. A snack was in order—perhaps even a full meal, with wine.

I watched from the arrow loops in my old apartment in the barbican as Cordelia entered the castle. She rode a great white warhorse, and both she and the horse were fitted with full plate armor, fashioned in black with gold trim. The golden lion of England was emblazoned on her shield, a golden fleur-de-lis of France on her breastplate. Two columns of knights rode behind her, carrying lances with the banners of Wales, Scotland, Ireland, Normandy, France, Belgium, and Spain. Spain? She'd conquered bloody Spain in her spare time? She was rubbish at chess before she left. Real war must be easier.

She reined up her horse in the middle of the drawbridge, stood in the stirrups, pulled off her helmet and shook out her long golden hair. Then she smiled up at the gatehouse. I ducked out of sight—I'm not sure why.

"Mine!" she barked, then she laughed and led the column into the castle.

Yes, I know, love, but bad form, isn't it, to march about with your own bloody army laying claim to random property, innit? Unladylike.

She was bloody glorious.

Yes, a snack would do nicely. I laughed a bit myself and danced my way to the great hall, indulging in the odd somersault along the way.

————

Perhaps going to the great hall in search of food wasn't the best idea, and perhaps it wasn't my real intention, which was just as well, since instead of a repast, the bodies of Lear and his two daughters were laid out on three high tables, Lear on the dais where his throne sat, Regan and Goneril below, on either side, on the main floor.

Cordelia stood over her father, still in her armor, her helmet tucked under her arm. Her long hair hung in her face, so I couldn't tell if she was crying.

"He's a good deal more pleasant now," said I. "Quieter. Although he moves about the same speed."

She looked up and smiled, a great dazzling smile, then seemed to remember she was grieving and bowed her head again. "Thank you for your condolences, Pocket. I see you have managed to fend off pleasantness in my absence."

"Only by keeping you constantly in my thoughts, child."

"I've missed you, Pocket."

"And I you, lamb."

She stroked her father's hair. He wore the heavy crown that he'd thrown on the table before Cornwall and Albany what seemed so long ago.

"Did he suffer?" Cordelia asked.

I considered my answer, which I almost never do. I could have vented my ire, cursed the old man, made testament to his life of cruelty and wickedness, but that would serve Cordelia not a bit, and me very little. Still, I needed to temper my tale with some truth.

"Yes. At the end, he suffered greatly in his heart. At the hands of your sisters, and under the weight of regret for doing wrong to you. He suffered, but not in his body. The pain was in his soul, child."

She nodded and turned from the old man. "You shouldn't call me child, Pocket. I'm a queen now."

"I see that. Smashing armor, by the way, very St. George. Come with a dragon, did it?"

"No, an army, as it turns out."

"And an empire, evidently."

"No, I had to take that myself."

"I told you your disagreeable nature would serve you in France."

"That you did. Right after you told me that princesses were only good for—what was it—'dragon food and ransom markers'?"

There it was, that smile again, sunshine on my frozen heart, it felt. And like a frostbitten limb, there were pins and needles as the feeling returned. Suddenly I felt the small purse with the witch's puffball heavy on my belt.

"Yes, well, one can't be right all the time, it would undermine one's credibility as a fool."

"Your credibility is already in question in that regard. Kent tells me that the kingdom fell before me so easily because of your doing."

"I didn't know it was you, I thought it was bloody Jeff. Where is Jeff, anyway?"

"In Burgundy with the duke—well, the Queen of Burgundy. They both insist on being referred to as the Queen of Burgundy. Turns out you were right about them, which again counts against your standing as a fool. I caught them together at the palace in Paris. They confessed that they'd fancied each other since they were boys. Jeff and I came to an arrangement."

"Aye, there's usually an arrangement in those situations—the arrangement of the queen's head and body at different addresses."

"Nothing like that, Pocket. Jeff is a decent chap. I didn't love him, but he was a good fellow. Saved me when Father threw me out, didn't he? And by the time this happened I'd won the guard and most of the court to my sympathies—if anyone was going to lose his head, it wasn't me. France took some territories, Toulouse, Provence, and some bits of the Pyrenees with him, but considering the territories I've taken, overall it's more than fair. The boys have a crashingly large palace in Burgundy that they perpetually redecorate. They're quite happy."

"The boys? Bloody Burgundy buggering froggy France? By the dangling ovaries of Odin, there's a song in there somewhere!"

She grinned. "I've purchased a divorce from the Pope. Bloody dear[1] it was, too. If I'd known Jeff was going to insist on sanction of the Church I'd have pushed to reinstate the old Discount Pope."

The sound of the great doors opening echoed through the hall and Cordelia turned, fierce fire in her eyes. "I said I was to be left alone!"

But then Drool, who had lumbered through, pulled up as if he'd seen a ghost, and started to back away. "Sorry. Beggin' your pardons. Pocket, I got Jones and your hat." He held up the puppet stick and my coxcomb, forgot for a second that he'd been shouted at, then resumed backing out the doors.

"No, come, Drool," said Cordelia. She waved him in and the guards closed the door behind him. I wondered what the knights and other nobles might think that the warrior queen would admit no one to the hall except two fools. Probably that she was merely another in a long line of family nutters.

Drool paused as he passed Regan's body and lost his sense of purpose. He lay Jones and my hat on the table

---

1. Dear—British colloquialism, expensive, costly.

next to her, then pinched the hem of her gown and began to raise it for a peek.

"Drool!" I barked.

"Sorry," said the Natural. Then he spotted Goneril's body and moved to her side. He stood there, looking down. In a moment his shoulders began to shake and soon he broke into great, rib-wrenching sobs and proceeded to drip tears upon Goneril's bosom.

Cordelia looked at me with pleading in her eyes, and I, at her, with something that must have seemed similar. We were shits, together, we were, that we didn't grieve for these people, this family.

"They was fit," said Drool. Soon he was petting Goneril's cheek, then her shoulder, then both her shoulders, then her breasts, then he climbed on the table on top of her and commenced a rhythmic and unseemly sobbing that approximated in timbre and volume a bear being shaken in a wine cask.

I retrieved Jones from Regan's side and clouted the oaf about the head and shoulders until he climbed off the erstwhile Duchess of Albany and slipped through the drape and hid under the table.

"I loved them," Drool said.

Cordelia stayed my hand and bent down and lifted the drapery. "Drool, mate," she said. "Pocket doesn't mean to be cruel, he doesn't understand how you feel.

Still, we have to keep it to ourselves. It's not proper to dry-hump the deceased, love."

"It ain't?"

"No. The duke will be here soon and he'd be offended."

"What 'bout the other one. Her duke is dead."

"Just the same, it's not proper."

"Sorry." He hid his head under the drape.

She stood and looked at me, turning away from Drool and rolling her eyes and smiling.

There was so much to tell her, that I'd shagged her mother, and we, technically, were cousins, and, well, things might get awkward. It was my instinct, as a performer, to keep the moment light, so I said, "I killed your sisters, more or less."

She stopped smiling. "Captain Curan said they poisoned each other."

"Aye. I gave them the poison."

"Did they know it was poison?"

"They did."

"Couldn't be helped, then, could it? They were right vicious bitches anyway. Tortured me through my childhood. You saved me the effort."

"They just wanted someone to love them," I said.

"Don't make the case with me, fool. You're the one that killed them. I was just going to take their lands and property. Maybe humiliate them in public."

"But you just said—"

"I loved them," said Drool.

"Shut up!" I chorused with Cordelia.

The doors cracked open then and Captain Curan peeked his head through. "Lady, the Duke of Albany has arrived," said he.

"Give me a moment, then send him in," said Cordelia.

"Very well." Curan closed the doors.

Cordelia stepped up to me then, she was only a little taller than me, but in armor, somewhat more intimidating than I'd remembered her—but no less beautiful.

"Pocket, I've taken quarters in my old solar. I'd like you to visit after supper tonight."

I bowed. "Does my lady require a story and a jest before bedtime to clear her head of the day's tribulations?"

"No, fool, Queen Cordelia of France, Britain, Belgium, and Spain is going to shag the bloody bells off you."

"Pardon?" said I, somewhat nonplussed. But then she kissed me. The second time. With great feeling, and she pushed me away.

"I invaded a country for you, you nitwit. I've loved you since I was a little girl. I came back for you, well, and for revenge on my sisters, but mostly for you. I knew you would be waiting for me."

"How? How did you know?"

"A ghost came to me at the palace in Paris months ago. Scared the béarnaise out of Jeff. She's been advising the strategy since."

Enough talk of ghosts, I thought. Let her rest. I bowed again. "At your bloody beckoning service, love. A humble fool, at your service."

ACT V

How I would make him fawn and beg and seek
And wait the season and observe the times
And spend his prodigal wits in bootless rhymes
And shape his service wholly to my hests
And make him proud to make me proud that jests!
So perttaunt-like would I o'ersway his state
That he should be my fool and I his fate.

—Love's Labour's Lost, Act V, Scene 2, Rosaline

25.

The King Shall Be a Fool

Alas, your humble fool is the King of France. Actually, France, Britain, Normandy, Belgium, Brittany, and Spain. Perhaps more, I haven't seen Cordelia since breakfast. She can be a terror when left to her own devices, but she keeps the empire in working order and I adore her, of course. (As has always been the case.)

Good Kent had his lands and title restored, and was also given the title Duke of Cornwall, and the attendant lands and properties. He's retained the black beard and glamour given him by the witches, and seems to have convinced himself that he is younger and more vibrant than the multitude of years he carries on his back.

Albany retained his title and lands and signed an oath of fealty to Cordelia and me, and I trust he will be true to it. He's a decent, if dull chap, and without Goneril in his ear, his will be the way of virtue.

We've given Curan the title of Duke of Buckingham, and he acts as regent of Britain when we are not on the islands. Edgar took his title as Earl of Gloucester and returned to his home where he buried his father in the walls of the castle temple built to his many gods. He's started his own family and will no doubt have many sons who will grow up to betray him or simply be dolts in the image of their father.

Cordelia and I live in a number of palaces around the empire, traveling with an embarrassingly large entourage that includes Bubble and Squeak, as well as Shanker Mary and other loyal staff from the White Tower. I have a crashingly large throne, on which I hold court with Drool on one side (who has been given the title of Royal Minister of Wank), and my monkey, Jeff, on the other. We hear cases of the local farmers and merchants, and I pronounce judgments, damages, and sentences. For a while I allowed monkey Jeff to pronounce sentences while I was off having lunch with the queen, giving him a little plaque with various penalties to which he could point, but that had to stop when I returned one afternoon from a protracted Cordelia bonking to find that the cheeky little bloke had hanged the entire village of Beauvois for cheese violations. (Awkward, that, but the French understand. They are very serious about their cheese.) Most of the time justice can be satisfied with a bit of verbal humiliation, name-calling, and pointed sarcasm, at which, it turns out, I excel, so I am viewed as a fair and just king and much beloved by my people, even the fucking French.

We are at our palace in Gascony now, near northern Spain. Lovely, but very dry. I was just saying to froggy Queen Jeff today (he and Queen Burgundy are visiting), "It's lovely, Jeff, but bloody dry. I'm English, I require dampness. I feel as if I'm drying out and becoming all crackly as we speak."

"It's true," Cordelia said. "He's always gravitated toward the moist."

"Yes, well, darling, we shan't speak of that in front of Jeff, shall we? Oh, look! Drool has sprouted an erection. Let's ask him what he's thinking about. Had his way with a knotted oak on the way here. A right spectacular tree-shagging it was, too. Knocked down enough acorns to feed the village for a week. They wanted to have a special feast day in honor of the git—declare him god of the tree-shag—more fertility symbols there than you can shake a stick at, innit?"

"*C'est la vie,*"[1] said Jeff, in perfectly incomprehensible fucking French.

---

1. *C'est la vie*—fucking French for "that's life."

Later, as I was holding audiences with the public, there entered the great hall three ancient, bent figures. The witches of Great Birnam Wood. I suppose I'd always known they'd show up at some time or another. Drool ran and hid in the kitchen. Jeff jumped on my shoulder and screeched at them. (Jeff the monkey, not the queen.)

"A year has passed for witches three,

And we are here to collect our fee," said Rosemary, the green, cat-toed witch.

"Oh, for fuck's sake, you're on with the rhyming again?"

"A need was filled, a promise made,

For service done we must be paid," the witches chanted in unison.

"Just stop the rhyming," said I. "And those rags are entirely too heavy for this climate. You'll get a rash on your warts and carbuncles if you're not careful."

"You've been made a king and enchanted your true love to be yours forevermore, fool. We only want what is our due," said Sage, the most warty of the three.

"Rightly so, rightly so," said I. "But Cordelia is not enchanted to love me. She is with me of her own free will."

"Balderdash," said Parsley, the tall witch. "We gave you three puffballs for three sisters."

"Aye, but I used the third to enchant Edgar of Gloucester, so he would fall in love with a laundress at his castle named Emma. Lovely lass with smashing knockers. She'd been mistreated by the bastard brother—only seemed just."

"Still, the spell was used. We will have our payment," said Rosemary.

"Of course. I have more treasure than you crones could carry. Gold? Silver? Jewels? But Cordelia doesn't know of all of your manipulations, nor that the ghost was her mother, and she mustn't ever. If you agree, name your reward, I've important kingly things to accomplish and my monkey is hungry. Name your price, crones."

"Spain," said the witches.

"Fuckstockings," said the puppet Jones.

You Cheeky Git—An Author's Note

I know what you're thinking: "Why, are you, an American comic novelist, thrashing around in the deep end of genius with the greatest artist of the English language who ever lived? What did you think you might possibly achieve besides peeing in the pool and drowning in your own shallow aspirations?"

You're thinking: "Shakespeare writes a perfectly elegant tragedy that functions perfectly well and you can't leave it in peace. You have to put your greasy hands all over it, befoul it with badger shagging and monkey spunk. I suppose we just can't have nice things."

Okay, first, good point. And second, I can't believe you think like that . . .

But you're right, I've made a dog's breakfast of English history, geography, *King Lear*, and the English language in general. But in my defense—well—I don't really have a defense, but let me give you an idea from whence one begins when trying to retell the story of *King Lear.*

If you work with the English language, particularly if you work with it as dog-fuckingly long as I have, you are going to run across Will's work at nearly every turn. No matter what you have to say, it turns out that Will said it more elegantly, more succinctly, and more lyrically—and he probably did it in iambic pentameter—four hundred years ago. You can't really do what Will did, but you can recognize the genius that he had to do it. But I didn't begin *Fool* as a tribute to Shakespeare; I wrote it because of my great admiration for British comedy.

I began with the idea of writing a story about a fool, an English fool, because I like writing rascals. I fired the first shot across the bow several years ago, over breakfast in New York with my American editor, Jennifer Brehl, on a morning after I had taken entirely too much sleep medication. (New York kind of freaks me out. I always feel like I'm a sponge mopping the anxiety from New York's brow.)

"Jen, I want to do a book about a fool. But I don't know whether I should just do a generic fool, or Lear's fool."

"Oh, you have to do Lear's fool," she said.

"Lear's fool it is, then," said I, as if that entailed no more effort than saying it.

Then she slowly melted in her chair and was replaced by a hookah-smoking caterpillar that said nothing but, "Wah, wah, wah, wah, wah," but did pay for breakfast. I've blacked out the rest of the morning. (Business traveler's tip: If you're still not asleep after a second sleeping pill, DO NOT take a third.)

So into the deep end I dove, spending nearly two years immersed in Shakespeare's work: performed live, in written form, and on DVD. I must have watched thirty different performances of *King Lear*, and frankly, about halfway into my research, after listening to a dozen different Lears rage at the storm and lament what complete nitwits they had been, I wanted to leap onstage and kill the old man myself. For while I respect and admire the talent and stamina it takes for an actor to play Lear, as well as the eloquence of the speeches, a person can take only so much whining before he wants to sign up for the Committee to Make Elder Abuse an Olympic Sport. Amid all the attractions at Stratford-upon-Avon, I think they should add one where participants are allowed to push King Lears off a high precipice. You know, like bungee jumping, only no bungee. Just, "Rage, wind, blow, crack your cheeks! Ahhhhhhhhhh!" Splat! Sweet, sweet silence. Okay, perhaps not. (They have a Shakespeare Hospice at Stratford, by the way, for those who ticked the "Not to Be" box.)

Once one decides to retell *Lear*, time and place become problems that must be addressed.

According to a history of British monarchs (*The Kings of Britain*) compiled in 1136 by the Welsh cleric Geoffrey of Monmouth, the real King Leir, if indeed he existed, lived in 400 B.C., or about the time between Plato and Aristotle, at the height of the Greek empire, when there were no great castles in England, the counties that Shakespeare refers to in his play were long from being established, and at best, Leir would have been some sort of a tribal leader, not the sovereign of a vast kingdom with authority over a complex sociopolitical system of dukes, earls, and knights. A mud fortress would have been his castle. In the play, Shakespeare makes references to Greek gods, and indeed, legend says that Leir's father, Bladud, who was a swineherd, a leper, and king of the Britons, journeyed to Athens looking for spiritual guidance, and returned to build a temple to the goddess Athena at Bath, where he worshipped and practiced necromancy. Leir became king rather by default when Bladud's essential bits dropped off. The battle for souls between the Christians and the pagans that I portray in *Fool* probably took place closer to around A.D. 500 to 800, rather than during Pocket's imagined thirteenth century.

Time, then, becomes a bit of a problem, not just in relation to history, but to language as well. (The time frame of the play seemed to bollocks up even Shakespeare, for at one point he has the fool rattle off a long list of prophecies, after which he says, *"This prophecy Merlin shall make; for I live before his time"* (Act III, Scene 2). It's as if Will threw his quill in the air and said, "I know not what the hell is going on, therefore I shall cast this beefy bit of bull toss to the groundlings and see if it slides by." No one appears to know what kind of language they were speaking in 400 B.C., but it certainly wasn't English. And while Shakespeare's English is elegant and in many ways revolutionary, much of it is foreign to the modern English reader. So, in the tradition of Will throwing his quill into the air, I decided to set the story in a more or less mythical Middle Ages, but with the linguistic vestiges of Elizabethan times, modern British slang, Cockney slang (although rhyming slang remains a complete mystery to me), and my own innate American balderdash. (Thus Pocket refers to the quality of Regan's gadonkage and Thalia refers to St. Cinnamon driving the Mazdas out of Swinden—with full historical immunity.) And for those sticklers who will want to point out the anachronisms in *Fool,* rest easy, the whole book is an anachronism. Obviously. There are even references to the "Mericans" as a long extinct race, which places our own time somewhere in the distant past. ("Long ago in a galaxy far away," if you get my meaning.) It was designed thus.

In dealing with the geography of the play, I looked for the modern locations that are mentioned in its text: Gloucester, Cornwall, Dover, etc. The only Albany I could find is now, more or less, within the London metropolitan area, so I set Goneril's Albany in Scotland, mainly to facilitate easy access to Great Birnam Wood and the witches from *Macbeth.* Dog Snogging, Bongwater Crash, and Bonking Ewe on Worms Head and other towns are located in my imagination, except that there really is a spot called Worms Head in Wales.

The plot for Shakespeare's play *King Lear* was lifted from a play that was produced in London perhaps ten years earlier, called *The Tragedy of King Leir,* the printed version of which has been lost. *King Leir* was performed in Shakespeare's time, and there is no way of knowing what the text was, but the story line was similar to the Bard's play and it's fairly safe to say he was aware of it. This was not unusual for Shakespeare. In fact, of his thirty-eight plays, it's thought that only three sprang from ideas original to Shakespeare.

Even the text of *King Lear* that we know was pieced together by Alexander Pope in 1724 from bits and pieces of previously printed versions. Interestingly enough, in contrast to the tragedy, England's first poet laureate, Nathan Tate, rewrote *King Lear* with a happy ending, wherein Lear and Cordelia are reunited, and Cordelia marries Edgar and lives happily ever after. Tate's "happy ending" version was performed for nearly two hundred years before Pope's version was revived for the stage. And Monmouth's *Kings of Britain* indeed shows Cordelia as becoming queen after Leir, and reigning for five years. (Although, again, there is no historical record to support this.)

A few who have read *Fool* have expressed a desire to go back and read *Lear,* to perhaps compare the source material with my version of the story. ("I don't remember the tree-shagging parts in *Lear,* but it has been a long time.") While you could certainly find worse ways to spend your time, I suspect that way madness lies. *Fool* quotes or paraphrases lines from no fewer than a dozen of the plays, and I'm not even sure what came from which at this point. I've done this largely to throw off reviewers, who will be reluctant to cite and criticize passages of my writing, lest they were penned by the Bard hisownself. (I once had a reviewer take me to task for writing awkward prose, and the passage he cited was one of my characters quoting Thoreau's "On Civil Disobedience." You don't get many moments in life; pointing that out to the reviewer was one of mine.)

A note on one of Pocket's prejudices: I know that the term "fucking French" seems to crop up quite a bit in Pocket's speech, but that should in no way be interpreted as indicative of my own feelings about France or the French. I love both. But the alliteration was very seductive, and I wanted to convey the sort of surface resentment the English seem to have for the French, and to be fair, the French for the English. As one English friend explained to me, "Oh yes, we hate the French, but we don't want anyone else to hate them. They are ours. We will fight to the death to preserve them so we can continue to hate them." I don't care if that's true or not, I thought it was funny. Or, as one French acquaintance put it, "All Englishmen are gay; some simply don't know it and sleep with women." I'm pretty sure that's not true, but I thought it was funny. The fucking French are great, aren't they?

Finally, I want to thank all the people who helped me in the research of *Fool:* The players and crew of the many Shakespeare festivals I attended in Northern California, who keep the Bard's work alive for those of us in the hinterland of the Colonies; all of the great and gracious people in Great Britain and France, who helped me find medieval sites and artifacts so I could completely ignore authenticity when writing *Fool;* and, finally, great writers of British comedy, who inspired my plunge into the deep end of their art: Shakespeare, Oscar Wilde, G. B. Shaw, P. G. Wodehouse, H. H. Munro (Saki), Evelyn Waugh, The Goons, Tom Stoppard, The Pythons, Douglas Adams, Nick Hornby, Ben Elton, Jennifer Saunders, Dawn French, Richard Curtis, Eddie Izzard, and Mil Millington (who assured me that while it was virtuous that I was writing a book wherein I aspired to call characters "gits," "wankers," and "tossers," I would be remiss and inauthentic if I neglected to call a few "twats" as well).

Also, thanks to Charlee Rodgers for her patient handling of logistic and travel arrangements for research; Nick Ellison and his minions for handling business; Jennifer Brehl for clean hands and composure in her editing; Jack Womack for getting me in front of my readers; as well as Mike Spradlin, Lisa Gallagher, Debbie Stier, Lynn Grady, and Michael Morrison for doing the dirty business of publishing. Oh, yes, and to my friends, who put up with my obsessive nature and excessive whining while I was working on *Fool,* thanks for not pushing me off a high precipice.

Until next time, *adieu.*

Christopher Moore

HARPER LUXE

THE NEW LUXURY IN READING

We hope you enjoyed reading
our new, comfortable print size and found it
an experience you would like to repeat.

Well – you're in luck!

HarperLuxe offers the finest in fiction and
nonfiction books in this same larger print size and
paperback format. Light and easy to read, HarperLuxe
paperbacks are for book lovers who want to see
what they are reading without the strain.

For a full listing of titles and
new releases to come, please visit our website:

www.HarperLuxe.com